I0546394

Also by Carole Walker Carter

Aztarian Series
AZTARA, The Mastel Kingdom
SURTEES, Science Rules
AZTARA, A Galactic Love Story
AZTARA, Secrets Revealed

Evers and MacFarlan Detective Series
Final Alumni
Shadowy Faces
Nine Points of a Circle

Fantasy Books
The Child Rowanda, Little Dragon
The Child Rowanda, Return to Arolsen
The Child Rowanda, Underworld
The Child Rowanda, Dragon Princess

Children's Books on www.walkercarter.com
Tinker Robot
Grandma's Magic Scarf
Granny Nell
Alec the Astronaut

AZTARA

The
Mastel Kingdom

Aztarian Series
Volume 0

Carole Walker Carter

WALKER CARTER PUBLISHING, LLC

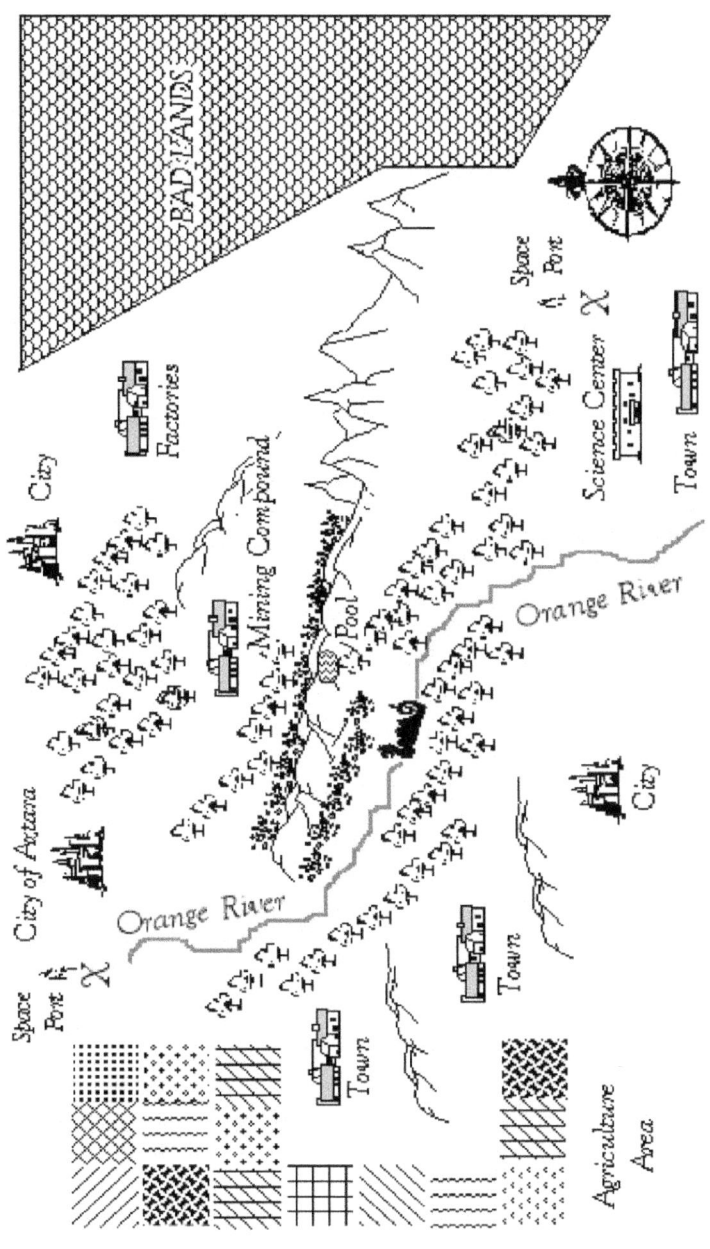

The sale of this book without its cover is unauthorized. If you purchased this book without a cover, you should be aware that it was reported to the publisher as "unsold and destroyed." Neither the author nor the publisher has received payment for the sale of this "stripped book."

This book is a work of fiction. Names, characters, places, and incidents either are products of the author's imagination or are used fictitiously. Any resemblance to actual events or locales or persons, living or dead, is entirely coincidental.

Copyright © 2018 by Carole Walker Carter
All Rights Reserved

No part of this publication may be reproduced, or stored in a retrieval system, or transmitted in any form or by any means, electronically, mechanically, photocopying, recording, or otherwise, without the written permission of the publisher. For information regarding permission, send an email to adminhost@walkercarter.com, Attention Permission Department.

Cover Design and Layout by Donald E Carter
Black Mountain Unicorn © Art of Sandra
Cover Lightning Photo © iStock by Getty Images

AZTARA, The Mastel Kingdom / by Carole Walker Carter

Aztarian Series / Volume 0

ISBN 978-1-947734-00-5

9 8 7 6 5 4 3 2 1 17 18 19 20 21

[1. Monsters, 2. Interspecies Telepathy, 3. Young Adult,
4. Alien Creatures, 5. Alien World]

WALKER CARTER PUBLISHING, LLC

Please check out my website at <u>www.walkercarter.com</u>

To my girls Jennifer and Lisa, my grandson Nixon, my granddaughter Alex and my husband, Don.

In memory of my mother and dad, Elda and Dean Walker.

I will always love you!!!

ACKNOWLEDGEMENTS

I wrote this book in cooperation with my best friend and husband, Donald E. Carter, author of <u>Concurrent Engineering, Product Development Environment</u> business books. Don's inspiration helped to create characters for the planet Aztara and Surtees, and he researched all the technical information.

Janis Lane supported me with my writing by cheering me on to tell my stories. Don and I worked diligently to edit this book over the past year.

My girls, Jennifer and Lisa Coyle, provided several useful resource books. Without their support and prodding, this book may still be in draft form. Jennifer, with a keen eye for graphics, helped Don with the cover art.

Without my older sister, Linda Sturgill, and younger sister Janel Walker, giving me love, support, and resources, I would not be able to write. They each spent hours proofreading and editing the *Aztarian Series* Books and *Evers & MacFarlan Detective Series* Books. I will forever be grateful for my family's encouragement and dedication to my creations.

Special Thanks to all those that donated to my GoFundMe page, Linda Sturgill, Elda Walker, Janel Walker, Judy Mathiesen, Linda Maddex, Afsaneh Fowler, and Carol Royce Davidson. These donations kick-started my venture by allowing me to acquire editing tools, printed proof copies, ISBN numbers, audio equipment, and final publication costs.

Table of Contents

CHAPTER ONE

The Aztarian mastel mare lay on the soft purple grass with the turquoise clouds moving gently in the breeze through the buttercream colored sky. Her ribs heaved with the strain of giving birth. The rhythm of contractions was evident with the undulating muscles of her abdomen as her body tried to push the foal out and into the world.

Standing guard was the stallion father. He was a strong, brilliant red mastel stallion with a flaming red mane and tail. The rest of the colorful herd grazed close-by, ready to form a protective ring if any threat appeared.

Geselle, a strawberry colored mastel with visible stripes on her coat and whirling green eyes that glittered in the fading light of the day lay exhausted. If she were not so preoccupied with giving birth, Geselle would have noticed the turquoise clouds gathering into a large dark mass in the distance. Her mate, Rydor, watched nervously and snorted from time to time. Rydor, torn between watching his mate straining to give birth, and keeping an eye on the advancing storm, finally trumpeted a warning to the herd to seek shelter.

Paws stomped, and claws tore at the grass. None of the other mares wanted to abandon Geselle as she lays helpless on the ground. A trechor could come upon her and kill her in her weakened state. Rydor noting the herd's confusion, took charge, and made the difficult decision.

With teeth snapping and paws giving warning strikes, the stallion ran circles around the herd until they were all facing in the direction of safety. Driving the pack forward, Rydor continued to bully the mares and their offspring until they all were racing away from the meadow where Geselle now lay alone and vulnerable.

The herd's safety was paramount, and Rydor knew he must protect the many and sacrifice the two, even though Geselle was his favorite, and she was giving birth to her first foal. Giving one glance back at the birthing mare, Rydor continued nipping to drive the other mares to a large cave nearby where they would be safe from the hideous, burning streaks of the red lightning bolts from the storm.

Geselle did not make a sound of protest. She knew, too, that Rydor must protect the herd at all costs. It was unfortunate that a storm approached at this time. There was no way Geselle could get to her feet as the front feet of her offspring made their appearance between her legs. Heaving and straining, Geselle pushed with all her might, and the foal's little head appeared for all the world to see. Continuing her efforts, Geselle flailed and kicked her legs as the contractions punished her body. She had no control over the spontaneous movements at this time. Wave after wave of muscular contractions continued as more and more of the tiny little body appeared. With one last muscle contraction, the foal plopped to lay on the purple grass beside his mother. Both lay on the grass, exhausted for many minutes.

Geselle struggled to get to her feet and sniffed the little colt. He was red as his father except with a gold mane and tail. He lay quietly for a few moments, exhausted from the demanding efforts his mother's body put upon him through to expel him into the world. The cord connecting their bodies remained attached. It would break naturally as Geselle moved around more.

Geselle nuzzled the little mastel and licked his little face and body. A deep rumbling purr emanated from Geselle's throat as she cuddled her newborn. The storm grew nearer, and Geselle knew the two would die here on her baby's birth day. It would be some time before her newborn son would be able to stand on his own four legs. Geselle would not abandon him to get to safety. Intuitively, she would stand guard and fight to the death to protect him from a predator. There was nothing; however, she could do to protect her colt from this approaching storm. Geselle, in her weakened state, believed the cave where the other mastels took shelter, was too far away.

Dropping to her knees and rolling onto her side, Geselle curled her body next to her little foal. She continued to nuzzle and lick his face while he searched for a nipple to suckle. Watching the sky turning darker as the storm approached, Geselle was resigned to her fate.

Trumpeting was heard as Rydor raced back to the place where he left his beloved mare. As he watched the sky, he saw the strikes of angry red lightning in the distance approaching fast. Time was not on his side.

Coming to a furious stop at Geselle's side, Rydor pawed at the mare to make her rise to her feet. Her resistance to leaving the foal made Rydor double his efforts. Grabbing the foal by his neck, Rydor gently lifted the newborn mastel in the air with his teeth. The foal dangled from the mouth of his father.

Geselle immediately got to her feet and protested. Rydor paid no attention and dragged the newborn in the direction he herded the other mastels. Geselle realized the stallion was trying to carry her baby to safety, and time was of the essence. Rapidly getting to her feet, she moved nervously beside her mate tearing the cord that attached the placenta to her foal. Mother and newborn were now separated into two individual entities.

Rydor moved more quickly, with the tiny hind legs of his son dragging lightly on the grass as the stallion increased his pace as fast as he could while carrying the foal gently between his teeth. Geselle followed dropping unexpectantly as her body gave way to strong contractions to expel the afterbirth.

Stopping suddenly, Rydor once again must decide whether to abandon his mate and take his offspring to safety or stay by her side. Geselle neighed her complaint that Rydor stopped his forward movement, and the stallion sadly carried the foal onward to safety. Geselle laid her head back onto the grass and allowed her body to proceed with the expulsion of the afterbirth.

CHAPTER TWO

Reaching the safety of the cave moments after abandoning Geselle, Rydor laid the foal onto the hard ground. Many mares came forward to sniff the newest member of the herd. The little colt struggled to get to his feet and stood wobbling on his unused legs. Falling back to the ground, the foal was content to lay quietly without attempting to stand again.

Outside the cave, a network of jagged red bolts of lightning filled the air. Rydor stood at the cave entrance deciding whether to venture out into the storm again to find his beloved mate. Looking to see that the colt was now safe and being guarded by many mares, Rydor leaped out into the threatening storm.

Geselle, upon dispelling the afterbirth, rose to her feet. Seeing the storm advancing at a rapid pace behind her, she raced, stretching her long body into a full run, hoping to make the entrance to the cave before she was pelted by the rock-hard hail that accompanied these storms. Many mastels bore the scars from the searing hail that accompanied the storms, and many perished when caught out in the open.

Running as fast as her exhausted legs could carry her, Geselle leaped upon boulders, clawing her way up the hill and to the safety of the cave. Rydor seeing her efforts to escape the storm, raced to her side. Staying on the downside, Rydor lent his strength to his mate by bracing her as she leaped from rock to rock as she made her way up the hillside to the waiting mouth of the cave.

Behind them, the hail could be heard as it pelted the grey and lavender colored boulders showering them with golden sparks. Lightning bolts followed by instantaneous loud thunder crackled in their ears, alerting them to the fact that the lightning was striking with great force all around them. With the opening of the cave only leaps away, Geselle raced into the cave with Rydor screaming in pain right behind her.

Rydor limped into the cave, with blood streaming down his vivid red hindquarters and golden tail. Sadly, searing hail pierced his rump before he made it to safety. The mares moved to make an opening into the cave where their leader dropped to the ground.

Panting and emitting moans of pain, Rydor thrashed and rolled, trying to dislodge the sharp piece of rock now embedded in his muscular hindquarters. Several mares came to his side. One mare licked the blood away to expose the gaping wound. The old matron mare extended her claws to rip at the wound, exposing the rock-hard shard of hail. With bellows of pain, Rydor strained to remain motionless, as the old mare extracted the piece of rock from his wound. The wound bled freely, and the mares licked at it until the bleeding stopped. The stallion continued to lay quietly on the hard ground, a few feet from his newborn son.

The strawberry colored mare, Geselle, stood between her newborn foal and her injured mate, torn between which to give her full attention. As Rydor, closed his eyes to get some much-needed rest, the young colt strained to get to his feet. The decision was made when the little foal nudged at the mare's belly to find his mouthful of life-giving milk.

Geselle stood in a stupor, reflecting on what should have been a glorious day. Instead, it became a day of dread. Being safe within the cave with her leader lying asleep, barely escaping death, made her both fearful and joyous that she and her colt were alive. There was a point where Geselle thought deep down that she and her colt would not survive. Only Rydor's determination to save them made it possible for Geselle and her colt to be standing in the cave at this moment. Now Rydor was in pain. He would live, and that is the only thing that mattered.

Another thought formed in Geselle's head. What should she call her new son? She knew she should wait and let Rydor name him. It should be his privilege of being the father and the herd's leader. As if her thoughts reached the stallions, Rydor raised his head and whinnied a response. The name Teetawn filled the air with his vocalizations.

Teetawn didn't stop nursing. He continued to nudge his mother's belly to make more milk drop-down for his nourishment. Geselle stood proudly as the other mares came to inspect the new baby. Several other colts and fillies came as their mothers stood in line to welcome Teetawn to the herd.

The storm passed violently, however, quickly, and the herd slowly ventured out of the cave. Rydor continued to lie on the ground as each attempt to stand caused pain. The wound remained open, and the movement made the bleeding start again.

The oldest and wisest mare put a restraining paw upon the stallion to block his attempt at rising. Food would be brought to him while he recuperated. Hour by hour, mares would bring mouthfuls of grass to the stallion allowing him to eat while remaining quiet. Geselle and Teetawn remained in the cave as well. Teetawn was making a nuisance of himself as he found he could jump and leap on his long, spindly legs. More than once, Rydor growled a warning when his son stepped on his tail or legs while he frolicked in the cave.

Geselle finally walked out of the cave with her energetic colt by her side to allow her mate time to heal without annoyance. Immediately, Teetawn ran towards another colt mastel. He, too, was a red male with a stubby little tail, and a short, fine, golden mane. Seeing Teetawn approach, the little colt arched his back and leaped straight up into the air, landing on Teetawn's back. Both colts went to the ground under the impact and rolled down the hill in a mass of long, knobby legs. Coming to a stop, the colts shook their heads, trying to clear their vision from the head over heel tumble. Slowly they got to their padded paws.

Teetawn's new playmate spotted a tree and was scurrying off at full speed. Teetawn remained in his spot for one moment, and then he followed at full speed. Teetawn stopped and watched his playmate extend his claws and pierce them deeply into the tree. Carefully, he retracted claws from one paw and placed this other paw higher on the tree, once again extending his claws to lock it into the soft bark. Gradually, the little mastel climbed up the tree to the lowest limb and sat precariously.

Teetawn mimicked the technique used by his playmate and found himself gradually climbing the tree until he, too, reached the lowest branch. Hesitantly and awkwardly, Teetawn crawled up onto the limb and sat down beside his new friend. Side-by-side, the two infant mastels viewed their new world from a different perspective.

The gentle rolling purple hills dotted with red and orange wildflowers extended an invitation for them to run for k-rods. The buttercream sky overhead with the soft turquoise clouds held no hint of the horrible storms that inflicted such pain on the lead mastel. The sun had barely cleared the horizon, and the rays were changing colors in a dramatic display of prismatic splendor. Looking beyond, dark mountains bordered the meadow where unbeknownst to the diminutive mastels, a ribbon of orange water leisurely flowed for many k-rods giving a false sense of security to any that stopped to drink.

Bringing his eyes back to the herd below, Teetawn saw a spectacular display of rich and soft colors as the mares grazed, some with colts and fillies by their side. Striping was obvious on some of the coats of the mares as dark strawberry brushed across the soft cream base color. Other mares seemed solid in color as the striping was barely discernable. The young stallions on the ground by their mothers' sides contrasted vividly with their rich red coats and splashy gold manes and tails. Two gold buds could be seen on every head as the sun reflected off the buds as the mastels dropped their heads to graze or raised them to alertly watch their surroundings. Without the lead stallion on guard, the mares and young stallions remain more vigilant than normal.

As minutes became close to an hour, the two little mastels decided to descend the tree with little knowledge as to how to do so. Should they go down backward and shimmy down or forwards with their heads looking to the ground. Since Teetawn was the last one up the tree, it was up to him to climb down first to make room for his buddy to descend.

Tentatively, Teetawn decided to shimmy back down the tree. He tried to hook his claws from one back leg into the tree. It stuck fast to the tree, but Teetawn was afraid to let go of the limb long enough to allow his other hindfoot to also grasp the tree fixedly. Half on the limb and half off, the tiny little mastel felt panic rising, and he started to bawl pitifully.

Geselle, grazing contentedly with the other mastel mares, heard her son's cry of fear. Looking around in all directions, she did not see the tiny little mastel. The loud wails were coming from above. Spotting her son clinging to a tree caused Geselle to leap into action. Finding barely enough space on the lowest limb, she jumped upon it without knocking off the other little occupant. Grabbing her offspring with her teeth, she shook him gently; thus, allowing him to dislodge his claws. Once freed from the bark of the tree, Teetawn swung sluggishly in Geselle's grasp. With one leap, Geselle was on the ground with her son safely in the grass. Geselle knew someday soon Teetawn would be as agile as the tree-dwelling gurlion with its long orange tail. Presently, the fresh mastel was clumsy and inept.

The other little mastel, who was several weeks older than Teetawn, climbed down the tree slowly. Once on the ground beside Teetawn, the little male swiped at Teetawn's hindquarters to start a new game of chase. The two were off and running in the field of grass, stretching their little legs out completely to find their top speed without a backward glance at their mothers. Catching up to each other caused a blur of fur as the two rolled head over heel somersaulting as one mass until they finally stopped with their dazzling eyes whirling unable to focus from the tumble. Once rested and oriented, the game would start again, and the two would bound off into another game of chase.

Geselle contentedly watched her son frolic with his new playmate. Her only concern at present was for her mate, who lay in the cave with a gaping wound. The bleeding stopped. The pain, however, was too great for the stallion yet to rise and renew his responsibility of guarding his herd. Younger stallions would take up his duty until he could return. Someday, these same young stallions would leave the herd in search of mares of their own.

Geselle sought out the most tender shoots of grass and grabbed mouthfuls to take to her mate. She knew he was unable to get to his paws to graze. Seeing the young mare carrying food to the cave, other mares joined in the service to their lead stallion. Soon a large pile of grass lay upon the cave floor within reach of Rydor. Raising his head and stretching his neck, Rydor begins to graze as more mares brought grass to replenish what was eaten.

Geselle gracefully walked to her colt, who was resting under a fragrant jicerian tree. A large grove of jicerian trees bordered the meadow on one side. Geselle knew a clean stream trickled through the grove, and she nudged Teetawn with her nose to get him to his paw. Geselle was thirsty, and she knew the nursing colt would not want to follow as his thirst was met by her milk. Geselle would not leave him alone. There were lessons he needed to learn. Soon he would stop nursing, and clean water would replace her milk.

When he did not make any effort to rise, Geselle used her paw to drag him from the comfortable spot he found under the tree. The young colt whined his complaint. He did not try to get to his feet. Swatting him hard on his rump, caused Teetawn to startle to his feet and tiny paws. Never before had his mother hurt him. Teetawn did not want to feel that pain again. He now knew that when his mother said to get up...he better get up.

Geselle turned and walked into the grove of trees. Overhead a troop of gurlion chattered in excitement. Geselle ignored their irritating noise. Teetawn strained his head upwards to watch the little-animated animals as they swung from tree to tree, following the progression of the two mastels heading towards the stream. Annoying as the little animals were to Geselle, she knew they would give the alarm if any danger were near.

Reaching the stream, Geselle dropped to her belly and lapped the cold, refreshing water. Teetawn mimicked his mother and fell to his stomach as well and began to lap the water. Not being thirsty, Teetawn stopped drinking and rose to his feet. Seeing a small fish swimming in the pool, Teetawn leaped into the stream to try to pounce upon the little fish. Instead of catching the fish, he managed to get his mother soaking wet with the considerable splash he caused.

Snarling a warning, Geselle got to her feet and shook her body, sending droplets of water in all directions. Teetawn, enjoying the freshwater on his warm hide, splashed merrily around in the stream, forgetting the little fish entirely until something grabbed his toe and Teetawn howled in pain. Jumping out of the water and shaking his rear foot in the air, Geselle saw the cause of her foal's pain. Attached smartly to his toe was a snapping hyddle who became incensed with the colt disturbing his hiding place amongst the river rocks. The hyddle's sharp claws were pinched tightly to Teetawn's smallest toe, and the creature locked his claws in place.

Shaking his leg did not detach the hyddle, and Teetawn bawled in pain and fear. Hopping on three legs and jerking the fourth leg did nothing to cause the hyddle to release its hold on the colt's toe. Geselle grabbed the hyddle with her teeth and bit down hard. Crunching could be heard as the hyddle was bitten in two. Before dying, the hyddle released its hold on Teetawn's toe. With Teetawn licking his injured toe, Geselle returns to fill her stomach with water. Glancing at her son, Geselle knew his injury would not cause him any serious problems.

The gurlion took up the chatter again as the two mastels retraced their steps back to the meadow. Swinging from limb to limb with long legs and prehensile tails, the gurlions seemed to mock the young mastel's pain. Teetawn limped along behind his mother, reluctant to place any weight on his painful toe. Coming to the edge of the trees, Teetawn totally forgot about his injury when he spotted his playmate. Rushing ahead of his mother, he was soon racing around in large circles beside his buddy on all four legs.

CHAPTER THREE

Subtle changes were in the wind. Weeks passed, and Rydor was back in top condition with only a large jagged scar to show that he was previously injured. No young stallion challenged him when he exited the cave, even though he was in a weakened state. Most of the young stallions were his own offsprings and respected his leadership. There would come a time when one would step up and try to take his place. It wasn't today.

Sniffing the air, Rydor decided it was time for the herd to move to higher grounds. The heat of the season would cause the purple grass to become dry soon. The meadows in the mountains would remain cooler and lush.

Slowly the stallion began to swing his head from side to side in a menacing manner to move the mares and young mastels in the direction he wanted them to go. When met with resistance, a swipe of a claw or a nip with his teeth would convince the animal to do as directed. The herd massed together and slowly started the trek towards the mountains.

Geselle called Teetawn to her side. As usual, Teetawn was playing with his buddy; the young mastel ignored her whinny. When Rydor came behind the young colt and swatted his hindquarters with his paw, claws retracted, the colt knew he was being warned. If he ignored the stallion, he would soon bear the marks of the claws. Squealing, the young colt bolted to the safety of his mother's side.

The herd walked for hours, only breaking for short periods to allow the youngsters to rest while the mares and young stallions grazed. Pushing the herd onwards, the level grounds started a gentle ascension. The going was noticeably more difficult as the day approached the evening.

Rydor halted the herd on a small level plateau. The herd dropped to the ground to settle down to sleep. Several young stallions surrounded the mares and foals to help keep watch while the lead stallion took his rest. The dangers were not as great in the mountains as near the orange-colored river. However, predators often ventured far from their normal hunting grounds, and guards were necessary.

As a calm wind started to blow, it carried the sounds of heavy breathing as multiple animals allowed themselves to sleep. Teetawn nuzzled close to his mother's side and rested his head on her ribs. His head moved slightly up and down with each of his mother's breath taken in or expelled.

Scuttling noises could be heard by the young stallions as weilks came out from their daytime hiding places amongst the rocks. The weilks had small pointy snouts with sharp teeth and large protruding eyes. Weilks main objective was constantly looking for rodents or smaller animals to feed upon at night. The mastels were too large to be their prey; thus, the young stallions gave them little notice.

Larters were well hidden with their puce color and rounded bodies, but their pungent, musky smell gave away their hiding place to the standing guards. Strong front legs and long sharp claws, were used for scratching out fremits from under the rocks. They, too, were no threat to the larger mastels. Only the rocks being turned over and tumbling downhill caused a slight alarm when a young mastel was startled to its feet by the noise.

Rydor woke to take his turn to stand guard in the darkest time of the night. He would rest more easily when his herd was in the mountain meadow and far from any dangers. Several of the young stallions dropped to their knees, allowing them to lie down to sleep for a few hours before the leader's bugle would signal the need for the herd to rise-up and continue their journey up the mountain. Tomorrow would prove to be more difficult as the landscape would become steep and the mastels would need to leap from boulder to boulder to navigate the mountainside.

As the first angular beams of color from the rising sun reflected between the turquoise clouds, brilliant multi-color hues changed rapidly from violet to fuchsia to pink. Also, mixed in this impressive aura were colors rarely found on the planet like green, blue, and yellows.

The trumpeting of Rydor could be heard by all the mastels. Getting to their feet, none of the mastels even gave the sky a glance. The kaleidoscope of vibrant colors rarely caught their attention. It was a normal occurrence of each morning, and the mastels never wondered from whence the splendor above them originated.

As Geselle rose to her feet, Teetawn butted her belly, forcing her milk to drop. All the foals took this short opportunity to suckle. The next time could be hours from now. As Rydor pressed the mares to start the day's journey, foals trying desperately to get one more mouthful of milk found themselves being pulled off the teat as their mothers moved onward.

The occasional whinnying complaints were heard briefly. The excitement of navigating the steeper path quieted the sounds quickly. Youngsters started to lag as the herd leaped from boulder to boulder. Mothers waited and encouraged their progeny to gather themselves for the difficult leaps. When the boulders were too far apart, the mothers took their sons and daughters by the neck and leaped, holding them in their mouths. Soon, all the mothers were exhausted and in need of rest.

Rydor pressed them to make several more jumps until they came upon a wide ledge where they could rest in relative comfort and safety. Immediately, the youngsters started to nurse with little milk available. With no water accessible on the trek thus far, the nursing mothers were becoming dehydrated, and their milk supply was diminishing.

Sniffing the air, Rydor followed his nose, leaving the herd to rest. He maneuvered the curvy pathway and found a small grassy area with a cave opening. Inside the cave, the stallion saw a large pool of fresh water. Moving closer to the pool, Rydor bent his head down to drink and found the water cool and delicious. As he lifted his head, tiny orange organisms clung momentarily to his muzzle and quickly fell back into the pool. Startled by the small creatures, but feeling no ill effects, Rydor retraced his path and called to the herd to follow him.

As the herd found grass to graze upon and water to refresh themselves, the mood lightened, and the youngsters once again began to frolic. Several of the older foals jumped into the pool and swam about until they were covered with small orange organisms. Climbing out of the pool, they shook the water off their coats, and the tiny creatures fell off, leaping into the safety of the pool.

Rydor watched the herd relax and refresh themselves. The herd would bed down in this spot for the night. As perfect as it was, the grass would be gone in less than a week if they stayed. The higher meadow remained their destination for the duration of the hot time of the year.

In the morning, Rydor raised his head and trumpeted the command to move on. The herd reluctantly obeyed. Backward glances were seen often as none wanted to leave the cool water. The day spent at the pool was like a vacation to the herd, who was tiring from the climb. Another two days would be required to reach the high grounds, and the two days would be the most punishing. The cliffs were sheer and the boulders insecure and ready to crash down the mountainside with the least touch. Knowing which boulder to leap upon and which boulder to avoid would be the risk Rydor would take alone to secure a safe path to the top.

Going slowly and picking the best route was stressful. Rydor leaped from boulder to boulder, testing each to see if it was safe. The herd remained on a ledge waiting for the command to proceed in the footpath the stallion had shown. Finding another secure ledge, Rydor shook his head up and down, whinnied, and the herd followed his lead to the next ledge.

The great stallion completed this task several more times, finding the footing more difficult each time. Once at the top, he whinnied for the herd to follow and watched with trepidation as the mares with foals seemed to struggle with the climb. Geselle steadied her colt as they leaped from boulder to boulder. When Teetawn missed his footing, Geselle was there to grab the young mastel by his neck and pull until Teetawn's hind legs scrambled and scratched to make contact.

Hearing a scream of terror, Geselle looked down to see one foal falling mercilessly to a boulder below. His screams of terror and pain filled the mountainside. Before Geselle could look up, Rydor was slipping past her in a blur of action. She watched as the stallion landed on a boulder next to his fallen offspring. As Rydor grasped the colt's neck in his mouth, the little mastel cried out in pain. His hind leg dangled at an odd angle, and Geselle knew his limb was broken. Each one of Rydor's leaps to the next boulder was agony for the colt, and his cries stopped when he became unconscious from the pain and shock.

Lying the colt down on the ledge, others joined the pair. The mother of the colt arrived and nuzzled her offspring. Minutes passed before the colt opened his green eyes. The usual dazzling, whirling gems were now motionless and dazed. He panted and struggled to get to his feet, but fell back on the hard rock faint from the effort.

Rydor looked to the top of the mountain, assessing whether he could reach the summit with the colt in his mouth. As strong as the lead mastel stallion was, the climb would be treacherous at best and near impossible if he leaped upon an unstable boulder. Knowing he could bring down half of the mountain upon his herd, Rydor needed to decide whether to abandon the colt and keep going or to try to save the young mastel who would be able in time to survive with the use of three legs.

Uneasiness filled the herd as they pawed the hard rocks and shifted their weight from leg to leg. Only the youngest had no idea of the dilemma and used the time to drink milk from their mothers. As the injured colt tried once more to get to his feet, Rydor made the decision not to leave the brave little mastel.

Grabbing the complaining colt with his teeth once more, Rydor looked to find the shortest distance from boulder to boulder, knowing he would not be able to make a long leap with the extra weight of his son. Finding the first boulder secured, Rydor carefully chose every rock to land upon until he was safe at the next ledge. The going was extremely slow, and the sky was changing from buttercream to the deep golden hue of the sunset before Rydor reached a ledge large enough for the mastels to lie down upon for the night.

The injured colt's mother leaped behind Rydor all the way to the ledge, where she dropped down beside her colt to sleep. The colt was too exhausted to try to nurse.

The morning found the herd ready to do the final climb with Rydor waiting the extra minutes to allow the injured colt time to get nourishment. Even trying to nurse was painful for the little mastel. His sucking instincts took over as his stomach growled its complaint from hunger.

Gently grasping the colt by the neck, Rydor looked to the next boulder and started his climb to the top. By late afternoon, Rydor placed the colt down in the soft grass next to his mother. One-by-one, the rest of the herd made it to the top. A sparkling-cold stream passed through the meadow, and Rydor waited for all his herd to drink before he, too, made his way to the water. This would be their summer home away from the hot and dry heat in the lower valley. Rydor looked towards the injured colt and wondered how he would make the descend when the cold winds of winter signaled the herd's return down the mountain. For now, the herd was safe.

CHAPTER FOUR

The summer was coming to an end. The foals were no longer tiny babies; they are now strong and full of life. Little Three Legs was now able to run with his playmates, though always a few steps behind. Teetawn often stayed behind to run beside him. As the other young mastels took to the trees to test their abilities to climb to the top, Three Legs only made it to the bottom limbs. Rydor watched the frolicking colts and made the decision to take the long way down the mountainside, knowing Three Legs couldn't possibly navigate the steep cliffs.

As the first flurries of snow made their appearance in the early fall on the mountaintop meadow, Rydor started to pace nervously. It was time to gather his herd and begin the long trip down the other side of the mountain. The drop was less dramatic, in fact, it was an easy climb down. The problem was that it would take the herd to the Orange River, and the only way to get back to their winter grazing land was to follow the river for days.

Rydor shivered, thinking about the monsters who dwelled in and near the river. The herd would be in grave danger from the minute they got within k-rods of the river until they reached the borders of the winter homeland. Three Legs would never make it down the mountainside the way they arrived, and he was now too large to be carried. Rydor looked to the forest that would be the first leg of their journey home. Even the forest held dangers.

As the herd entered the narrow forest path, Rydor positioned young stallions at the back of the herd. Any attack would be met by these strong, formidable mastels. The herd blended into a mass, almost impossible to tell where one mare mastel begin, and another ended. The camouflage of stripes worked in the herds favor to confuse any predator that may try to take an individual. The vivid colors of the stallions made them stand out from the herd, making them an easy choice for a predator, who unwittingly would find itself met with a challenging match as the golden buds would transform into spiraling horns to defend. Along with claws and teeth, no mastel was defenseless, though huge savage monsters lurked in the darkness.

Rydor's keen eyes and sense of smell guided the herd through the forest. The sun was blocked by the dense foliage making the day seem more like dusk as they trudged along the narrowing path. Soon the mares no longer could travel in mass. They moved in a single file through the thick forest.

Rydor could smell the strong acidic odor the nervousness of his herd produced. Mastels enjoyed open spaces where they could see for k-rods. Tree climbing was fun for the young. The copious forest contained trees whose branches were impenetrable, crossing in a network more web-like than scattered stems and lateral forked branches of normal trees and was foreboding, lacking any pretense of fun even for the youngsters.

Skittering sideways, one mare looked to the trees where she heard sounds. Before she could react, dropping onto her back was a fierce yuari, who lived high in the trees. Its compact head, full of sharp teeth, bit down on the mare's neck while she stepped quickly to the side. The yuari's teeth raked the mare's neck. Not finding the killing hold it intended, the yuari struggled to try to take down the mare. With the trees extremely thick and the path narrow, Rydor and the other stallions found it difficult to move to the mare's aid.

All the mares simultaneously produced spiraling horns where their buds once emanated. The mare in front and behind the injured mare, immediately lowered their heads to defend their herd member. Snarling and charging at the yuari, the shielding mares continued to jab and stab while the injured mare gathered her wits to join in the attack.

Closest to the yuari, and with blood streaming down her neck, the mare clawed at the weakened yuari as he screamed his defiance at the three mare mastels making their attack. As Rydor entered the fray, the yuari tried hard to retreat to the nearest tree to make its escape. A mastel stallion with horns extended to full length could kill a yuari with one powerful stab. The yuari leaped to the trunk of the nearest tree. It found itself immediately impaled before it could scamper up to the lower branches. As Rydor retracted his horns, the yuari fell to the ground dead, mouth agape to show the razor shark weapons the stallion immobilized.

Raking their claws through the yuari's body to make sure it was dead, the mare sniffed the animal to keep its scent within their memories. From this point on, each mastel would recognize the approach of a yuari and be on guard for future attacks. As the herd moved passed the dead creature, the strange ritual of each animal sniffing or clawing at the yuari's remains continued silently and almost reverently until the last mastel passed and the yuari was savaged and unrecognizable.

The journey through the forest took on a more fearsome trip as eyes constantly looked to the branches above. Rydor quickened the herd's pace to shorten the time they would be in the dark, dense forest. Mares relaxed as they found themselves leaving the danger behind, entering a more open space. Rydor's stance became even tenser as he approached the land near the Orange River.

Moving out of the forest, Rydor found patches of grass that were edible. The herd relieved, stopped, and grazed. All were content to eat and relax except Rydor, who stood vigilantly on guard, tearing up the purple grass with his claws in a mock challenge.

Slowly, mares stopped grazing and watched the stallion whose horns were at full length and claws extended. Rydor nose lifted to sniff the air with thick black lips pulled back in a grimace. The lead stallion's red eyes whirled, spinning so fast that the color appeared sparkling black instead of red. Even the foals knew something was dangerously wrong.

CHAPTER FIVE

Mares allowed their foals to nurse, and many of the young mastels lay down to sleep restlessly. The sun was dropping out of sight, and the last rays were spectacular as they shimmered vibrantly in ever-changing colors.

Rydor knew the mares and foals were exhausted from the long trip down the mountainside. They were a long way from their winter home, and Rydor wanted to keep moving. Going near the Orange River during the day was going to be dangerous enough, being close to it at night meant a member of his herd would most likely die. He allowed his herd to settle in the grass to sleep. Sleep was not something Rydor would get until they were well past the Orange River.

Prowling endlessly around the sleeping herd, Rydor moved quietly with purpose. His keen eyes constantly searched in the direction of the river, while his nose, lifted in the air, sniffed for the horrendous smell of the river monsters.

Rydor's mind flashed to memories of being a colt alongside his majestic father. In his nightmares, Rydor could see the blurry vision of the dreaded monster coming at full charge towards the stallion. The memory remained hazy. However, the stallion's memory was that the monster was huge. Possibly, Rydor reasoned; it only seemed huge because he was small at the time. Rydor allowed himself to relax momentarily, realizing the river monsters may not be as horrible as his young memory played them out to be in his mind and dreams. Cautiously, being on guard was necessary since the monsters could be as deadly as his instincts said they were.

Occasionally, Rydor allowed himself to gather a mouthful of the lush grass. As the morning light appeared, Rydor would push the herd at a quick gait to get as far from the river as possible in one hard push. Once away from the dreaded river, Rydor would be able to eat and sleep.

As the first rays of light broke through the trees and brightened the meadow, Rydor was racing around the sleeping herd, demanding them to get to their feet. Mares and young stallions alike protested. Seeing Rydor's savage intent to get the herd moving, the mares and younger stallions quickly got to their feet. The foals protested the most as they wanted to nurse or play. Mares nipped at their babies' hips to get them stirring with the rest of the herd. The tension felt by the stallion was apparent, and no one wanted to challenge him.

The pace set by their leader was fast. If Rydor could get the whole herd past the river at a stampede, he felt their chances of survival were greater. None of the herd knew of the river monsters since Rydor never allowed the herd near the Orange River. Only because of Three-Legs, Rydor needed to get the herd frighteningly close to the river.

With a young stallion in the lead, Rydor moved behind nipping or swiping his claws at any mastel that dawdled. An occasional snarl was enough to keep the herd moving at the fast speed. Rydor could smell the putrid Orange River, and he knew they would be passing by at the only gap that would allow the herd to move north towards their winter meadows. Knowing this was the most dangerous leg of the trip, Rydor spurred the mastels on with greater determination to keep the herd running quickly through the gap and away from the dangers of the river.

Leaving several young stallions at the rear of the herd, Rydor positioned himself between the river and the fleeing herd. The other young stallions at the lead continued their rapid pace as they directed the herd along the narrow path close to the river. The flurry of fur as the herd ran close to each other, caused the herd to look like one large entity with stripes blending from one mare to the next. Only the brilliantly colored stallions were identifiable as an individual as well as the dots of color from the young male foals interspersed within the herd. If none of the mares lagged, Rydor was sure the mares would be safe from attack. The stallions and male foals would be more likely the target.

Behind Rydor, the stallion heard the burbling noises of something rising from the water. Trumpeting, the lead stallion encouraged the mares to run even faster, as Rydor turned to face the churning water as horns made their appearance from the murky depths of the orange water.

Golden horns spiraled from Rydor's buds on his head as he prepared to meet the challenge of the river monster. The beast waded slowly up from the river revealing his mass, and Rydor knew that his nightmares were not distorted. The creature was enormous with spikes along his entire body.

Rydor met his challenge in the shallows of the river, not wanting the monster to come upon dry land until his herd passed safely. Screaming a challenge, Rydor lowered his head and braced his body for an attack.

The monster, not able to get his feet totally under himself for a charge, continued to plod along the bottom of the riverbed until he was standing firmly on all four of his legs in the shallows. With a snort and head lowered, the creature charged Rydor meeting him head-on with a crashing sound that terrified the last mares as they squealed and pushed above on the path, past the two animals locked in battle.

Seeing the monster attacking their leader, several young stallions broke away from the stampeding herd to come to Rydor's assistance. With extended horns glinting in the sunlight, each stallion approached from a different direction. Their efforts were met with spikes.

Rydor's horn was deep within the hide of the monster. If he allowed his horn to recede back to a bud, he would be gored by the beast, he now was locked into battle. Pushing with all his weight and trying to drive the monster back into the river was proving to be too difficult for the stallion.

The younger stallions took turns driving their horns into small gaps between the spikes with little damage done to the monster. Rydor feeling his strength waning from the long trip from the mountains, lack of sleep and little food, found his legs slipping backward as the beast continued to push against him to get to dry land where all the mares and foals were passing.

Rydor, exhausted, found one more determined drive and gathered his strength to push the beast back into the water. As the last of the mares passed the river, Rydor snorted for the younger stallions to retreat. Rydor wanted to push the animal into the water deep enough that he could release the beast and move away from the water quick enough to be out of reach. Rydor could not do that until all the younger stallions were safely out of the way.

Snarling a warning to the last young stallion who continued to try to prod the water monster, Rydor felt his strength leaving his body. He knew he must release the monster now or be dragged into the water, where he would have no chance of winning. When the young stallion did not heed his warning to move away, Rydor had no choice but to release the monster or die.

Spiraling horns disappeared, and Rydor leaped aside as the river monster was now free to attack forward. The beast's forward momentum from the sudden lack of resistance, caused the huge, lumbering animal to fall forward on the ground. With the animal at a disadvantage, the young stallions attacked from all sides, driving their horns into small unprotected openings in the hide between the spikes.

As the dying monster's beady eyes closed, a long tentacle from yet another monster could be seen to reach out for its tail, slowly dragging the beast beneath the water where he could be consumed. Rydor shook his head and quickly looked in the direction where the herd passed by earlier.

Growling one final time, Rydor leaped in the direction of the fleeing mares and raced after them with the young stallions at his heels. The mares would not stop running for k-rods no matter how tired they were due to the fear that the monster was behind them.

Rydor needed to catch up to the herd and make them stop before the foals were run into the ground in a panic to flee the feared Orange River. Pushing with adrenalin and his last ounce of energy, Rydor passed mare after mare until he finally reached the front with the young stallion leading the stampede. Snarling and biting, Rydor turned the herd into itself until they came to an uneasy stop.

Lather from extreme exertion dripped from each mastel's body. Muscles twitched from exertion. Rydor nuzzled noses with mares and gave them reassurance that they could stop, rest, and nurse their young. Slowly the mastels started to relax, and the smell of fear diminished.

Rydor noticed that one of the young stallions who helped to kill the river monster did not return. Moving his head slowly from side to side, Rydor tried to assess what happened to the young stallion. The other stallions were unable to convey anything.

Leaving the herd to rest and graze, Rydor backed down the trail to the river. Getting closer to the dreaded orange river, Rydor sniffed to get wind of the young mastel. The stench of the river filled his nostrils. It overwhelmed his senses, and he could not detect the scent of the young stallion.

Rydor moved closer to the river, staying alert to what may come from the water or even from the trees on his side. Moving his head continuously to catch even the slightest movement, Rydor looked desperately for his offspring. In the sand near the water, Rydor spotted blood. Carefully, he came to the spot and sniffed it. It was mastel blood. There was no sign of the young stallion, not even a drag mark. Rydor looked to the water to see if he could see the tentacle that pulled the dead monster into the water. There was no evidence. Nothing was visible through the dark orange of the river.

Calling out, Rydor hoped to get a response from the young injured stallion. Looking at the trees, and back to the ground, the mighty stallion sniffed the land hoping to catch some evidence where the young stallion left the river once he was injured. Ever looking back to the river to make sure there would be no surprise attack, Rydor continued to move along the tree line looking for tracks, blood droppings, or a whiff of a familiar scent.

A faint odor caught his attention, and he moved towards it. The smell became stronger as he left the bank of the river and moved deeper into the trees. Listening intently since his vision became diminished in the darkness of the closely entwined branches full of leaves, Rydor sniffed constantly.

The crack of a fallen branch being broken brought Rydor to full alert. As his eyes adjusted to the darkness, he searched the forest for any movement. Scanning in the direction of the noise, the stallion tensed, not knowing what he might meet in the tangle of trees. He lifted his head, knowing a yuari could live comfortably in the meshwork of limbs above. Having one drop onto his neck from high above could cause his neck to be broken or his juggler to be severed. Moving cautiously, knowing an attack could come from above or from behind the next tree, Rydor proceeded towards the sound he heard.

A familiar smell affronted his nostrils. It was the smell of pain and fear. Again, the sounds of twigs breaking and dried leaves rustling drew Rydor onward slowly. Seeing a mass on the ground, Rydor stopped. The smell of pain and fear was stronger, and Rydor was sure it was coming from the form on the ground.

Standing in the darkness of the forest, Rydor watched as the animal struggled, kicking the dried leaves he lay upon. Breathing was labored, and as Rydor approached cautiously, Rydor sniffed and could make out the familiar smell of his son.

Moving quickly to the injured mastel's side, Rydor's horns filled the space in the thick forest, blocking his movement forward. Realizing his horns were not going to protect him, but hinder him in the thickened brush, Rydor retracted his weapons and moved closer to the young mastel.

Blood was oozing from the young stallion's shoulder. The wound was deep and painful. The young stallion's eyes were glazed over with pain and fear. Rydor lowered his muzzle to his son and sniffed him gently. When the young mastel showed no signs of recognition, Rydor realized his son was close to death. He could only stay by his side to try to give him comfort and to protect him while he continued to breathe.

Time passed slowly, and Rydor was uneasy. He worried about his herd. He could not leave his dying son to be eaten while he was alive. Dropping down into the leaves beside the dying mastel, Rydor allowed his own body to help warm the injured mastel. Licking the blood from the wound, Rydor knew he could offer nothing more than his body as comfort.

In the trees above, Rydor heard chirping and raised his head towards the sound. Birds this close to the Orange River seemed unlikely. The water was not clean enough for birds to drink. Rydor strained to see what kind of birds might be perched above him in the treetops.

Flittering down and landing barely beyond the reach of the mastel, a jade-colored bird twittered as it hopped around the ground. Rydor felt no threat from the small bird and watched it with some interest. The bird held a small berry in its mouth. Rydor looked around to see if he could see a bush that held berries and saw none. The little jade bird dropped the berry and pushed it with its beak toward the mastels.

Rydor watched the berry roll close to his body and looked to see if the bird was going to come close enough to retrieve the berry. Instead, the colorful bird chirped constantly and flapped his wings. Suddenly, several more jade-colored birds descended from the treetops. Each carried a berry, and each dropped the berry at Rydor's paws. Soon a small pile accumulated.

Rydor watched as the small birds continued to fly away and return with more berries until the pile was paw high. Rydor did not understand why the birds were bringing berries. One brave little bird hopped closer to the injured mastel and plucked up one of the berries in its beak and placed it on the wound. Pecking at the berry, it burst open, and juice spilled into the wound.

Rydor immediately knew what he was supposed to do. Opening his mouth, the stallion gathered the berries and chewed them until the juice was spilling from his mouth and dripping into the wound of his injured son.

The young stallion stirred for the first time and moaned in pain. Rydor stopped chewing and watched to see if he was hurting the young mastel. To his surprise, the blood stopped seeping from the wound. The blood started to clot. The young stallion's breathing started to become more regular, and his moaning ceased.

The birds flew away in mass, and Rydor laid his head gently on his son's rump to continue to provide warmth and assurance. The afternoon passed, and the night was upon them with Rydor staying alert to any sounds in the woods. He knew the river monsters became active in the night, and they were very close to the river. The smell of blood would draw the monsters to them, and Rydor would need to fight to the death to protect his son.

A flurry of activity overhead caught Rydor's attention once again as a mass of jade-colored birds swirled to a landing close to the mastels, each carrying twigs with lavender leaves with tiny coral flowers in their beaks. Soon a pile of leaves and flowers were lying at the mouth of the sleeping young mastel. Twittering and chirping, the little bird grabbed one small branch and flew right up to the mastel's mouth. Pushing the small twigs into the lips of the mastel, the bird kept prodding and pushing the leaves and flowers into the closed lips.

Slowly, the young mastel opened his eyes. Too weak to raise his head, he seemed to know that he was to eat the leaves and flowers offered. Taking the small branch between his teeth, he chewed carefully. Stopping to breathe between bites, the young mastel ate everything offered to him by the little birds and seemed to raise strength from each morsel. The little flock of birds flew away and out of sight. They returned shortly with more lavender leaves, blooms, and berries. As the young mastel continued to eat the leaves offered, Rydor chewed the berries and allowed the healing juice to flow from his lips into the wound of his son.

As darkness descended upon the dreary forest, the birds took to the branches above, and quiet cooing sounds could be heard as they fell asleep. Rydor stood to guard his son as the young mastel slept soundly for the first time.

Evening sounds gave way to howls and growls as the night creatures came out of their dens, from under rocks or dragged themselves from the river. Rydor stiffened and stood his ground, wondering from where the attack might come. One little jade bird flittered down and sat upon his back. Cooing softly, Rydor found himself relaxing. It was as if the bird was keeping watch with him.

Even though snuffling and grunting sound continued through the night, nothing came close enough to cause Rydor's horns to extend. Rydor was sure something would follow the blood trail that night.

Relieved when the ashen light of morning barely broke through the dense forest Rydor found the young mastel rising on wobbly legs. Rydor went to his son and nuzzled him. Knowing they must travel back to the herd for their own safety, Rydor pressed his son forward. The flock of jade birds flew through the branches to guide the way, each carrying a gift of branches full of lavender leaves and blooms to offer to the mastels once they reached the safety of the meadow where the herd waited.

The going was slow, and Rydor sniffed the ground often to find any traces of the blood trail that his injured son left behind the day before that may cause monsters to follow. Rydor found no trace of the blood trail at all. Instead, he found large amounts of bird droppings covering the spots where he previously smelled blood the day before. The unusual odor from the droppings completely erased any other smells.

With his limited understanding, Rydor realized the birds were more than guardians. They were their protectors, and without them, neither of the mastels would have survived the night that close to the river. Allowing the tired birds to ride upon his back was the only way he could thank them.

CHAPTER SIX

Returning, Rydor pushed the herd towards their winter grazing lands. Jittery and nervous from the stallion's absence through the night, the mares and foals followed their leader far away from the Orange River. The young stallions took up their posts at the rear to protect the herd from any monster that may have strayed from their usual hunting grounds. The injured stallion stayed in the thick of the herd for added protection even though he was growing stronger each minute from the added benefits of the leaves, blooms, and berries his guardian birds supplied.

Not until the herd was far away from the river and happily grazing on the lush purple grass did Rydor or the younger stallions relax. Putting their heads to the ground to graze was a moment of pure pleasure. Rydor took few opportunities to nourish himself since leaving the high meadows. Dropping to the ground, Rydor rolled, kicking his legs to the sky like a frisky colt.

The foals seeing the stallion rolling in the grass mimicked his actions, and before long, many long legs were wriggling and kicking in delight. Teetawn rolled to his feet and raced towards Three Legs, knocking him off balance as they tumbled in the grass. Jumping to their feet, the games began, and the horrible fears of river monsters vanished as they frolicked in the meadow.

Geselle, flighty and fearful, watched her son playing. As the colt approached the imaginary border limit of safety in the mare's mind, she called her son to halt and return to the safety of the herd.

Reluctantly, the two colts circled back and continued their play closer to the herd.

Days passed, and Geselle was finally able to graze calmly without watching her colt at every moment. Teetawn took her passivity as a sign that he could explore a bit further from the grazing herd. As dusk approached, Teetawn found himself out of sight from the herd. Sniffing the air, Teetawn caught the scent of an unfamiliar animal and walked in the direction of the unknown aroma. As the odor became stronger, Teetawn snorted to remove the scent from his nose as it was offensive.

The musky scent was strong and ripe. It hurt Teetawn's sensitive nose. Despite the offensive odor, he was too intrigued not to follow. Teetawn wanted to know what caused such a smell. He continued to sniff the air and follow the scent until he heard a gruffly, snuffling noise that stopped him in his tracks.

In the dim light, Teetawn saw a dark, compact animal digging in the rocks. Its sharp claws were apparent as it scratched and carved its way around large stones. Its small beady eyes were half-closed as if the receding light of the day was too harsh. The animal seemed determined to root out the small creature who lived under the rock, and Teetawn stood mesmerized by the action.

Trying hard to determine what the creature was that stood before him, Teetawn took inventory of other smells he knew from his short life on this planet. This animal was not a larter, even though both had long, sharp claws. The larter was larger than this creature, however, not near as offensive in smell. Weilks could also be found amongst the rocks. Teetawn knew them to be much smaller than this creature. A weilk might be the target of the excavation going on before him.

As rocks rolled left and right, rolling out of the way of the animal, a squeaking could be heard as a small animal was dragged from the safety of a boulder. Growling fiercely, the predator dragged the smaller animal out into the open where sharp claws held the prey to the ground.

A challenging snarl was heard as another one of the smelly creatures scampered to the scene. Rushing towards the first creature, a fight pursued with vicious biting and clawing, and terrible piercing cries filling the air. Teetawn, startled, turned and ran as fast as he could to find his mother and the protection she would provide from the hideous creatures.

Visibly shaking, Geselle knew her colt was frightened and raised the alarm. Rydor immediately answered with horns spiraling to the night sky. Sniffing the air, the stallion found no threat in the breeze of the wind and came to Geselle and his son to comfort them.

For several days, Teetawn stayed close to his mother's side. He was aware there were more scary creatures than the river monsters to worry about. Having no way to ask his mother what the creatures might have been, Teetawn's curiosity forced him to slip away from the herd as the light started to fade. To discover for himself what they might be was too alluring.

Gingerly walking the same path as he had several evenings earlier, Teetawn found himself near the same groupings of rocks. He sniffed and found no scent of the dreadful creature who scared him from the lower rocks. Pushing himself further, Teetawn scaled the rocks and stood upon a boulder where he could see for k-rods in any direction. Scanning his surroundings in the fading light, Teetawn waited for his eyes to adjust to the diminishing sunlight.

Not far from where he stood, Teetawn saw an opening in the rocks that suggested a cave or den of an animal. Watching carefully, Teetawn saw a dark creature emerge from the opening. His senses told him it was the same type of creature he witnessed fighting. The animal moved warily away from the cave entrance and headed towards the rocks where Teetawn stood.

Jumping lithely to higher ground without a sound on his soft padded paws, Teetawn looked for a safe perch to continue his surveillance. Spying a tree limb, the colt sprung up onto the lower limb and quietly maneuvered to a higher perch.

More creatures made their way from the cave opening. Spreading out, the animals hunted independently of each other, looking for food. Teetawn reasoned he was probably too large to be considered prey for these creatures. He was not willing to come down from the tree to test his theory. Instead, he watched and waited to see what the creatures might do.

Occasional snarls filled the air as the animals fought each other for smaller creatures to eat, as Teetawn witnessed the first time he encountered these beings. Catching glimpses of dark shadows moving around the rocks, Teetawn knew he must remain motionless to avoid detection. He waited, and he watched throughout the night.

As the first signs hinted of the morning, Teetawn watched a parade of creatures scampering back into the dark cave to escape the burning rays of the approaching sun. Soft colors spread out across the sky, and not a trace of the dark creatures remained outside of the cave opening. Becoming braver, Teetawn leaped from the branch of the tree and stealthily stalked closer to the cave entrance. Listening intently and sniffing for fresh odors that may announce the arrival of one of the creatures, Teetawn grew more confident. Smelling nothing more than the lingering scent of the creatures and hearing, not a sound, Teetawn approached the cave entrance. Peering inside, he saw nothing but darkness and knew not to take another step closer.

As Teetawn started to leave, he stepped on something that crumbled under his paw. Lifting his leg, Teetawn saw pink powder clinging to his paw. Licking it, Teetawn discovered that he liked the salty taste and licked some more. Putting his head down between his front paws to the ground, the colt lapped up every bit of the crushed mineral on the ground. Sniffing to find more, the colt was gratified to find several more pieces of the mineral scattered about the opening of the cave. Eating each piece, Teetawn realized the morning was unfolding, and he had been away from the herd all night.

Running in the direction where the herd was bedded down for the night, Teetawn was met by Rydor, who gruffly cuffed him on his head as he nipped and swatted at the colt all the way back to the herd. Disobedience was not taken lightly, and the stallion was angry at his son. Teetawn rushed to his mother's side, hoping for protection from his boisterous sire. He found only angry growls emitting from her throat as well. Taking another cuffing, Teetawn shrank away to find comfort in his playmates.

Three Legs inhaled the unfamiliar scent on Teetawn's mouth and licked at Teetawn's lips to taste the pink powder that clung to his playmate's mouth. Continuing licking, Three Legs begged for more. Teetawn had no way of telling Three Legs what the powder was and where he got it.

The day was spent with Three Legs and the other foals far away from their mothers. Teetawn did not wish for another cuffing. As the daylight lessened, Geselle walked towards her colt and pressed him to stay near for the night. Teetawn looked towards the rocks and boulders and wanted more than anything to slip away. His mother watched his every move all night long.

It was days before Teetawn could slip away again. This time Three Legs was right behind him. The young colt remembered the pink powder and wanted more. Walking softly, Teetawn showed Three Legs the way to the caves and where he found the pink powder. Sitting upon the high perch of the tree, the two colts waited impatiently for the vicious animals to leave the caves as they seemed to do each night. Once the colts were sure all the creatures had left the cave, the two jumped down and ventured quietly to the opening outside of the cave. Putting their heads to the ground, they sniffed for the pleasant odor associated with the mineral. Finding several pieces, Teetawn and Three Legs devoured them greedily.

Not wanting to be chastised again, the two ran back to the herd at a full run before the night was totally upon them. Rydor nor Geselle didn't seem to notice that the colts were gone. Relieved, the two colts settled down side by side for the night.

CHAPTER SEVEN

Three Legs and Teetawn craved the pink mineral. The watchful mare's eyes made it difficult to leave the herd again for many days. A time came when many of the mares were starting to foal. The other mares were excited about the new arrivals, and their attention was on the upcoming births. The stallions' attention, too, was averted. They all stood guard, knowing that the mares and newborn foals would be easy targets for any predators lurking in the forest.

With maternal eyes on the newborn foals, the two young mastels slipped away into the evening shadows. Excited for the prospects of finding more minerals at the entrance to the cave, Teetawn and Three Legs leaped from boulder to boulder up onto their usual perch in the tree. Watching the cave-dwelling creatures leaving to find food made their cravings for the mineral intensified. It was only a matter of moments before they could go down and scavenge for the pink mineral.

Watching closely, Teetawn was about to jump down to the ground from the limb when one last creature emerged, looking backward into the mouth of a cave emitting a piercing warning snarl to two smaller creatures. To Teetawn's surprise, he received mental pictures from the yowling complaints of one of those smaller creatures.

'Mommy, I'm hungry. I want to go hunting with you,' came a whining complaint. The yowling was met with a snarl and a bite on the flank by the older, larger creature. Teetawn knew instinctively that the larger one was the mother of the smaller two creatures.

As the last adult creature was out of sight, Teetawn and Three Legs gingerly walked to the opening. As Three Legs sniffed to find the mineral spread out upon the ground, Teetawn poked his head into the cave. Small snarls emanated from within.

"You better not come in here, or I will eat you!" came sounds accompanied by the mental pictures of the same little creature.

Hearing this challenge within his head, Teetawn answered. "You can't eat me because I am bigger, smarter, and faster than you."

Silence. Teetawn mentally reached out again. "I can understand what you are thinking? Why?"

A small dark creature came forward into the entrance to gaze upon the mastel. "What are you?" the creature asked.

"I am a mastel. What are you?" Teetawn sent out to the little creature.

"I am a griswell, and I am hungry! Mommy won't let me go hunting because she says I am too young, and it is dangerous to go out of the cave. I don't want to wait until she comes home to eat. I want to eat now!" demanded the little griswell.

"If I bring you something to eat, will you bring me more of the pink mineral?" answered Teetawn.

"If you bring me meat, I will," projected the little griswell.

Turning away from Three Legs, Teetawn trotted off to the trees. He remembered seeing gurlion flitting around in the treetops. Now, as an experienced agile tree climber, Teetawn was sure he could grab one. Three Legs, having devoured every morsel, and wanting more, followed Teetawn half-heartedly, looking back in hopes he would see one final piece of the mineral lying on the cave entry.

Sitting at the bottom of the tree, Three Legs watched as Teetawn leaped from branch to branch until he cornered a gurlion. Nabbing it in his teeth, Teetawn dropped to the ground and raced back to the cave entrance with Three Legs hot in pursuit.

"I brought you meat. Where are my pink rocks...I mean...mineral?" asked Teetawn.

Both little griswells came to the opening, one pushing the pink minerals towards Teetawn. Piles of mineral lay before Teetawn. Three Legs looked confused.

Teetawn pushed the gurlion towards the little griswell who eagerly jumped upon the dead animal, snarling a warning to his sibling not to try to get any of it.

"It's mine. My mastel brought it to me. Not you!" Snarling a warning, the little griswell continued. "Mine...mine...you ask that other mastel to bring you...your food and leave my food alone."

Three Legs was startled when he heard a voice in his head asking for food. Looking to Teetawn, he saw him greedily eating the pink mineral the griswell cub pushed towards him.

Searching everywhere for why he saw visions in his head of a griswell wanting him to bring a gurlion, Three Legs became aware that the hungry little animal was staring at him keenly.

Three Legs vocalized a muffled sound of confusion until he realized this little animal was communicating with him. He wanted food, just like Teetawn supplied for his sibling. Moving towards the tree, Three Legs sprung to the lower branch, faltering a bit he managed to succeed in catching a small gurlion in his jaws. Returning with the prey, Three Legs dropped it on the ground, where he found a pile of pink mineral waiting for him. The two greedy little griswell cubs dragged their food deeper into the caves for their safety and the protection of their bounty without even a goodbye.

Teetawn and Three Legs were surprised to find that they could communicate silently with the little griswells. Unexpectedly, the realization that they too could visualize each other's feelings when Teetawn thoughts indicated 'they must return to the herd quickly.' Three Legs simultaneously completed Teetawn's feelings by expressing 'before we are missed.' The two ran side by side with a new glee in their hearts. Their minds, feelings, and thoughts were one. They could sense each other's thoughts. They knew what the other was thinking.

"Watch out for that tree limb!" Three legs visualized as Teetawn raced forward without looking where he was going. The thrill of connecting minds with his buddy was euphoric and made the mastels careless.

Barely missing having his head knocked hard by the low hanging limb, Teetawn snorted his gratitude, and the two continued running back to the herd. No one missed them as the herd circled several mares who now stood nursing their newborns. Giving each other a knowing glance, the two young mastels joined the herd to look on in awe at the newest members.

'Silly looking little mastel,' thought Three Legs to Teetawn.

'At least it has four legs,' joked Teetawn.

Leaving the herd to lie down in the grass with their heads together, Three Legs indicated that it was going to be hard to explain to the other mastels that they ate a pink mineral, communicated with griswells, and can also communicate with each other mentally. Teetawn snorted again and indicated it would be impossible for any of the other mastels to understand on any level. They would need to continue sneaking out in the evenings and not get caught.

Three Legs' final thought to Teetawn was 'maybe, just maybe, for the benefit of the herd we should get caught.'

CHAPTER EIGHT

Intense growls met the young mastels as they ventured close to the opening of the cave. The little griswells left piles of pink mineral crystals laid out at the entrance and were fighting for dominance as to which griswell would receive their gurlion first. Barred teeth and snapping jaws seemed almost comical when the young griswell cubs displayed their aggressive behavior. Their odor intensified as glands from beneath their tails emitted a foul slime.

Teetawn and Three Legs stayed back watching the scrapping of the sibling griswells. Each mastel carried a recently killed small animal in their mouths.

"We aren't coming closer until you stop fighting," Teetawn announced mentally to his bonded griswell. "You both stink badly, from your aggressive play, and the odor hurts our noses."

Immediately the two griswell cubs stopped their tussling. Food was far more important than the territorial disputes they were displaying. Backing slightly from the piles of mineral, each griswell seemed almost docile as they awaited their food.

The mastels dropped the food, and each griswell rushed forward, grasping the small animal into their jaws and backed quickly into the opening of the dark cave. Contented mews and ferocious growling were heard as each griswell tore their food into pieces to be eaten while guarding it against their sibling.

Stepping out from the trees, Rydor snorted his displeasure at what he had seen his offsprings doing. Lowering his head, with his ears pulled back to show anger, he swung his head menacingly from side to side. Rydor attempted to herd his two willful young sons back towards the herd and away from the cave.

Teetawn refused to move. Standing his ground, he used his muzzle to push some of the fragile pink morsels towards the stallion. Throwing his head up in surprise, Rydor stred at the little pink rocks on the ground and wondered what Teetawn was trying to convey.

Teetawn took one piece between his teeth, and as the crystal broke into powder, the colt licked his lips in great pleasure. Once again, he pushed several rocks with his muzzle towards the great stallion.

Rydor used his paw and gently pulled one of the small pink crystals closer to him. Sniffing it, he raised his head to look at his son. Teetawn grasped another crystal and repeated the operation. Joining in, Three Legs pushed a few of his coveted prizes towards his sire as well.

Rydor sniffed once again, and then he allowed his tongue to softly lick the surface. Tasting the sweet and slightly salty morsel, Rydor gently grasped the whole crystal and let it break apart in his mouth. Savoring the taste for only a moment, Rydor gobbled the remaining crystals that were placed before him.

A thought popped into his mind. "What is this delicious rock?"

Rydor was alarmed when another thought slammed into his mind that was not his own. "It tastes wonderful, doesn't it, Father?"

Startled by the sound in his head, he moved backward for several steps. Rydor snorted and allowed his spiraling horns to protrude from his forehead. Sure, that some creature was about to pounce on his back, Rydor swirled in a defensive circle to see from where the danger would come.

Chuckling sounds came from his two sons, and Rydor glared at each one. "You can hear us in your mind, can't you?" Teetawn asked.

Rydor shook his head to clear it and stamped his paws in confusion. This was something he never felt before in all his years living on this planet. It was frightening to have another's thoughts invade his mind even if it was his own son's.

"Why can I feel you in my mind?" Rydor demanded of his sons.

Three Legs stepped forward and tried to close the gap between himself and his sire. Rydor found himself moving backward with each step Three Legs took towards him.

"Papa, this is a good thing, not a scary thing. Teetawn and I can communicate with each other, and only good has come from it. It is wonderful, and now you can hear our thoughts in your head. Think, if all the herd could hear each other's thoughts, you could tell the herd quickly when there is a danger, and everyone would know at the same time." All these thoughts were expressed as pictures showing a storm coming and Rydor telling all the herd at once to flee for shelter without having to nip and bite to move the herd.

Rydor stopped backing up as he processed the thoughts whirling through his head. "But how can this happen?" the stallion inquired.

Teetawn moved two more crystals close to his father and mentally showed how he and Three Legs discovered the minerals-- how they hunted for food for their griswells and how the griswells brought minerals in exchange from the caves. Rydor snorted several times in displeasure as he was shown the griswells and his sons killing small animals for the greedy little beasts.

Torn between wanting to show his displeasure and wanting to eat the delicious minerals that Teetawn offered, the minerals won out, and Rydor lapped up the powder that formed when the fragile mineral was pushed too hard. Sniffing the ground to see if he could find any trace of the mineral, Rydor raised his head and stared hard into the dark entrance of the tunnel.

"Can we go in and get more?" Rydor visualized himself marching into the dark cave and eating all the pink mineral on the ground.

Three Legs allowed his mind to show how his bonded griswell needed to go deep down into the cave and dig out the precious treats. Teetawn joined the mental connection with his visualizations of the nasty little beasts willingly bringing minerals in exchange for the small animals that they could not get by themselves.

The darkness completely settled around the three mastels, and Rydor indicated it was time to return to the herd. His mind was full of images of his sons, and he was weighing the unique benefits against the natural order. Picturing his mastels hunting small game to feed griswells in exchange for the mineral was difficult to grasp. Would being able to communicate with the whole herd at once be enough of a benefit to risk mastels hunting for the cave-dwelling beasts? Would it be worth changing the way the herd lived, and for that matter, how the other creatures in the forest lived autonomously, for the many past generations?

The two young mastels did not intrude on their father's thoughts as they raced back to the safety of the herd. They knew their father lived in their world for many more years than they had, and this new idea would be harder for him to accept.

As they saw the herd in the meadow, Three Legs and Teetawn broke away from their father. Each touched their nose with their mothers' nose, wishing they could communicate the way they could with each other and now their father. How fun it would be to show their mothers what they were doing all day long and to receive her approval in their mind. The young mastels lay down in the grass, exhausted from the day, and fell asleep.

The next day Rydor stayed far away from the two young mastels. Teetawn and Three Legs spent the day together playing far from the other young mastels. Neither thought it was fun to spend time with the others now that they could communicate with each other. The only fun part of being with the other mastels were teaming up against them when they played. Soon the other playmates grew tired of the tricks Three Legs and Teetawn would play on them, and the two were excluded.

Neither Teetawn or Three Legs cared if they were excluded. The games of racing to the top of the boulders were no longer a challenge as Teetawn showed Three Legs the easiest way to the top before the other young mastels could figure it out. Teetawn, like his father, was proving to be athletic and clever. He figured out every obstacle long before anyone else, and he passed on his findings to his buddy. The other mastels resented the fact that Three Legs, the weakest of all the mastels, could figure out how to navigate the trees, boulders, and cliffs far ahead of the others. None knew that Teetawn was showing Three Legs pictures in his head.

As evening approached, Teetawn and Three Legs looked for Rydor. They were afraid the stallion would stop them from venturing back to the cave. As they started to slip away from the herd, they found Rydor waiting along the rarely used path for them in the trees.

"Okay, show me what you do to bond with a griswell?" Rydor commanded.

Teetawn and Three Legs bolted into action. They raced to the treetops and chased gurlions through the branches to catch their prey. With the small animal dangling from their mouths, they leaped back to the ground and encouraged Rydor to do the same.

Knowing he needed to fully understand the implications, Rydor swiftly bounded into action and returned in a flash with an adult gurlion, several times larger than either of the animals that his sons captured. Standing by their side, he showed them he was ready for the next step.

The three raced towards the caves and arrived as the mother griswell was snarling her goodbyes to her offsprings. Seeing the adult mastel coming from the forest, the adult griswell's raucous barks of alarm sounded, and she expected her two cubs to move rapidly into the cave for protection. Instead, her offspring raced to meet two of the smaller mastels enthusiastically.

"Mama, these are our friends. They are bringing us food in exchange for the pink mineral. Isn't it wonderful? We don't need to go out of the cave and be in danger. Our food is brought to us."

The adult griswell's hackles stood on end down her neck and spine. She was unsure as to whether to attack or stand her ground and watch. One of her litter raced into the cave and returned with crystals carried gently in its mouth. Dropping them in front of one of the smaller mastels, the mother griswell was surprised to see a gurlion placed on the ground in front of her cub.

Rydor came forward carefully and placed the larger gurlion within reach of the mother griswell. Suspicious but hungry, the adult griswell snatched the meat and retreated to the cave opening where she was heard to rip, tear, and crunch bones.

"I thought she was supposed to bring me minerals," Rydor said in his mind as he looked to his sons, who were happily eating the minerals placed before them.

"You should consider reaching out to the mother griswell with your mind and see if she will accept you as her bonded friend," Three Legs said without looking up from his tasty treat.

Rydor tried picturing himself, bringing more food in exchange for the pink mineral. He waited for some response in his head and was about to give up when a picture flashed suddenly in his mind. He saw the adult griswell heavy with litter and not wanting to go hunting. He saw himself bringing gurlions, glemee, and other prey to the cave and piles of pink mineral waiting for him.

Coming from the depths of the cave, the mother griswell returned with a large mouthful of pink mineral. Placing them on the ground in front of Rydor, the stallion knew he was bonded to this griswell for life. As he ate the mineral, he was surprised to feel the griswell rub against him while making a strange little purring sound. Rydor felt intense pleasure and warmth that penetrated his soul. He needed to understand more about this new experience.

.

CHAPTER NINE

Days passed with three mastels slipping away off into the forest each night. Rydor posted young stallions on watch while he and his two sons went to the caves. The bond between the three griswells and the three mastels was strengthening with each day. Rydor was privy to the feelings his beloved mother griswell felt for her son and daughter as the mother griswell could feel Rydor's pride in his sons.

Searching for an image to visualize the mother griswell, Rydor's bondmate, he came up with Flint. The mother griswell's coat gleamed like the hardened black rock that could be found along paths on the rocky cliffs. Rydor pictured Flint anytime he wished to convey his griswell to his sons. They, in turn, kept mental pictures for their griswells as well. Three Legs little female griswell was imaged as Sunshine, even though she never ventured out into the bright light. However, Three Legs felt her personality was much more bright and cheery than her brothers. Teetawn agreed that his male griswell was far from cheery in any respect. Teetawn pictured him as a marshy bog. Bog became the name Teetawn gave to him when communicating with his father or Three Legs about the bad-tempered little griswell.

Once back with the herd in the late hours of the night, the three mastels continued their communications with snorts, and what often sounded like laughter. The other mastels found the new comradery odd even for sire and offspring.

Several older stallions vied for the position of the head stallion when Rydor would leave each night. Upon return, Rydor was angered; he needed to break up these fights between them. Teetawn sent a mental picture to his father, where all the herd could communicate together. 'Either, you could stop fights from afar, or you could leave one stallion in charge while you were away. You would always know what was going on with the herd without having to be with them', Teetawn conveyed through these mental images.

Rydor contemplated his son's reasoning and found it valid. Rydor didn't know how to cause bonding between the other cave-dwelling beasts and a large portion of his herd. There were fewer griswells than mastels--not all would bond. Could the griswells be convinced of providing enough minerals for the whole herd? Many thoughts traversed Rydor's mind as he tried to problem solve the dilemma.

Crashing images into Rydor's brain, seemingly out of nowhere, arose a distress call from Flint. She was picturing a griswell badly injured lying at the cave entrance, bleeding to death. Rydor startled visibly, causing the little jade bird to fluttered from his perch on the stallion's back, and fly to a low branch on a nearby tree. Without another moment's hesitation, Rydor leaped into a full-out run towards the cave, leaving Teetawn and Three Legs the mental picture he received.

Coming to a halt at the cave, Rydor saw the injured griswell on the ground, as Flint portrayed in his mind. The other griswells were in the cave hiding from the glaring sun. Flint's pain from being in the sun was evident, yet she stayed by this griswell showing Rydor he was her mate and the father of Bog and Sunshine. Pleading for help, Flint mewed pitifully.

Rydor paced, not knowing what to do for the injured griswell. To make matters worse, the little jade bird kept fluttering in his face, distracting him and making him uncomfortable. Rydor tossed his head, trying to make the bird fly away until finally, Rydor realized the bird was trying to get his attention. She flittered off a few rods away and chirped frantically. When Rydor took steps closer to the bird, the jade bird would fly a bit further until Rydor understood he was to follow the bird.

The little bird flew quickly with Rydor gathering his muscles in a burst of speed to keep pace. Rydor leaped from boulder to boulder and bounded over the ground quickly until the bird came to a stop on top of a fallen log.

Puzzled, Rydor wondered if the little bird led him on a merry chase until the bird pecked on the log, and several insects scurried out of the open end. One insect crawled to Rydor's toe and bit down hard and would not let go. Inspecting the insect, Rydor saw that he cut his toe while steering around sharp rocks. The little insect was holding the cut together.

Dawning on the mastel what the little bird intended, Rydor carefully lifted the log in his mouth, keeping it as level as possible, he rushed back to the cave entrance. The griswell remained where he was dragged by his fellow griswells. His breathing was unsteady, and the pool of blood grew significantly.

Lying the log down upon the ground with a thump, insects scattered out of the log. Quickly they zeroed in on the dying griswell with speed. Locking their jaws on the wound, the insects closed the wound, and the bleeding ceased.

While the insects were doing their job, the little jade bird pecking on the ground found the pink mineral much to his liking. Keeping one eye on Rydor and the griswell, the little bird continued to peck up all the residual minerals left behind from the comings and goings of the griswell band.

Chirping happily with a song in the air, Rydor could make out a word associated with the insects. 'Feigons, feigons, feigons,' chirped the little bird.

Rydor understood that the little bird had a name for the insects. He called them feigons. Rydor realized he could understand the little jade bird and reached out to thank him. Flint also wanted Rydor to convey her appreciation that the bird saved her mate.

"What do you call yourself, little jade bird?" Rydor tried hard to convey in mental pictures.

The bird sent out a blurred picture of himself and chirped a response. *Jade Harbinger* would be hard to form into a picture. Thus, Rydor continued to use the picture of a little jade bird when referring to his newest bond friend.

"Can anyone else read your thoughts?" the big stallion wanted to know. The bird chirped a negative. The little bird conveyed to the big stallion that this special bond was between them alone. The rest of his flock communicated fine with chirps and whistles. They had no need for the pink mineral. The little bird liked Rydor, that was all, and wanted to stay close to him. He pictured himself happy upon the back of the stallion even when his flock flew away.

Testing his ability to bond with the little bird, Rydor pictured the healing berries. The little jade bird immediately took flight and was gone in a flash. Returning within minutes, carrying a branch full of berries, the bird laid them at Rydor's paws. Flying to his perch on the highest golden bud on Rydor's head, the little jade bird continued to sing a melodious song, signaling he did something good for his new friend.

Rydor looked down upon the motionless griswell. Reaching out to Flint, Rydor showed juice from the berries having healing qualities. Knowing that Flint received his mental instructions, Rydor took the next step to help the griswell. Pulling Flint's injured mate closer to the tunnel of the cave with his claws retracted, Rydor pulled him out of the blazing sun. The other griswells could now reach him without experiencing pain from the brilliant sunlight and continued pulling the injured griswell into the safety of the cave. Hearing the scuffling and scrambling of many feet, Rydor knew that griswells were coming to do just that. Rydor backed off, allowing the rescue. Flint would now do what was needed to help her mate. Rydor's work was done.

Walking quietly through the forest back to the herd, Rydor was amazed by what happened that day. Beasts, insects, birds, and mastels worked together for the better good. The pink mineral would be necessary for a better life for the mastels. Rydor's thoughts worked on a plan to get more mastels bonded with griswells.

CHAPTER TEN

Rydor was back with the herd and on the watch when Flint sent a message that her mate was conscious and doing better. She conveyed that she would like Rydor to bring two prey animals this evening since her mate would be unable to hunt for himself for quite some time.

Rydor responded with a mental picture of himself bringing enough food for both. Rydor, ever curious, asked if Flint's mate told her what happened to him. Flint immediately stormed Rydor's mind with sequences vividly animated; it was as if Rydor was there himself.

Flint showed her mate in his usual hunting grounds with his eyes half-closed. Even the moonlight or starlight was painful for the griswells. Using their super sense of smell for hunting, and keen hearing, most griswells were able to find prey amongst the boulders and dig them out without incidence. However, more often than the griswells liked, injuries or death occurred when larger creatures caught the griswells unprepared to defend themselves. This is what happened to Flint's mate.

Flint showed her mate, Greyble, digging out a weilk, who took refuge in a deep crevice of a rock formation. Intent on burrowing the rock-dwelling creature from the protection of its hole, Greyble was unaware of the yuari in the treetop above him. Without a sound, the yuari dropped from its perch to Greyble's back, sinking its teeth deeply into the griswell's shoulder blades, barely missing the spinal cord. Infuriated by the pain, Greyble flipped to his back and clawed frantically at the underbelly of the yuari, disemboweling the creature and leaving it for dead. Greyble dragged himself to the mouth of the cave, where he collapsed from loss of blood.

The powerful stallion conveyed his plan to his bond friend and showed how the mastel and griswell could benefit each other. If the mastels, who were able to hunt in the dark or daylight without pain to their eyes, would hunt for meat for the griswells, would the griswells supply the pink mineral for the mastels allowing communication with each other directly?

Flint showed the other griswells as mean, nasty, irritable creatures who barely got along with each other. Rydor countered with how well her cubs and she got along with Rydor's sons and himself once they bonded. Picturing each griswell bonded with a mastel in a like friendship may be the answer, Rydor thought. Possibly, since the two creatures were not natural enemies, bonding may be more feasible.

Flint's plan became obvious to Rydor as she showed the time of evening when the griswells left the caves in search of meat. If Rydor had as many mastels as there were griswells, each waiting at the mouth of the cave with meat, Flint was sure that the griswells would be willing to go into the cave and bring back as many minerals as they could carry in exchange. Flint expected only two or three nights of exchanging food for minerals before bonding would take place.

Rydor, excited at the prospect, communicated to Flint that her idea would be put into action that very night. Now, Rydor pondered how he could communicate what he wanted the mastel herd to do without the telepathy he now enjoyed with his sons. Reaching out to Teetawn and Three Legs, a plan was hatched. It would only work if Rydor could impose his will upon the chosen mastels for this experiment.

By mid-afternoon, Rydor was chasing the younger stallions and some of the older mares into the forest. The mares with foals would continue to graze or nurse their young in the meadow. The mastels being herded were confused and anxious, not understanding why the mighty stallion was nipping at their rumps to move them towards the woods.

Once in the woods, Rydor told his two sons to take to the trees to catch gurlions as the stallion stayed on the ground to make sure the mastels were watching. As Teetawn and Three Legs descended with the gurlions in their mouths, Rydor nipped and bit at one mastel after another to take to the trees. Soon most of the mastels were in the treetops, puzzled as to what they were expected to do.

Once again, the two young mastels climbed to the treetops snatching their prey until one after another mastel seemed to understand what they should do. As the mastels descended the trees with prey in their mouths, Rydor once again nipped at their rumps until the herd was heading towards the caves.

Reaching the cave opening, Teetawn, Three Legs, and Rydor each spread out and dropped their offering on the ground. Looking at the herd, Rydor shook his head and vocalized his dominance to make sure each mastel, in turn, did as Rydor demonstrated.

First, Flint emerged from the cave with her offsprings. Rushing to the meat, the three griswells deposited a large mouthful of minerals besides the meat. Other griswells timidly exited the cave and understood quickly that the meat was for them. Looking at the minerals Flint and her children deposited beside the meat, each griswell raced back into the cave to do the same. Soon only piles of the pink mineral were lying upon the ground as the greedy griswells grabbed their meat, scrambling back into the comfort of their dark cave.

Rydor lowered his head as did his sons and ate the minerals. Each mastel stepped forward to a pile of mineral and sniffed it suspiciously. Watching their leader lick his lips in appreciation of the delicious taste, the other herd members ate the minerals with relish.

The mastels sniffing the ground and wanting more, were unhappy when Rydor once again pushed the herd to leave the area. As the mastels raced back to the rest of the herd, Rydor went in search of a glemee to present to Flint for her mate. Sending a message to his new bonded friend, that he would be back shortly with more food, Rydor turned and headed towards the high ground where the glemee could be found.

Standing grouped together, the glemee like sheep placidly grazed on the lush purple grass. Rydor found it easy to pluck one glemee from the flock. Carrying it back to the cave, he found Flint waiting for his return. The glemee, much larger than a gurlion, would feed her mate for several days. By the time that more food would be necessary for her mate, Flint envisioned the need for another mastel from the herd to bond with Greyble.

Rydor only knew of one other stallion available to bond. This stallion left the herd several days ago, wanting to find his own mares to form a new herd. Rydor knew this stallion would be trouble. Already Rydor fought him twice for dominance. Rydor was not willing to search him out and try to bring him back to the herd. That meant that one of the nursing mares would need to join the hunters. Watching his herd, Rydor decided which one of the mares would be the best candidate. Geselle, his favorite, even though having barely given birth to Teetawn's new sister, was his choice. She would join the hunt as soon as Greyble improved.

CHAPTER ELEVEN

Morsian enjoyed his solo excursions into the unexplored parts of Aztara. He was many rods away from the factory city, where he invented tools and equipment for the citizens of his planet. The holidays were a special time when he could put on his backpack and traipse into the unknown parts of the planet. Until now, Morsian never crossed the mountains in the direction of the Orange River, where one scientist warned him not to ever approach. Tales of monsters with tentacles and beasts with spines were horrible but intriguing to Morsian. Knowing there was not enough time to go as far as the Orange River on this holiday, Morsian spent the time studying the wildlife and flora in the western valley. Daylight began fading with its spectacular display of colors dramatically changing second by second, Morsian watched the beauty while setting up his camp. Morsian was never tired of the display of rays from the setting sun as the colors changed from purple to red to gold to orange then shades of green and teal before becoming dark. It seemed the colors never were the same any night but presented a kaleidoscope show that entertained him until the last ray dimmed out of sight. Picking up his new invention, Morsian zoomed in on that last ray.

This instrument was one of Morsian's favorite invention of his own design that allowed him to watch faraway places as if he was close. Special thermal imaging allowed him to even watch the movement of wildlife at night. Scanning the valley below, Morsian caught sight of a large herd of animals. Their movements were graceful and powerful. Time passed with his Allsight instrument to his eyes as he watched the animals stop moving and settle down for the night. All but one large animal slept. The one largest animal stood above the herd, turning his head often, probably watchful of any danger. Morsian was sure this was the boss's animal.

As his eyes tired from constant vigilance on the herd of animals, Morsian finally crawled into his tent to sleep. His last thought was that he would move closer to this group of animals, thus allowing him to observe them better in the morning.

The daylight interrupted his sleep, and Morsian yawned and stretched. He crawled out of his tent and prepared a cold breakfast of an assortment of grains, nuts, and berries that he placed in his backpack for a quick and easy meal. Morsian knew if a pool presented itself, he would find fish for another meal. If not, rehydrated food would work.

Finding a path down from the plateau proved difficult with the backpack. It was mid-morning before Morsian reached the foot of the hill. Morsian wanted to find another place to camp closer to the herd. It needed to be high enough that he could observe them without being seen or smelled by the animals.

A perfect spot presented itself. It was on higher ground than the valley where the animals grazed. It was also tree-covered with sweet-smelling bark from the jicerian tree which concealed his presence. Morsian was pleased with his new campground. By early afternoon, his tent was pitched, and the Allsight instrument was handy. Seeing a tree with a strong limb, Morsian decided the higher perch would be perfect for his afternoon observations. Taking a notepad with him, Morsian climbed the tree and settled himself into a comfortable crook.

Morsian sketched the animals and wrote descriptions beside each drawing. Without colored pencils, Morsian used expressive words like fiery red, soft beige, strawberry, striped, golden buds, golden manes, golden tails, sharp claws, strong jaw with a long muzzle, and erect ears. Along the column, he added words like intelligent, alert, and social. He also added a question...'Are they dangerous or harmless?' He would need to find this out.

As the afternoon settled into the time before dusk, Morsian watched as the leader herded most of the animals, and they left as a group leaving mother and infants to graze. Watching the powerful animals sprint out of sight caused Morsian great anguish. He wanted to know why they left in a rush and where they were headed.

Dropping from the tree, Morsian ran in the general direction of the herd. Moving quickly through the cover of the jicerian trees, Morsian heard in the distance the chattering of a large troop of tree-dwelling animals from high above. The small animals moved in fear as a louder crashing noise followed. Taking cover as best as he could, Morsian watched the trees fill with the grazing animals he was observing and now followed. Each scampered as easily through the trees as the little beasts they chased until the smaller animals were cornered and caught. Morsian recognized the prey as gurlions. Surprised by this seemingly uncharacteristic action of a grazing animal, he now had no idea of how to describe and catalog this apparent meat-eating predator.

Morsian, amazed at the sight of meat between the larger animal's teeth, found himself puzzling why grazing animals were hunting meat. From his position hidden behind a larger, faraway tree, he watched the muscular, graceful animals drop to the ground, each carrying a small gurlion. As the herd raced off with the gurlions dangling in their mouths, Morsian, once again, took up the pursuit.

As the forest started to thin, Morsian slowed his pursuit. He began sneaking from tree to tree to hide from the animals that stopped in front of a cave. Taking out the Allsight as the light of day diminished, Morsian watched in total surprise as cave-dwelling beasts exited their dwellings with mouthfuls of pink rocks. He watched spellbound as the smaller, dark beasts spat out the rocks and scurried back into the cave carrying the dead prey. Even more surprising, Morsian watched the herd animals lick up every single pink piece of rock and even lick the ground where the rocks crumbled into powder.

Morsian knew instantly that the pink rocks were not rocks at all, but minerals from the cave. Questions bombarded his mind as Morsian tried to connect the dots. Why would grazing animals kill little game and carry them to cave-dwelling beasts, which in turn provided them with minerals? Nothing made any sense to him.

As the herd animals retreated as a group, to return to the females and young, Morsian supposed he was alone. Wanting to see if there was a trace of the coveted mineral, Morsian quietly made his way down to the cave opening. Not a speck of mineral remained. Morsian was disappointed not to be able to see this mineral first hand.

Gathering his nerve, Morsian decided that he might be able to find some minerals that dropped from the cave-dwelling beast's mouths as they carried it above ground. His Allsight made it possible to see how far he could trek into the cave with the moonlight, lighting his path.

Walking slowly inside, Morsian took only one small step at a time and listened carefully for any sound of the beasts who lived within. Not hearing any scuffling or snarling, Morsian took another step and another with his eyes downcast searching for any little piece of mineral that might have dropped.

As he descended deeper into the cave, Morsian's hair on the back of his neck rose. He could hear breathing. There was no way Morsian would go deeper without more light. Backing away carefully, Morsian was almost at the cave opening when he felt a small crunch under his foot. With the added light from the moon,

Morsian lifted his foot to see pink powder that his boot must have smashed. Scooping it up in his hands, Morsian was about to leave when a crushing force hit his leg, and Morsian howled in pain.

Biting down hard on his booted ankle was one of the cave-dwelling beasts whose fierce, shrill, snarls filled Morsian's ears. Kicking and beating the beast with his fists, Morsian managed to bring his night vision instrument down hard on the beast's head, stunning the animal enough that he let go momentarily. That was all the time Morsian needed to run out into the bright moonlight, leaving the animal growling his warning to never return.

Limping as quickly as possible for fear that a whole pack of the nasty tempered little animals would follow and devour him, Morsian ran limping for his life. Reaching the perceived safety of the forest, Morsian stopped long enough to see if he was bleeding.

Relieved that his tough hiking boot took the brunt of the attack, Morsian continued to limp back to his campground. More fears wracked his brain as he crawled into his tent. What if the fearsome beasts tracked his smell along his path of retreat? What if his ankle was broken? What if…?

Trying to calm himself, Morsian breathed deeply. Once breathing normally, he became aware that his fist was clutched tightly, and he continued to hold the pink powder within his grasp. Slowly opening his hand, Morsian observed the properties of the mineral. Fine crystals were difficult to see in the darkened tent. Putting his Allsight to his eyes, Morsian tried to see the crystals better but decided the instrument was inadequate for the kind of observation he wanted. Gathering a bag, Morsian put the pink powder inside to keep it for studying when he returned home. With residual dust on his palm, he licked it off his fingers to see if it was bitter or sweet. It was amazingly sweet and a bit salty. Just that small amount was indescribably delicious, and Morsian was illogically tempted from scientific reasoning to consume the rest out of the bag where it was stored.

The rest of the night was a battle between wanting to eat the mineral and wanting to study it upon his return to his lab at home. Taking his boot off, Morsian discovered that there were no bite marks, however, his ankle was swollen. It hurt, and he wanted to take his mind off the pain. His thoughts returned to the pink mineral, and finally, the memory of how good it tasted won out, and Morsian licked up the rest of the mineral. He figured he could possibly get more if he went into the cave with a lantern and some sort of weapon. Morsian's scientific mind reasoned that this cave-dwelling creature must be light sensitive due to its tiny beady eyes and its desire to remain within the darkness of the cave. A risky plan formed in his mind as he fell asleep.

CHAPTER TWELVE

The sun was shining, the birds were chirping, and Morsian woke feeling anxious. He decided to enter the cave. His weapons were limited. He carried a knife on his belt. Looking at the short blade, he knew it would be of little use against one of those nasty creatures. The light source would help him find the mineral, and it would help to blind the creatures. Again, as a weapon, it was a weak choice, he thought. He needed something that would keep the animals away from him. His backpack yielded nothing promising.

Whittling a spear as Morsian cooked a meager breakfast, he wished he brought along his luminescence powders. He thought about making a stick that when placed on an object, it would ignite in a painful burn. If he had the chemicals needed, he would have done so. In the unfamiliar wilderness, it would take way too long to locate the three chemicals needed, if there even were sources in this area. The spear would need to suffice, along with a bright light source. Maybe that would be enough, Morsian speculated as his desire for more of the pink mineral lurked in his brain.

Morsian's ankle was swollen, where that horrible beast had bit down hard. He imagined seven or eight of those creatures swarming all over him and the damage they could do. He knew he would never survive such an attack.

'Best to go in the middle of the day when the creatures would be deep within the cavern and sound asleep,' Morsian told himself.

'Even if a guard were posted, it would be deep down a tunnel and not close to the entrance where the sunlight would burn its eyes.'

'Odd that I am craving something that I barely tasted,' Morsian thought to himself. Speaking out loud now, Morsian said, "Maybe it is addictive. Now wouldn't that be horrible if I became addicted to something that is far from where I live and is guarded by nasty, horrible beasts? Too late now to consider the consequences, I guess."

With that, ambivalent thought rolling around in his mind, Morsian gathered the items he would need and proceeded to the cave. Coming upon the entrance, Morsian gathered himself and gave himself a pep-talk about going into the dark cave armed on with a light source and a hastily made spear.

'Okay, here it goes,' Morsian thought. 'There is no turning back. You've got this Morsian. Chances are you won't encounter a single nasty creature. Come on, let's go,' and the pep-talk heightened.

Putting one foot in front of the other, Morsian tightened his grip on his spear. He held it ready to thrust if a creature should come snarling towards him. The light source was illuminating the cave, only a footstep or more in front of him. Watching and listening, Morsian inched his way deeper into the cave.

Morsian found the temperatures in the cave to be relatively cool and dry. He decided to see if it would be pitch black if he turned off his light source and was surprised by a very gentle shimmering from the cave walls. The dim light source from the walls was not enough to see very far into the cave. It gave him comfort, though, since he felt as though he would not be totally blind if his own light source should fail. With his own brighter light source in hand, Morsian swept the beam over the walls of the cave, looking for traces of any of the coveted mineral.

When the cavern split into two tunnels, Morsian decided to go to the left. Slower than before, Morsian barely took a step without stopping to listen for any sounds that meant one of those creatures was about to spring upon him. Shining the light above, below and on both sides of the tunnel walls, Morsian's attention was caught by scratches etched into the one side of the wall. Walking quietly to the spot, Morsian touched the scratches to feel how deeply they penetrated.

Taking out his knife, Morsian scratched deeper into the grooves the claws of the beasts made in the tunnel wall and was surprised to see a few pink crystals deep within. Excited by the prospect of having found a few minerals, Morsian kept scratching at the sandstone, which gave away easily.

Spiking his spear into the soft ground, Morsian placed his free hand directly below where he was digging, hoping to catch the fragile crystals before they broke into powder. Several crystals tumbled into his hands as he etched around the pink mineral to excavate it. Quickly, he placed several of these crystals into his bag. Digging a little too forcefully, Morsian saw the mineral turn to powder and cupped his hand to catch every little grain.

As his hand filled, Morsian ate it quickly, allowing his hands-free to be filled once again as he dug deeper into the little vein of minerals that he found. So, intent on getting more minerals, Morsian was unaware of the scratching sound coming closer from deeper within the tunnel where he stood.

Giving a warning growl, the griswell scurried up from the depths of the tunnel. The growl gave Morsian enough time to grab the spear from the ground. Prodding the animal to keep it at a distance, Morsian backed out of the tunnel, ever watchful of the advancing beast.

Warily the beast approached the intruder, not knowing what he was. Feeling angry and defensive of his territory, the furious creature menaced the human, making serpentine movements back and forth, trying to find an opening past the man's defense. As more growls could be heard coming from deep within the earth, Morsian knew he would soon be outnumbered. His only hope was to dispatch the one griswell and run for the safety of the sunlight before the other griswells attacked in force.

Lunging with the spear pointed at the advancing creature, Morsian impaled the griswell and dropped him to the ground. Seeing the glint of eyes reflecting off his light source, Morsian knew he must run as fast as possible.

Screaming in pain, the injured griswell was soon surrounded by many griswells. Some ran after the human who attacked a den member, and a few remained by the wounded griswell. Morsian could see the opening ahead and doubled his efforts to run hearing the snarls, grunts, and growls close behind him. Breaking out into the sunlight, Morsian continued to run at full speed until his lungs could no longer pull in air.

Falling to the ground, Morsian's ribs heaved from the efforts of running on a swollen ankle. The adrenalin would leave him shaky and nauseated. Slowly getting back to his feet, Morsian limped back to his camp, knowing he would need to move long before dark when the cave-dwelling creatures would hunt him.

Taking a few minutes to settle his stomach and rewrap his ankle, Morsian stood and started to break camp. Feeling ambivalent about leaving the source of the pink crystal, Morsian started to hesitate. However, Morsian let his better judgment make the decision to leave quickly before evening and return home. With all his belongings packed in his backpack, Morsian decided to check out the fascinating herd once more before leaving the valley.

Slowly trudging up the hill where he last saw the herd, Morsian was happy to see the herd gathered below him. The stallion kept watching from an adjacent hill. Morsian was aware the wind was in his favor, and the stallion was not aware he was there. However, Morsian retreated behind a boulder so as not to be observed.

Never tired of looking at the blend of colors amongst the herd, Morsian settled down to watch, thinking he had hours before the evening sun would descend, leaving him vulnerable to an attack from the nasty cave beasts. Intrigued by the play of the foals, Morsian was caught off-guard by the bellows coming from the hill where the stallion now stood, tearing up the ground with his claws. To Morsian's surprise, long, golden, spiraling horns now appeared where previously seen were golden buds.

Wondering why the stallion was alarmed, Morsian's attention was riveted to the magnificent animal. Soon, the threat was clear as another red stallion advanced up the hill. Shrill, screaming challenges came from the young red stallion as he leaped upon the guardian of the herd.

Screams of pain and roars of anger filled the air, causing the herd below to panic. The mares and younger animals circled in confusion as their leader engaged in a battle to the death. Fighting with horns and claws as well as teeth, the two large males continued piercing screams into the air. Dust swirled around the two combatants as they battled for supremacy.

Morsian rushed from boulder to boulder to get closer to the action. As he finally found himself where he could view the battle at close range, the sounds of squealing, groaning, and yowling were ear-piercing. The horns clinked and clattered as they met each other in parry to get the advantage. Deflecting horns with vaulted leaps from side to side, the two animals jousted for the upper position. Thrusts of horns and swipes of claws continued the duel with banging and gashing of bodies in the assault. One stallion advanced, and the other stallion retreated to gain the advantage of its opponent. Bright red blood could be seen flowing from multiple wounds on each stallion where a slashing horn or sharp claws made contact. Moving apart, the horns sparkled in the sunlight with tips crimson from the blood.

Morsian peered out from behind the boulder, unable to take his eyes off the battle before him. Cracking, crunching, and snapping sounds indicated the shattering of bones of the young stallion as it finally lay on the ground breathing its last breath.

Morsian could swear he saw the sadness in the eyes of the victor as he stood over the younger stallion, bright red blood flowing over its dark red coat. Suddenly, the mighty stallion dropped to the ground beside the loser of the battle.

Laying his head on the ground, the stallion was motionless. Morsian wondered if both animals died in the fight, he observed moments ago. Quietly, Morsian stood and walked cautiously towards the animals. He could see the ribs barely moving up and down on the victor's side. He could tell at a glance that the animal was badly injured. Slowly moving to his side, Morsian took inventory of the wounds. Bending down to inspect the most serious gash, Morsian knew he could repair it if the animal remained unconscious.

Removing contents from his backpack, Morsian found the kit he carried for injuries while traveling alone. Disinfectant, needle, and thread were carefully packed in sterile containers. Two vials of painkillers, as well as a large dose of antibiotics, were also in the hard-shelled box that contained other medical equipment.

Morsian worked quickly to disinfect the wounds and suture them, keeping an eye on the herd below who continued to mull around nervously. About to give an injection of antibiotics, he was startled to hear threatening snorts behind him. Circling him were several young stallions from the herd, which had come to protect their leader from the new enemy. The herd knew to stay clear when their stallion was fighting the other stallion challenger for the rights to the herd. This new animal was a different threat and was not to be tolerated near their leader.

Morsian stood slowly to face the spiraling horns that now encircled him from all sides. There was no escape. Morsian knew he would be stabbed from all angles if he moved one more inch as growls increased with even the subtlest movement.

One young stallion stepped closer with his head lowered, his gleaming horns inches from Morsian's chest. Morsian tried to find his voice to make some calming utterances. The only sound that came out of his mouth was a squeak. Closing his eyes, not wanting to see the moment of his death, Morsian was surprised when the whole herd moved away as one.

Opening his eyes and watching the herd walk down the hill, back to the purple grass below, Morsian found he could release the breath he was holding inside.

"Whew, that was close," Morsian said out loud.

'Thank you,' came a voice within his head.

Morsian swung around to see where the voice was coming from and realized it was in his head. Was it his own unconscious thanking God for saving him? He was not aware he was offering a prayer at that moment, even though it should have occurred to him to do so. If it was not a conscious thought, then it must be an unconscious thought. Nothing else made any sense.

'I said, thank you. It is only polite to respond with your welcome,' a new thought intruded upon Morsian's mind.

"Who is taking over my mind?" Morsian said out loud, not expecting an answer. Looking around and feeling foolish, Morsian decided the stress of the past two days was making him a bit crazy.

'You aren't crazy. I am trying to get your attention. Will you look at me for a moment?' the mental intrusion continued.

Morsian spun around and saw brilliant green gem-like eyes twirling into his own. The stallion was awake and trying to raise his head.

Morsian bent down to the animal to soothe him. Saying out loud, "Don't try to get up yet, or your sutures might burst. I did the best I could to sew your wounds. Unfortunately, I am not a doctor. Please lay back and rest." Thinking how crazy these words must seem to a dumb animal.

'You saved my life. I am indebted to you,' came a peculiar thought into Morsian's head. Shaking his head, Morsian looked around to see if someone was speaking to him. Not seeing anyone, Morsian's eyes locked on the stallion whose eyes whirled, holding Morsian's gaze intently.

"Is it really you who is inside my head? How can that be?" Morsian asked in disbelief.

'You ate the pink dust, didn't you?' came the stallion's mental pictures in response.

"I did. How did you know?" Morsian quickly answered.

'You don't need to speak out loud unless you want to do so. I can see your thoughts in my mind,' continued the stallion's thoughts through image after image cascading into Morsian's mind.

"This is not possible!" Morsian said out loud. To test the theory, Morsian continued the questions non-verbally. 'What are you called, and why can I hear your thoughts?'

'I am called Rydor. I am the leader of the herd that I just sent away to protect you. It is now your turn to thank me for saving your life.'

"Oh my gosh! You can read my thoughts. How is that possible?" Morsian said, in disbelief.

'You ate the pink crystal. That gives you the ability to understand certain being's thoughts. However, you can only read my thoughts because I decided to honor you. We are now bondmates.'

"Well, if you are bonded to me, then I need for you to lie motionless while I inject the antibiotic into your hide. This will sting a bit, but it will keep you from having an infection in that wound. I did my best to clean it. Claws and horns can be filthy things," Morsian said as he prepared the syringe.

'Don't waste your medicine on me. We have natural remedies that work. My little friend, the Jade Harbinger, will lead you to berries that will work better for me. You can keep your medicine for yourself as you may need it someday.' The stallion pressed mental pictures into Morsian's mind of the little bird and what berries he needed to find.

A little green bird fluttered down from a tree, pecking at small seeds that fell from wild grasses near where the stallion lay. Periodically, the little bird stood frozen in its tracks, seemingly listening to something.

"Can you communicate with that little bird," Morsian asked of Rydor.

'Yes, this little bird has bonded with me as well. Right now, my little friend will lead you to the berries that I need. I want you to bring more than you think I will require because I have something else that you must do,' insisted Rydor.

"What must I do?" asked Morsian aloud.

'You must repair the damage you did to the griswell. My bond friend in the cave informed me of the injury you caused one of their den members. You must mend his wound as you did mine, and you must provide him with berries.'

"I can't go back to the mine. Those beasts will kill me. They already tried to kill me twice!" Morsian said in alarm.

'You will not be hurt by any of the griswells. Members of my herd are bonded with the griswells. They will protect you while you return to mend the injured griswell. This is important if you are to remain in this valley. Besides, I am the only safe way for you to get pink minerals. I will expect you to do this favor for me,' Rydor demanded.

The little bird started to fly in the direction he needed Morsian to follow. Seeing the bird leave, Morsian did not try to argue with his new bondmate. Later, he could try to sway the argument in his favor. Going back into that cave with those blood-thirsty beasts was not something he was willing to do. Right now, the berries were a priority in keeping Rydor alive.

The trip seemed endless, as Morsian's ankle was not healing well. Needing to run on it to escape, as well as the time spent walking up and down hills, did not help the injured ankle. Grabbing a downed branch from a tree, Morsian used it as a walking stick to take some of the weight from his injured leg. Even with the pain, most of the trip was spent in wonder and bewilderment. The reality of his situation was beyond incredible. Even though he was a man of science, Morsian couldn't wrap his mind around anything that just happened.

When the bird landed at a bush in a clearing, Morsian broke from his reverie and noted berries growing upon the bush. The little bird picked one and dropped it on the ground. Morsian supposed that was his clue to start picking the berries. The sooner he filled his bag, the sooner he could return to the stallion. Filling his knapsack with berries took longer than anticipated. Feeling exhausted, Morsian slumped his shoulders, feeling too tired to walk all the way back.

Immediately a new thought popped into his mind from Rydor, 'You may ride upon Lattee's back. She is willing.'

'What is a Lattee?' thought Morsian.

As the mental transfer was made, a marvelously beautiful strawberry mastel came from out of the nearby trees. The contrast between the strawberry coat and the red mare's mane and tail was striking. It was obvious the mastel was female from the subtle striping of cream with the luscious pink tones of her coat. The unusual vivid red of the mane and tail were unique from the other mares.

As the mare mastel dropped to the ground, Morsian climbed upon her supple back, yet another mental picture popped into his head, 'Hold on tightly, or you will be unseated, and don't pull on her fur.' With that warning, the mastel sprang to her feet and leaped into a full gallop. Not being prepared for the soaring bounds from boulder to boulder, Morsian found himself landing hard on the ground.

'Lattee says she is sorry. She will go slower. Get on your feet and climb onto her back, ...again.' Rydor conveyed.

Rubbing his sore hip, on which Morsian landed, he walked cautiously back to Lattee. She was waiting patiently, making a whimpering sound. Patting her softly on her shoulder, to soothe her, Morsian slipped upon her back and was trying to decide where to hold.

'Use your legs and squeeze gently—I do mean gently,' Rydor instructed from afar.

Morsian gripped with his legs as the mastel walked back in the direction where the stallion laid. As Morsian became more comfortable, Lattee increased her speed until she was loping slowly across the countryside. Morsian laughed with glee at the exhilarating experience.

'One day, will I be able to ride upon your back, Rydor?' sent Morsian to his new bondmate.

'Don't get too cocky. I am a stallion. You can't even sit on a mare; how do you think you could sit on me as I leap into trees and over boulders?' the smirk somehow translated into a mental message.

A smile crossed Morsian's lips as he realized his life would never be the same. Excitement filled his head and heart. A strange deep, satisfied feeling that he could only describe as a new form of love entered his mind.

CHAPTER THIRTEEN

Morsian returned to Rydor to find him standing tall. The herd dug a grave or hauled the dead mastel someplace since the stallion was no longer in sight. Morsian decided not to intrude on Rydor's grief to ask him the question as to what happened to the dead mastel. Somehow Morsian knew the dead mastel was Rydor's son, and even though it was not unusual for a son to challenge his father for the right to rule the herd, it was entirely a sad event for the whole herd.

Bringing out the knapsack filled with berries and thanking Lattee with another pat, Morsian was trying to decide how he could get out of the next part of what Rydor expected him to do. He really did not wish to go down into the cave again. Somehow, Morsian did not think that the mastels would be able to keep the griswells from attacking him. He saw the murderous look in their eyes as he ran for his life.

'The herd is ready. The members who have bonded with griswells will accompany you closer to the cave to give you the confidence you lack. I will remain here. Flint has connected, and we are communicating. She has assured me that none of the griswells will attack. They each are in contact with their bond friend. You will enter the cave and repair the damage you did to the griswell,' Rydor commanded.

Lattee, once again, moved to Morsian's side to offer him a ride to the mouth of the cave. Reluctantly, Morsian climbed on her back with his backpack in place. Many berries remained from his knapsack even though Rydor ate his fill, and some were squeezed upon the wound directly.

'The herd will stop once to allow you to gather feigons to close the wound. The jaws of the insect work better than the thread you used on me. I caution you to work fast. The griswells do not like you at all. They complain that you are a killer and you smell bad,' Rydor chuckle-snorted.

"I do not smell bad!" Morsian said as he lifted his arm to sniff his armpit. "Okay, maybe I do need a bath."

Rydor instructed the herd, and they left without giving voice except for the mares who neighed to their youngsters. Lattee was one who joined in and called out, and Morsian felt her vibration under him as she vocalized.

Coming upon a rocky area, Morsian received a mental note to move aside logs to find the feigons. Finding several of the insects, Morsian gently placed them inside a deep pocket, hoping they would remain inside and not climb out to bite him. Keeping one hand on the flap at the top of the pocket to ensure the insects remain in place, Morsian remounted and rode on.

At the mouth of the cave, Lattee and the other mastels stopped. Morsian noted one mastel with only the use of three legs. He saw that one hind leg dangled uselessly. Marveling at how well the young mastel maneuvered the trail with the rest of the herd, Morsian dismissed the thought.

As Morsian was instructed to dismount and go into the cave where the injured griswell lay where he dropped, Morsian noted the intent stares on the mastels' eyes. Each seemed almost in a trance. Morsian wondered if it took that much concentration to keep the griswells from attacking him and feared to go in.

Lattee nudged Morsian from behind, pushing him to the entrance. Morsian dragged his feet and walked cautiously into the cave as if walking to his execution. The backpack weighed upon his shoulders, causing him to slump forward as he took one step at a time toward what he felt was his impending doom.

Once inside, Morsian lit his light source and took the left tunnel to where he knew the injured griswell lay. He did not need to go as deep as he first walked into the tunnel as the pursuing fight with the griswell forced him back closer to the entrance. That was one thing for which Morsian was thankful.

A growl emanated from the griswell as Morsian's approached, halting him. Fear froze him in his tracks.

Rydor sensing Morsian's fear reached out, 'He won't bite you, but I think you should not dawdle. He does not like you one bit. He feels you are a thief and a ruthless killer of griswells. Do what you need to do and leave.'

Quickly, Morsian reached into his knapsack and squeezed berry juice upon the wound. The flap of his pocket was open, and Morsian noted the feigons traveling down his leg to attach to the griswell's wound, closing it completely. Morsian was relieved not to need to handle the large-jawed insects. Morsian was sure their bite would hurt and wondered how long they would cling to the injured griswell without letting go.

'Feigons will stay on the wound until it is completely closed. Once there is no longer blood or dead tissue to feed upon, the insects will drop off and return to the logs,' Rydor educated.

Laying the remaining berries close to the griswell--not so close that the beast could snap off a finger, Morsian bowed and backed out of the cave and returned quickly to Lattee. Jumping on her back, he waited for her to spring into action. When she did not move, Morsian became concerned that his life was in jeopardy.

'Why aren't we leaving?' Morsian reached out with his question to Rydor.

'Wait and see. You are very impatient,' came the mental response.

At the mouth of the cave, Morsian saw a griswell pushing a pile of pink crystals barely out of the shadows. The griswell would go no further in the bright light of day.

'I am afraid that you will need to dismount Lattee and retrieve the phyrium, as the pink crystal is named by the griswells.' Rydor announced.

'Oh, no! I am not going back into the cave with a griswell lurking in the shadows,' thought Morsian.

'Stop acting like a coward and be humble. Remember what you have done to earn the contempt of the griswell. Our mission is to assist you in undoing the damage you caused. Teetawn, my son, is saying Sunshine, his bond friend who provided the mineral, has already descended back into the cave. It is safe for you to go inside and pick up the phyrium. Now go!' Rydor insisted.

Morsian slid from Lattee's back and whispered for her to stay close if only to boost his confidence, as he once again walked cautiously back inside the cave. Not seeing, hearing, or smelling a griswell, Morsian carefully gathered up the mineral, taking several into his mouth before pocketing the rest. It was the largest amount of phyrium that he had ever seen. The knapsack that was filled with berries was now filled with the special pink mineral that he craved.

Thrilled to be gone from the cave, Morsian munched a few more crystals while riding back to the herd. Reunited with Rydor, Morsian decided he never wanted to leave his bondmate and should go about making a permanent shelter. As the stallion was on the mends, Morsian limped off to find a suitable place, close by the herd.

With only a hatchet, Morsian was unsure how he would cut enough trees to make a small cabin. By the end of the day, Morsian only had five small trees cut. At this rate, it would take all spring to get enough logs. Setting up his tent, Morsian ate and sent a mental message to Rydor, thanking him for the phyrium that he knew Rydor acquired for him.

Peeking out of the tent, Morsian saw the band of mastels leaving to hunt meat to take to the griswells. Morsian noted that Rydor did not go this time. He stayed with the mares and young.

'I have extra phyrium, thanks to you. Shall I bring some down to you?' Morsian reached out to Rydor in question.

'Thank you, my bondmate, but Geselle, my favorite mare, will bring my share. She and my sons will hunt extra for a few days to allow me to regain my strength and not rupture my sutures. Sleep, I am on guard,' came the soothing thought of Morsian's beloved new best friend.

CHAPTER FOURTEEN

Tiring of cutting logs for his new home, Morsian went about finding the perfect caulking for between the logs. Chinking to seal the logs from the weather was needed since strong storms seemed to come out of nowhere in this part of the country. Noting jicerian trees not far from the area, Morsian knew the resin from the tree could provide a type of glue that would be fragrant as well as practical. The only problem was that the glue formed from the jicerian tree could not withstand the most severe storms.

Hollowing out a stump from a tree, Morsian made a bucket to collect the sap. He knew the resin would be running at this time of the year and considered gathering enough to make a sweet syrup as well as the caulking. Taking his walking stick, since he did not wish to intrude on Lattee for a ride, Morsian limped off to the forest. His thoughts were on how he would strengthen and create a useful polymer. In a strange flash of thought, Morsian wondered what phyrium might do to improve the polymer.

Filling his wooden bucket with resin that was acquired drip by drip from the tap, gave Morsian time to think about the proportions he might use. Experimenting would be the only way he would know. By the time he got home, Morsian's ankle was quite swollen. Removing his boot, Morsian sat and massaged his ankle as he examined it to make sure there wasn't any infection. Relieved not to find red streaks moving up his leg, Morsian decided it was soft tissue damage and would heal eventually if he could brace it.

Sitting for a short time, Morsian got out another hand-carved bowl and pour the resin into it. Mixing some warm water in a 3:1 proportion to thin the resin, Morsian took some of the phyrium powder and diluted it to a solution using the same proportions. Mixing the two solutions together, Morsian found that he created a thick rubbery material. Taking it into his hands, he rolled it into a ball and then stretched it out as far as his arms allowed. Laughing as the material sprung back into shape when he released his hold on one end, Morsian wondered if he invented a child's toy.

Distracted by a sharp stab of pain in his ankle, Morsian thought that it would be nice to create a foot splint of some sort for it. The thought passed his mind when the goop he made, seemed to slip from his hand and landed on his ankle, wrapping itself completely around.

Startled, Morsian looked down at the violet-colored goop formed from the resin and phyrium, finding that it was pleasantly warm. 'Maybe I invented a heating device,' Morsian laughed to himself. Reaching to gather the bowl that held more of the same goop, Morsian found he needed to stand to reach it. Once on his feet, he found that his ankle did not hurt at all. Each step he took was pain-free. Curiously, Morsian walked around his campsite to test the theory that what he made could be used in a medical application. The goop clearly created an exoskeletal brace for his ankle. More amazing to Morsian was the fact that the goop truly responded to his thoughts. Wanting to share this newest invention, Morsian reached out to Rydor.

'Come and see what I created,' Morsian conveyed through the distance between his camp and where Rydor stood nose to nose with Geselle.

'Why must you disturb me at the worst time possible.' a scolding thought came to his head.

'This is really worth seeing. You can nuzzle with Geselle later! Come here, please.'

A resigned sigh was what Morsian felt in his mind, and he knew Rydor would be pawing up the ground to see what his bondmate thought was that important. The thought barely left Morsian's mind when Rydor stood before him with a glint of sweat on his luxurious coat.

"It is getting warm, isn't it?" Morsian said out loud, wanting to hear his own voice. Rydor snorted his agreement and then pushed his muzzle into Morsian's shoulder for physical closeness as he was doing a few minutes earlier with Geselle.

Morsian rubbed Rydor's neck, knowing that the stallion was expressing love for him as he did with his own herd members. It made Morsian feel accepted and less lonely. Being out in the wilderness for weeks, Morsian was starting to feel very much alone until he connected with Rydor. All thoughts of his human home were minimized since being with Rydor. Where Rydor lived was now home to Morsian.

Looking down as Morsian raced around to show off how well his newest invention supported his ankle, Morsian was delighted when Rydor flashed a mental picture into Morsian's mind showing Three Legs running and jumping on all four legs.

'It might work, Rydor. I am glad you immediately thought of an application that will benefit the herd. Let's give it a try. Summon Three Legs, and I will mix up a larger batch of polymer,' Morsian said in reply to the mental picture Rydor produced.

Sitting down with a bowl in hand and ingredients assembled, Morsian mixed another batch of polymer with the results being exactly as before. Delighted, Morsian plied the goop between his hands to further mix it as he had previously done. As Three Legs bellowed his greeting, Morsian approached the young mastel with the goop in hand.

Snorting and backing away, Three Legs showed his suspicion towards the violet glob of goop. Rydor commanded the colt to stop moving and to stand still while Morsian applied the substance to the entire hind leg using careful molding techniques as if he were sculpting a statue. The polymer transformed itself into the mental image Morsian saw in his mind.

Giving Three Legs permission to move around, Rydor watched as his son walked on his fourth leg. Sending a mental picture to Three Legs to try to run, jump and then climb a tree, Morsian and Rydor puffed with pride at seeing the young colt display new athletic abilities that were lost to him when on three legs. The colt, too, became ecstatic and frolicked towards Teetawn, trumpeting his successes.

"I will call my invention an exoskeletal prosthesis," Morsian said more to myself than to Rydor. Rydor puzzled asked what a prosthesis might be. This sent Morsian into a teaching mode.

'Enough! I wanted a simple explanation, not a whole lecture,' Rydor revealed to Morsian.

Morsian laughed. He remained excited by his newfound uses for the mineral that up until now was only consumed. 'Think about what we might be able to do with the mineral.'

Stopping only momentarily to think things through further in his head, Morsian started conversing with Rydor. 'I will need a whole lot more of the mineral with which to experiment. At present, the griswells only supply enough for the mastels to eat. How can we get the griswells to mine more? What can the incentive be for them other than more food? They can only eat what meat can be consumed in each day without it spoiling, thus, what might motivate them to mine more minerals for me when they hate me?'

Rydor pictured the griswells eating Morsian, and Morsian knew he agreed that they hated him. 'That did not help the matter, Rydor. I was hoping for you to come up with something the griswells might want badly enough that they would excavate more phyrium. Can you maybe put your mind to that instead of graphic pictures of my demise?'

Looking at Three Legs running with the other colts and fillies, Rydor wondered if any griswell deep within the cave may have disabilities. 'It is a slim possibility that some of the griswells may have old injuries or birth defects that have left them disabled. I can reach out of Flint to see if she will return my inquiries.'

As Rydor seemed lost in thought, Morsian enjoyed watching Three Legs, now renamed Frisky by his peers, playing joyfully in the meadow. Even the mares caught the young colt's enthusiasm and were joining in the merriment. A contented smile crossed Morsian's lips as he felt pride that he improved one of the herd member's life. Morsian knew that even though the young mastel was doing well at present, that as he aged and put on weight, his abilities to keep up with the herd would have been diminished greatly if the leg had not been treated. Now, if his prosthesis remained viable, he could be sound like all the rest.

The thought, *remaining viable* caused Morsian to pause. What did he really know of the properties of phyrium? How long would this polymer last? Would it disintegrate over time? Would it cause the circulation to slow or the skin to break down? Looking down at his own ankle support, Morsian looked for any telltale signs that his body was reacting negatively to the substance. Seeing nothing at present, Morsian added another task to his day. He would need to check Frisky's prosthesis daily as well as his own. How would he get it off quickly if he needed to do so?

Thinking of the word *off*, his ankle support dropped to the ground into a bouncy ball. With both eyes popping open in astonishment, Morsian thought *ankle support* once again, and the ball wrapped around his ankle.

"Whoa! The mineral reacts to my thoughts! Amazing!" Morsian exclaimed loudly. "I wonder if Frisky can control the prosthesis as well?"

Calling out to Rydor, who once again showed irritation that he was being interrupted while communicating with Flint, Rydor sent an abrupt message for Morsian to be patient and wait. Morsian found himself pacing back and forth while he waited for the stallion to give him the attention he was seeking.

'What was so important that it couldn't wait for me to finish communicating with Flint? I thought the extra phyrium was important to you.' Rydor's irritated thoughts entered Morsian's mind, making the man flinch.

'It is important. I am sorry, I guess, in my eagerness to show you something else exciting, I forgot you were in contact with Flint. Forgive my rudeness?' Morsian asked and demonstrated with humbled body language.

'What was that important?' Rydor asked, showing forgiveness and compassion towards his excitable human. 'If you were a mastel, I would have nipped you for your insubordination. Since you are only human, and fortunately for you, my bondmate, I will let it pass this time.'

Morsian all but wiggled in his excitement. 'Watch,' Morsian said as he demonstrated how he could command his ankle support to let go of his ankle and then command it to go back into place. 'Isn't that incredible? I want to see if Frisky can do the same. Will you call him back here again?'

Interested in what Morsian demonstrated with his ankle brace, Rydor reached out to Frisky and summoned him back to where

Morsian stood. Reluctantly, Frisky left his playmates and the herds' celebration to return to the stallion and the human.

'Ask Frisky to think the command for the prosthesis to be removed,' Morsian requested of Rydor. As the stallion conveyed the mental picture of the prosthesis dropping to the ground, Frisky seemed to understand what was expected of him. Doing as commanded, Frisky found his prosthesis drop to the ground forming a ball, and his hind leg once again was dangling uselessly where he stood.

Turning a puzzled and sad eye towards his leader, he pleaded for the prosthesis to be restored. Rydor told him to think it back on his leg. In a blink, Frisky found the polymer clinging to his hind leg as before, and he bounded around once again.

Dismissing Frisky, the colt raced back to the herd with an even lighter step to his gait. He discovered that he could control the goop on his leg. Not knowing why he would ever want to remove it, he felt thrilled that he had that ability.

'My gosh! Frisky can control the polymer on his leg as well as I can control my ankle support. Do you know what this means? Whatever we make from this polymer will be under our mental control. If I build my house with it, I will be able to communicate with my house. If I build a barn for the herd, you will be able to control the barn!' Morsian said in excitement.

'Why would I want a barn that I can tell to drop into a ball at my request? Would I roll it to a new location and tell it to become a barn again?' the stallion pictured in his brain.

Laughing, Morsian admitted, 'I don't know what the ramifications may be--the possibilities could be endless. Maybe we could find a way to control the temperatures within the barn, that way, it is warm in the winter or cool in the summer. Maybe we could even store grass in the barn and have the building distribute the grass when you wanted to eat it. There could be endless possibilities with the properties of the mineral, phyrium. I will need to continue my experiments to see. The only thing that may limit the phyrium could be our lack of imagination! Isn't it exciting?'

'Speaking of grass, I will leave you to your thoughts and experiments. I am hungry.' With that parting mental vision, Rydor galloped away and back to the herd.

Morsian, too exhilarated to care that Rydor was putting his stomach before the future, went back to the bowl to mix up more polymer. Remembering that Rydor had not told him what Flint's impressions of how the polymer might benefit the griswells, Morsian almost interrupted Rydor again. Thinking better of it, he returned to stirring together the two solutions.

Looking at the logs piled up to make a cabin, Morsian started thinking of making polymer bricks and posts instead of logs to build a cabin. Morsian took goop and shaped it into rectangles and set the several bricks aside that he made from one batch of the polymer. Before mixing up more batches with the limited amount of phyrium remaining, Morsian decided to test whether he could build with the bricks he already made. Stacking them upon each other, Morsian saw that each brick bonded with the brick below and above to create a solid, strong wall. There would be no need for caulk or chink of any kind with the new phyrium polymer. Desperate for more phyrium, Morsian braved, interrupting Rydor.

'Did Flint respond to your question about obtaining more phyrium than normally supplied? If yes, did she say what the den members may want in return?' Morsian pushed for an answer.

'Yes, and yes,' Rydor responded without further explanation.

'Do I need to come to you to get the answer?' Morsian thought in exasperation.

'Yes,' was Rydor's only response.

Getting up from his important experiment, Morsian started to grab his walking stick when he remembered he had no need for it. With more enthusiasm for the walk down the hill to where the herd was grazing, Morsian set off at a quick pace, whistling a tune.

Arriving, Morsian found Rydor playing with some of the youngest members of the herd. Somehow Morsian found the playfulness out of character for the proud stallion.

'I never thought of you as anything but serious,' the mental picture conveyed by Morsian was more an image of being stern than serious.

'I often play with my offspring. It keeps the foals busy; that way, the mothers can graze in peace without worrying about them,' Rydor tossed his head to indicate the beautiful mares munching at the delicate purple grass.

'Couldn't the young stallions babysit? Then you could do your job,' Morsian asked.

'They are my foals, not the young stallions,' Rydor replied with annoyance.

Dropping the subject, Morsian repeated the questions regarding Flint and the griswells. 'I need more phyrium and lots of it if I am going to build a cabin and eventually a barn for the herd. Will the griswells excavate the crystals for me?"

"Not for you! For the mastels, they will," Rydor said while rolling in the grass with several small mastels swarming all over him.

'As cute as your playtime might be, this is serious. Could you possibly stop the mastel playtime and communicate with me?' Morsian said a bit offended that Rydor was not paying close attention to him.

"Rydor, you are giving me a headache. I need to know how we can get more phyrium and what it is going to take to get it?" Morsian said, reverting to the spoken language in frustration.

Snorting his chuckle-snort, Rydor was about to ask what a headache might be to further torment Morsian when he thought better of it.

'Thank you for not asking what a headache might be. I appreciate the fact that you have that much self-control,' Morsian said when he caught Rydor's little joke.

'Flint showed me several griswells who have been badly damaged by predators while hunting the past several seasons. Most have damaged limbs. I believe she said that repairing the damage done to the griswells would be payment enough for a rather large amount of phyrium. After that, I don't know what incentives the griswells might demand. They will provide you with enough phyrium to make prostheses like you made for Frisky and enough for you to build your cabin, even though the griswells don't like the fact that you plan to stay in this valley,' Rydor transmitted between their minds.

Happily, Morsian said, 'It's a start. How am I to go about mending these limbs.' The smile drained from his face when he thought through the whole process. 'I don't need to go down into the cave alone again, do I?'

Rydor stood, dumping the little mastels on the ground. 'Yes, you will need to go down, and there is a major problem. These are griswells who have not bonded with a mastel. The only restraint upon them will be by the griswells who have bonded with one of my mastel herd. It will be a bit difficult to manage.'

Morsian was feeling very uneasy. 'How so?'

'Each of the bonded mastel will be communicating with their bond friend. The mastels will propose that each griswell help to suppress the unbonded griswell while you are mending their limbs. The bonded griswells conveyed they will try their hardest to keep their fellow griswells from attacking you. No guarantees. There could be some mishaps. Are you willing to take the risk in exchange for phyrium?' Rydor communicated with an intense stare.

Morsian covered both of his eyes with his hands. His head really was hurting now. The thought of going down into the cave with angry griswells controlling angry griswells did not seem in his favor. He knew the mastels would try their best to keep their bond friends calm and not reactive. Morsian couldn't imagine how the bonded griswells were going to control the unbonded griswells. It seemed likely he would be walking into a trap.

'Well...?' Rydor pressed. 'Shall we arrange it or not? We need to leave soon to hunt meat for the griswells in exchange for our own phyrium. If they are to gather extra for your polymer goop, we need to know soon.'

'Okay, yes. I will take the risk. Once there is enough phyrium to make the polymer, I need to know how many injured griswells there are.'

'That information will be known when we return from the caves. I believe you should meet us there with many wooden buckets or other containers to carry the phyrium. We usually eat our fill at the cave." Rydor then pictured Morsian carrying several buckets filled to the top with phyrium from the cave entrance.

Morsian indicated he would be at the cave before dark with as many buckets as he could carry. Walking back to his camp, Morsian's steps were no longer jaunty. He dragged himself back up the hill, dreading having to go into the cave alone the next day.

CHAPTER FIFTEEN

Morsian watched as part of the herd left to hunt for glemee or gurlions or whatever prey might be available in the area. Gathering as many empty wooden buckets as he could carry and putting his empty backpack upon his shoulder to carry even more phyrium, Morsian started towards the cave, moving slowly. He certainly did not wish to arrive earlier than the mastels. Knowing the sun would set by the time Morsian arrived, the last thing he wanted to do was to get there before the meat was dragged back down into the depths of the cavern. He would sit on top of the hill in a tree, waiting for the mastels before he would go down and pick up the phyrium that should be waiting.

Coming to the top of the hill and looking down on the cave opening, Morsian was relieved to see many of the mastels eating phyrium. Not seeing Rydor, Morsian was unsure whether it was safe for him to go down and start to fill the buckets and backpack.

Reaching out to Rydor, Morsian asked where he was. The mental picture of Rydor dragging a very large glemee popped into his head. He knew Rydor would be along soon and chose to stay on the hill and wait. If Rydor was bringing meat, that meant more griswells were waiting out of sight inside the cave entrance. There was no way Morsian would go down the hill until Rydor said it was safe.

Mastels started to leave the area after consuming the phyrium left for them. Morsian knew they would return to the herd. He did not know whether the mastels carried extra phyrium back to herd members who had not yet bonded with a griswell. There was no question that the phyrium was essential for the herd to communicate telepathically with each other. Morsian wondered why he never broached the subject with Rydor. It was understood that Rydor could communicate with all the mastels who were bonded with a griswell. Morsian would ask Rydor at some point, but not right now.

Right now, the only important thing on his mind was getting as much phyrium as possible. He needed more bucket loads than he could carry this one trip. Would there be enough for him to return? Would he return in the dark knowing the griswells had him at a disadvantage? Would they attack him before he could mend the injured griswells? All these questions continued to plague him until he saw Rydor coming into view with an enormous stag glemee.

Dragging the dead animal to the cave entrance, Morsian watched as half a dozen griswells came out from the shadows of the cave and swarmed on the stag, tearing him into manageable pieces to be carried below. Watching the horrific sight, Morsian almost decided the phyrium really was not necessary to live and was going to end the deal.

Rydor, sensing his indecision and fear, came to his side. 'It will not be you who is torn to pieces. I will protect you.'

'How can you? You can't come down into the cave with me. It is not big enough,' Morsian said, sizing up the cave opening.

'You do not need to worry,' Rydor stroked Morsian's mind comfortingly. 'Flint, Greyble, Sunshine, and Bog will fight to the death against their own den members to keep you safe. It is part of the bond between us. You will be okay, I promise.'

Morsian walked down the hill with Rydor and proceeded to pick up each crystal on the ground until all his buckets were filled, and his backpack was full. There were enough crystals to fill all his buckets again, plus his backpack and maybe even more. Looking at the extra, he was pleased since he would need all the phyrium laying on the ground to complete his plan, but Morsian did not care to return for the rest in the dark.

'Can I wait until the sun is blazing hot tomorrow before I return for the rest? I have no desire to return tonight. I know the mastels will not want to accompany me to make sure their bond friends do not come out and attack me,' Morsian played the scene in his head.

Rydor simply nudged him to pick up the buckets and to follow him. 'Get on my back if you are able, and I will walk slowly enough that you won't drop a single crystal.'

"You are offering me a ride on your back? I thought stallions did not do such things," Morsian said in a delighted, surprised voice.

'Shut up and get on before I withdraw my offer. You will get off before we reach the herd,' Rydor said, once more aware of his image.

Wishing Rydor would have carried him up the hill, Morsian lugged the buckets the rest of the way home. No mastel had seen Morsian riding on the stallion's back. Thus, Rydor could continue to act proud. Getting right to work, Morsian made batch after batch of polymer with the phyrium and resin. Realizing he would run out of resin before he ran out of phyrium, Morsian made the trek to the jicerian tree forest to tap into several more trees. The buckets loaded with resin were heavier than when the buckets were loaded with the fragile crystals. The trip took longer than anticipated with the heavy load. Morsian returned home very late at night. Only the stallion on duty knew Morsian left his campsite that evening as Morsian did not send out any mental images to his bondmate.

In the early morning hours, Morsian decided to take a nap. He wanted to be awake by noon; that way, he could return to fetch the remaining phyrium. He counted the number of bricks he made from his solutions made from resin and phyrium. He marveled at how the polymer shimmered in the light of day. Watching it quiver made Morsian feel queasy and a bit uneasy. He was not sure why the polymer would jiggle as if it had a mind of its own. He was too tired to care or try to think it through now. Instead, he headed to his sleeping mat.

Unsure why the thought came to his mind, Morsian got up and took several polymer bricks and laid them on the ground, covering the stack with his mat. With some caution, Morsian lay down upon the bricks. They instantly enveloped him, which made Morsian afraid. As he struggled to get away, the bricks unfolded to allow him to stand. With increased curiosity overcoming his fear, Morsian decided to lie down again. The bricks once more folded gently around him. This time, Morsian did not struggle. He relaxed when he realized how comfortable he was when lying upon the bricks. Letting his eyes close, Morsian slept better than he had since he was a child.

Feeling completely refreshed with only a few hours of sleep, Morsian woke by early morning. With the smallest wiggle of his shoulders, the polymer bed unfolded, allowing Morsian to sit up. He almost felt the bed was assisting him to his feet when he got up since it was entirely too easy to rise. Now, Morsian was sure he was fantasizing about the properties of his newest invention since beds did not lift people to their feet. However, it was worth trying one more time.

Morsian laid back down, became absorbed within his bed, wiggled enough to be released, and started to stand when he felt the bed assisting him to his feet. Again, and again, he laid upon his bed and got up, and each time, it was the same. The bed did help him get to his feet. Morsian was over-joyed at the prospects of the discovery of this mineral. He thought of the elderly and how much this polymer could assist them in their daily routines. Assistance in getting out of bed alone could ease their suffering and pain. What else could the polymer be used for on his planet? Morsian decided the prospects were boundless.

His thoughts were interrupted by Rydor, who reminded him that the sun was straight up in the sky, and if he wanted to make several trips to and from the cave to gather phyrium, they had best be leaving. Morsian indicated the grove of trees out of sight from the mastel herd where they could meet. Morsian was sure that Rydor was making an offer to carry him. The problem with the stallion was making assumptions could be risky. He would meet Rydor there and hope he would carry him back and forth to save time and energy.

Morsian was not disappointed. Rydor dropped to his belly and allowed him to climb upon his back. Morsian scratched behind Rydor's ears to thank him and was greeted with a purr. 'A little to your right...aww, that feels good,' Rydor sighed.

"I promise to give you a good brushing after we get back, but I think we should gather the phyrium before it gets trampled or eaten by the mastels," Morsian said.

'Alright, you promise!" Rydor pressed for a commitment.

"I promise," Morsian said when Rydor got to his feet and leaped into action. Morsian was impressed with Rydor's strength compared to Lattee's and told him so. Rydor puff with pride.

Making several trips back and forth to retrieve all the phyrium, Rydor asked if he had enough polymer to mend the injured griswells as it was time to return to apply the prostheses. Morsian felt his heart thump so hard in his chest that he could hear it. He was not ready at all. However, a promise is a promise; he would do what he said he would do.

Gathering several buckets of polymer, Morsian walked down the hill to meet the herd members who would accompany him to the cave. Lattee indicated she would carry him and the buckets, which Morsian gladly accepted. Teetawn stepped up to carry a bucket in his mouth, and Frisky took yet another. Before long, Morsian's hands were free, and several other mastels formed a bucket brigade of sorts.

Arriving at the cave, each mastel carrying a bucket set it gently down on the ground even though the polymer seemed to cling to the inside and was not in danger of spilling. Forming a semi-circle around the cave opening, Rydor sent a message saying all the griswells were in contact with their bond friend, and it was fairly-safe to enter.

'Fairly safe?' Morsian stated.

'Go and get the job done quickly,' Rydor demanded. 'Flint will meet you in the left tunnel entrance. Take your light source and shine it down directly at your feet. Do not wave it around. It will hurt her eyes if you are not careful.'

Morsian walked into the cave and turned to look back at his beloved bondmate. He knew Rydor would not send him into the cave if it were unsafe, but he remained afraid. He knew how much the griswells hated him. Some of the griswells were not bonded and, therefore, dangerous. Entering their world was reckless and stupid. However, he needed to do it.

Keeping the beam of his light on his feet and no further ahead, Morsian soon heard a grunt. Flint was waiting at the left tunnel as Rydor indicated she would be. Turning, she led Morsian deeper into the tunnel and down to the belly of the cave. A terrible dread weighed him down as he followed Flint deeper into the dark, musky cave.

The buckets were getting heavy, and the lack of humidity was affecting his breathing. Trying to keep his light source pointed down only made the task more difficult. Finally, Flint came to a stop. Morsian could hear scampering noises and low growls close by. Afraid to proceed, he felt Rydor touch his mind to give him comfort momentarily. Morsian knew Rydor needed to keep his full attention on Flint at this very moment to ensure his safety.

Flint turned and barked for Morsian to follow her. A few steps further into the cave, she stopped. There was a griswell, growling menacingly. The beam of his light was pointed directly on the griswell's body, who showed his yellow teeth with saliva dripping to the ground, in an exaggerated grimace of pain...or maybe a threat.

Flint stepped over the griswell, placing her paws to either side of his head to block his teeth from biting Morsian, who bent to examine his hind leg. The leg, which was obviously badly fractured some time ago and healed in a disfiguring malunion, was useless to the griswell.

Nervously he took a handful of polymer and placed it gently upon the crooked leg. Picturing how the leg should look in his mind, they watched as the polymer wrapped around the deformed limp, snapping it into a natural position. Whether the bone was straightened or the polymer compensated for the maladjustment, Morsian could not tell in the dim light. All he knew was that once Flint stepped back from the griswell, the injured griswell stood on all fours perfectly.

Flint and several other griswells stepped in front of the recovered griswell and backed him deeper into the cave as another griswell limped pathetically towards the human, snapping his jaws in resentment. Again, Flint placed herself between the injured griswell's teeth and Morsian. This time, Morsian saw he would need to work on a front leg, which meant the danger of being bitten was greater.

Shining the light source onto the injured leg caused a beam to hit the griswell directly in the eyes. A howling squeal of pain escaped his mouth, and he instinctively snapped at Morsian, who leaned back quickly out of harm's way. Knowing that he must have light to see what needed to be done, Morsian knew he needed padding on his arm and was rewarded immediately by a ball of polymer sliding upward onto his forearm, making a protective barrier. With the protective padding in place, Morsian reached for the animal's front leg a bit too quickly, causing the aggravated griswell to push Flint aside, to bite down hard on Morsian's arm. Thanks to the padding, he felt no pain. Without another thought, he grabbed a ball of polymer from the bucket and placed it onto the determined griswells leg. Instantly, the griswell let go of his arm. Stepping back to see his handiwork, he was pleased the leg was set in a normal position.

Checking his arm, he discovered it was completely unharmed. A smile crossed his face as he realized the importance of the polymer's ability to protect.

Griswell, after griswell, was brought before him, some more belligerent than others. The last griswell was born with a deformity, which caused his one front leg to be several inches shorter than the other, making it impossible to do anything but limp along on three legs. Morsian evaluated the situation and knew the polymer would need to replace the lost inches between his leg and the ground. Wondering whether the polymer could artificially create the joints missing in the foot would be an extreme test for the substance.

Balling the polymer between his hands, Morsian stretched the goop several directions thinking how he would best attack this situation. Closing his eyes and picturing the other foot in detail,

Morsian released the polymer and watched it extend itself from the top of the leg to the ground below.

Amazed and feeling some disbelief that the polymer could take on any shape needed and still have the strength and flexibility was unbelievable yet incredible. Covering a limb or supporting it, as with a fractured bone, was one thing, but replacing a part of a missing limb was impossible…except that Morsian had just seen it done.

The griswell could walk. The polymer imitated the other foot, bending when it needed to bend and locking when it needed to lock. Morsian continued rubbing his head in bewilderment when Rydor suggested that he return quickly to the surface and don't look back. Rydor showed how difficult it was becoming for the bonded griswell to keep the non-bonded griswells from attacking his person, especially since this form of communication was entirely new and difficult for the mastels and the griswells.

Morsian didn't let a single flash of time-lapse under his feet. Letting the light source shine fully about the cave, he ran to the surface. 'Run faster, Morsian! The bonded griswells could not stop three of the non-bonded griswells from following you. The excitement of your running away has elicited the prey drive in them. Run! I will be at the entrance, and you will jump on my back. I will carry you swiftly to safety!'

Morsian could hear the growls and low-pitched grunts and knew the griswells were closer than he hoped. Not wasting an ounce of energy on looking backward, Morsian dug down with his heels to accelerate faster. With lungs burning and a stitch in his side, Morsian pushed through the pain, holding his ribs. Continuing to run like a lunatic until the drastic incline of the cave and his exhaustion, slowed his pace. Tripping, Morsian found himself scrambling on all fours until he could right himself. Inspired to push himself to his limits as his hearing heard the clicking of nails on the cave floor, he knew the griswells were closer than he realized.

Snapping jaws were close to grasping his trousers. He knew the griswells were inches from him. He wanted to turn and fight, but without weapons, he knew there was no chance against three griswells. He wondered why the bonded griswells had not given pursuit to protect him. The answer was clearly that they hated him no matter what he did for the disabled cave dwellers. They would never trust him, ever.

The light at the opening of the cave was before him. The light should have given him hope. However, Morsian knew he was not going to make it to the opening before he was hamstrung and crippled by the pursuing beasts. Giving one brief look back, Morsian was about to be impaled by the horns of Rydor, who ducked his head and squeezed into the cave opening.

'Get behind me. I will protect you. If these griswells are smart, they will retreat. If they aren't smart, I will kill them,' Rydor's intentions flashed into Morsian's mind.

'I hope you don't need to kill them,' Morsian reflected as he ran behind his mastel. 'I only just mended them. I would hate to see all my hard work go to waste.'

The three griswells stopped suddenly at seeing the extended horns and long claws between them and their prey. They stood their ground and continued to show their bared teeth. Having not bonded with a mastel, they lacked the respect and love that their fellow cave dwellers felt for the animals. With limited room in the cave, the three griswells could not fan out to attack the mastel from all sides. Rydor stood his ground and refused to back up where the tunnel opened into a larger space. Rydor, too, knew he had the advantage by keeping the griswells in a confined area.

With his head lowered and horns aimed at the vicious beasts, Rydor directed Morsian to go out into the sunlight. 'I can fight better if I know you are safely out of the way. Move to the sunlight. Better yet, go climb a tree.'

Morsian didn't want to leave his mastel to fight three griswells alone. Rydor's logic, as presented, was sound. Unless Morsian could find a weapon, he would be of no help to his mastel. Turning and running for the safety of the glaring sunlight, Morsian looked for a weapon as he headed for the trees. Only seeing a limb lying on the ground to be used as a weapon, Morsian decided to climb the tree as instructed.

Rydor advanced forward, pushing the griswells deeper back into the cave without going too much further himself. Seeing the horns, the griswells gave way and backed a few steps.

Rydor could hear many feet pounding coming from within the cave as Flint, Greyble, Bog, and Sunshine came to Rydor's aid. Scrambling on to the backs of the three menacing griswells, fur started to fly as biting, clawing, and shrill cries echoed throughout the cave. A flurry of black griswell bodies intermingled in frenzied fighting as Flint and Greyble attacked with the two youngsters rushing in to grab a mouthful of fur.

Rydor backed out quickly to get into the sunlight knowing that the bonded griswells now had the situation in control. Morsian ran down the hill with a small limb held over his head in both hands to be able to bring a killing blow if any griswell should come out of the cave after Rydor.

Morsian could hear Rydor's laughter in his mind. 'What's so funny?' Morsian asked while standing like a statue with the limb held over his head.

'Really, do you think you were going to save me with that little stick? If I can't dispatch three griswells with my two mighty horns and claws, what do you think a stick will do?' the stallion said mockingly.

'Get on my back. I will take you home where you can sleep and dream of being a warrior,' Rydor continued to mock.

Morsian slipped onto the mastel's back. His pride was hurt shortly until he saw himself through Rydor's eyes. He did make a rather comical spectacle. The limb really wasn't as big as he thought. Rydor was right; it was more of a stick. Laughter erupted from Morsian's mouth, and Rydor joined in with a snort and a chuckle.

CHAPTER SIXTEEN

Several of the mastel mares that weaned their youngsters were available to bond with the griswells that Morsian healed. Most of these griswells were more than willing to form a bond with the mastel mares just to end their nights of hunting. However, there were three of the once disfigured and injured griswell's that Morsian healed that refused this bonding.

The three who chased Morsian out of the cave were leary of mastels due to Rydor threatening them while protecting Morsian. The reasoning for why Rydor protected the human was something the three griswells could not comprehend. Refusing to bond with a mare, these griswells remained as they were for generations.

Coming out at night to hunt, the three-banded together. Usually, solo hunters, the three stayed together to eliminate the possibility of injury again. Finding Morsian alone at night was something they all hoped would happen. They continued an intense hatred for the human. Morsian couldn't understand why the beasts hated him that much when he was the one who made it possible for them to hunt. It was senseless.

'Can you explain why the griswells hate me so much and why the three who tried to kill me would try to do so when I am the one who fixed their legs?' Morsian asked of Rydor as he brushed his fiery red coat to a brilliant sheen.

'You smell like death to them,' was Rydor's only answer.

Puzzled, Morsian said, 'Do I smell like death to you?'

'You smell, but not like death. You smell more like dirty water,' Rydor's mental picture conveying stagnant water.

'I don't smell like stagnant water…do I? I take baths in clean water most every day. Why would I smell like dirty water? That doesn't make any sense to me,' Morsian said a bit offended.

Rydor checked his mental pictures until he could convey water not flowing quickly. He pictured a stream, barely moving, and let the image project to Morsian's mind.

'Well, that is different. You think I smell like a slow-moving stream. I can live with that. That is not the same thing as stagnant water. I thought you were comparing me with a sludgy, algae-covered pond. I don't know why I would smell like death to the griswells. Why wouldn't I smell like a slow-moving stream to them?' Morsian pondered.

'Noses are noses. My olfactory senses are quite keen. I can smell things from quite some distance if the wind is blowing in my direction. Griswells are cave dwellers. Their senses are developed differently and unique for their situations. Just as you can't pick up the odor of other creatures like yourself, for example, you, humans, are very sadly restricted with your nasal abilities,' Rydor tried to explain.

'You are right. I can't tell when another human is close unless they have perfume or haven't bathed in quite some time. I guess my nose is not as enhanced a sense as yours. I could not smell a human from a long distance, that is for sure," Morsian conceded.

Taking a long deep breath, expanding his chest greatly, Rydor threw his head up alarmed at the new odor he caught on the wind. 'Is that why you cannot smell the humans who are over that hill from us? I am going to take the herd to the forest and out of sight why you find out who they are and why they are here,' Rydor said as he stretched out his tail while running down to the herd.

Morsian scratched his head and wondered what Rydor was picturing. His picture was of multiple images of Morsians in a group. Rydor said that more humans were on the other side of the hill. Morsian could only decipher that Rydor had never seen another human beside him. He assumed all humans would look like Morsian. Putting on his boots, Morsian started the long walk up the hill to see who or what was on the other side.

Reaching the top, Morsian saw several familiar faces from his town. Calling out, Morsian stopped them in their tracks.

"Hey, Kellyn, Branley, Sturjen, I am up here!" yelled Morsian from on top of the hill.

Seeing Morsian running down the hill to meet them with a wide grin on his face gave the three travelers pause. When Morsian finally reached them, hugs and handshakes were exchanged.

'We were starting to think you were dead when you did not return to town after the time you said you would be home. We came looking for you. We are sure glad to find you well and healthy. Puzzled, Sturjen added, "Why have you stayed away so long?"

"It is a long story, and I don't want to bore you now. I do have some interesting discoveries to share with you that I think will astound you. Come to my camp, and I will tell you everything," Morsian said excitedly.

"Can't you tell us some of it on the way to your camp? We are really curious," Kellyn asked.

Branley, young, tall, and willowy, the introvert of the group withheld any comment. He smiled warmly at his mentor. Morsian noted his silence and gave him another big hug.

"How is my favorite apprentice? What have you been doing in my absence? Have you invented anything that I will claim credit for its making?" Morsian laughed good-naturedly.

"No, sir, without your direction, I fear not much has happened in the lab other than what you instructed us to do. I would be home right now, doing nothing, if it were not for the fact that Kellyn and Sturjen said I could be useful in finding your path through the forest and meadows. They said that I think like you...I don't mean to say that I am as smart as you, only that we think alike...sometimes," said the young man fumbling his words.

Morsian laughed at the young man's embarrassment. "We do think alike, that is why I picked you as my apprentice. It would be difficult to train a young man who doesn't think at all."

Kellyn, always straight forward, broke into the conversation, "You said you would tell us why you remained out in the wilderness as we walked back to your camp. I can't wait to hear what you will say. There has to be a good story in here somewhere to keep you out in this wilderness for this long."

Morsian took a deep breath before starting. "There are some really interesting dynamics in this part of the world. Let me start with my finding a herd of mastels."

"Okay... what are mastels?" Branley interrupted, always wanting the details.

"Hard to describe these beautiful creatures. They have the prowess of a big cat, the stamina of cart-pulling beast, and the most incredible eyes you will ever see. Their eyes glimmer and sparkle like gems. You will need to see one to believe it. They are amazing. Oh yes, and they have gold-colored buds on their foreheads that can become horns....and did I say they can climb trees.

"At any rate, because of phyrium, I can understand the stallion in my head. I can even read his thoughts from a k-rod away or maybe even further. We have never put it to the test to see how far away we can communicate with each other." Excited, speaking quickly, Morsian rambled on, unaware that the three men stopped walking and were looking at him as if he was crazy.

Abruptly becoming aware that his companions were no longer walking with him, Morsian turned and asked if something was wrong. The three could only stare at him.

"Oh, you don't believe that I can communicate with an animal in my head. I can sure understand your skepticism. Until you achieve this bond yourselves, it will be hard to explain. You will understand more soon enough."

Branley, not wanting the others to think his mentor and teacher was crazy, jumped to Morsian's defense. "What Morsian is trying to say, I think, is that he has figured out a communication system that allows him to understand this mastel creature. Is that right, Morsian?"

"Thank you, Branley, for trying to defend me. I know it sounds a bit crazy. I won't say I have figured out a system to communicate, really, what happens is that the mastel sends me pictures into my mind that conveys what he is thinking. It isn't spoken words as much as mental visuals. I can relay what I am thinking in some abstract form that Rydor can understand. Like I said, you must bond with a mastel to comprehend what I am saying."

"Why would I want to bond with a mastel, and what is phyrium, and who is Rydor?" Sturjen asked gruffly. Sturjen, large framed and strong, always opinionated and lacking imagination, never believing anything that he could not see with his own eyes looked at Morsian with an almost blank stare.

"You can't get phyrium if you don't bond with a mastel. There is no going down into the cave to get the phyrium with the griswells there," Morsian said enthusiastically, not realizing that nothing he said made any sense to his three fellow townsmen.

Kellyn spoke up, "You are not making any sense. I don't know what phyrium might be or what a griswell is either. Why would I want phyrium, and why would I need to go into a cave to get some?"

"Let me back up a bit. I see you are confused," Morsian said. "Phyrium is a unique mineral that has astounding properties. You won't believe what all it can do. I haven't even scratched the surface of what I think I can create. I am positive it will revolutionize our whole world.

For one thing, it is the reason I can communicate with my mastel." Kellyn was about to interrupt; Morsian stopped him. "I am not finished yet. Let me finish.

The mastels can bond with the griswells who live in the caves where the phyrium can be found deep within the walls. The griswells trust the mastels and bond with them easily since the mastels bring them food. That way, the griswells won't need to come out of their caves, which is dangerous for the beasts."

Shooting glances back and forth that indicated they were listening to a crazy man who had been out in the woods alone far too long, the three stopped listening to Morsian as he talked. It was obvious that they thought Morsian needed a doctor. Each was trying to figure out if Morsian was dangerous and how they were going to get him back home.

Morsian did not notice the looks passing between his friends and continued his explanation, "I can bond with my mastel because I have a source of phyrium thanks to Rydor. The phyrium can be used for other things as well, and that is why it is going to alter our world totally. Once we get to my campsite, I will be able to show you what all I have discovered about the phyrium. Oh wait, I can show you my ankle brace right now."

Lifting his trouser leg, Morsian showed his companions the glittery, shimmering brace around his ankle. "Now watch this. I am going to *think of* my brace falling off." As he did this, the brace slipped into a ball of goop at his feet.

"My ankle was bitten by a griswell, and it was terribly swollen and sore; I could barely walk on it. That is how I discovered phyrium's ability to do as I commanded in my mind. I will now *think* brace and watch the phyrium polymer return to my ankle." Thinking the chosen words, the polymer returned to Morsian's ankle to the surprise and amazement of the three men.

"Isn't that wonderful? It can do that much and more," Morsian said, seeing the disbelief in the eyes of his companions. "Wait until you see what I have been able to build with it." Morsian continued, almost dancing a jig in his excitement to share what all he discovered.

Branley was the first to fully understand what he had seen and said enthusiastically, "Morsian, that is amazing. I can't wait to get to your camp to see more. Come on, hurry. Show us the way!"

The other two men rubbed their eyes in disbelief. Each thought their eyes were playing tricks on them. As the two men raced to catch up with Morsian and Branley, they continued the climb to the summit of the hill. At the top, the meadow below was visible.

"Usually the mastels are grazing down below, however, for right now, Rydor has hidden them in the forest. He is unsure what humans might be, even though in his mind, you all look like me. At any rate, I will have him come out and meet you when I think the time is right. For now, let's go down to my camp. I can show you more of my discoveries and inventions."

Morsian continued to jabber, while the three men followed him down the hill. Morsian stopped and froze in his tracks. Finally, he said out loud, "I am not jabbering like a crazed bird. I am excited to share how special everything is here in your valley. I can't help it if I sound like a fool. That is really quite unkind of you."

Sturjen said under his breath, "He really is mad."

"Morsian is not crazy!" Branley said vehemently. "You saw his ankle brace. There is no explanation except what Morsian is saying is true. I think you should hear him out."

Morsian turned and said to the three, "I am sorry. That was Rydor being rude. He can be arrogant sometimes. I hope the mastels that you bond with are nicer than my stallion."

Morsian looked at the three men, one after the other. "I know this is all hard to believe... you will understand soon. Right now, we are close to my home. I think you will be astounded by what you see."

Leading the men to his home, the first thing the observers noticed was the small cabin seemingly shimmering and shimmying in the light. "Is that cabin moving? In fact, is that a cabin?" Kellyn asked as he shaded his eyes against the glare of the sun.

"Yes, and no," answered Morsian. "I mean, it stays on the provided foundation, but it can move a reasonable amount to accommodate certain fundamentals. It can sway that way the wind does no harm to the building, and the walls move to allow more space within the structure, but it doesn't move off the foundation unless...I need it to."

No one said a word in response to what Morsian just said. Instead, they followed Morsian inside his cabin like lost glemee. Once inside, the cabin looked twice as large as it did from the outside.

"This cabin inside looks bigger than it looks from the outside," offered Sturjen, turning his body in circles to take in the whole building at a glance.

"It will look even bigger when it expands to make room for the three of you. I, personally, have very little need for space. With the three of you staying here, we will need more space. The cabin can allow for three extra rooms. On which side of the cabin would you like your room?" Morsian asked, not realizing that he sounded irrational to the men in front of him.

"Come on; don't be shy," Morsian asked. "Who would like a room at the right rear of the cabin? It isn't there yet, so stop looking for it. The cabin will make the room as soon as I ask it to do so."

Branley stepped up quickly to show his faith in his mentor, "I will take that room, sir."

"Then it is yours," Morsian said as he mentally communicated with his cabin. In an instant, the cabin walls expanded to allow for another room. Stepping back in astonishment, Sturjen and Kellyn were ready to bolt from the cabin. They were completely distrustful of a structure that could expand since that meant it could also decrease in size, trapping them in a violet-colored goop.

The traveler's sudden change in mood was misinterpreted by Morsian, who decided it meant the travelers were exhausted and needed to sleep. "I will make mats for you to sleep on right now. Branley, you might want to help me. I think you will find the process fascinating."

"Thank you, sir, I would be glad to assist you with the experiment," Branley added quickly.

Kellyn and Sturjen didn't like hearing the word experiment used for the item they would be sleeping upon in a room that could snap closed at any time. Both were thinking it might have been a mistake to come looking for Morsian.

As the two travelers nervously ate a snack prepared by Morsian, not knowing one of the ingredients contained phyrium, Branley went about mixing up the two solutions, as directed by Morsian, to make more polymer. Bricks were placed side by side, and Branley watched in amazement as the bricks conjoined to make the sleeping mats. Once three mats were completed, Morsian and Branley joined the other two men for a meal.

"Would you like to meet Rydor this evening or wait until the morning?" Morsian asked his guests.

Branley voted to meet him yet this evening, whereas the other two voted to delay the meeting. Contacting Rydor mentally, Morsian told his friends that Rydor agreed with the decision to delay the meeting until the morning. It was decided that Rydor would come to the cabin once the humans finished their morning meal.

Relieved not to need to deal with Morsian imaginary friend that evening, the men settled down to enjoy their meal. Taking a small bite, Branley said, "This is quite delicious. There is a subtle taste that I have never tasted. Did you find some new herbs in the valley? I wouldn't mind having some to take home to my mother. She would really love this meal."

"Thank you, Branley," Morsian said, quite pleased that his company was enjoying the meal. "I hope to send lots of the ingredients home to you sometime soon. It will take some doing, though. The mineral is not the easiest to mine."

"Are you referring to phyrium? You mean there is phyrium in this meal?" Sturjen said, spitting out the mouthful of food into the palm of his hand.

"Why yes," Morsian replied. "The mineral is good for many things, and it is edible. I have been eating it for weeks. It is the reason I can communicate telepathically with Rydor. Eat enough of it, and you and the whole village will be able to communicate in the same way. By tomorrow, I suspect you will be able to read the thoughts I send to you without speaking. It is great. You will love it."

With sudden anger swelling up, Sturjen replied, "You had no right to feed us phyrium without our permission. That was wrong, and I am about ready to leave here." Sturjen abruptly stood to his feet.

Branley suddenly announced, "Did you just say that Morsian is a crazy fool, and you will report him to authorities?"

Sturjen looked at Branley in horror. "My thought was exactly that, but I did not say that out loud. How did you know what I was thinking?"

"My gosh! I can actually hear you thinking that as well. I can read your thoughts. This is amazing! Think about how much this will benefit us as a community. No more wondering what people think of you...well, maybe it could be bad...." Kellyn announced.

Morsian stopped the conversation before it got out of control. "No, that is not the way it works. Sturjen hasn't learned how to control his thoughts yet. With phyrium, you will have the ability to share what you want to share and keep to yourself things that you don't want others to know. It is quite simple. I see no drawbacks. I have no ill-effects from eating the mineral, and I have consumed my share. The griswells have eaten it all their lives with no problems, and the mastels have eaten it longer than me. It is safe, I promise."

Morsian was amazed that the larger dose of phyrium he put into the meal would affect his companions as quickly as it did. He looked around the table in amazement to assess each one individually.

Sturjen was feeling defensive. Finally, his shoulders started to relax as Kellyn remarked that he saw benefits in being able to communicate telepathically. "I will be able to let my wife know what I want for lunch, and it will be ready when I walk through the door. I will also be able to let someone know that I have been injured in the field and not lie out there for hours before someone comes to find me. Why I can even show my son how to do a job without having to stand over him. This means much more work will get done in a day. I love the idea!"

Branley beamed with his new-found ability. He remained quiet and observant, as was his nature. Secretly, he was shouting in joy. Only Morsian could hear his neurons crackling with excitement.

Being late and knowing the men had many new thoughts to process, Morsian suggested that they go to bed. Sleeping on the decision as to whether to mine the mineral for the village and discussing it in the morning seemed like the thing to do. Causing two more rooms to be added to the cabin was simple enough. Asking each man to take their sleeping mats, Morsian started to leave to go to his room where he could communicate the ups and the downs of his interactions with the three men to Rydor.

Morsian was in the middle of telling Rydor about his day when he received an alarm from Kellyn. 'The mat is trying to eat me! Help!'

Morsian laughed and communicated to Kellyn to relax. 'If you want out of bed, all you need to do is wiggle a bit, and the polymer will release you. You will have the best sleep of your entire life if you only relax.'

Morsian received no reply. Alarmed, Morsian went to Kellyn's room and found him fast asleep. Sturjen and Branley were privy to the communication. Because of being forewarned, neither felt afraid when their own sleeping mats cradled them to sleep.

The next morning, Morsian served breakfast a la phyrium. There was nothing that Morsian would not add phyrium to these days. The mineral was delicious and subtly flavored when mixed with berries, roots, meat, or whatever Morsian ate. The three friends did not complain about phyrium being placed in breakfast. Eating heartily, the three men talked about mining the mineral.

'This is where it gets tricky," Morsian confided. Mentally, Morsian showed his friends how the griswell dig out the phyrium from deep within the earth and how the mastels trade meat for phyrium.

"Now, we are the third part of this triangle. The griswells hate me and will probably hate you as well. I get phyrium from Rydor. He shares his phyrium because we are bonded, and I can do things for him that he can't do for himself. It would benefit the village if more of you could bond with a mastel. Many of the mastels who are bonded with a griswell find the little beasts willing to bring more phyrium to the surface for their mastel bondmates."

"How do we go about bonding with a mastel?" Kellyn asked directly.

Morsian sat quietly for a few seconds. "Rydor is coming to the cabin now. I will ask him. Wait until you see how magnificent Rydor is. I am in awe each time I see him, and I see him several times a day. Oh, I did caution you that he is rather rude. I don't believe all mastels are as rude as Rydor can be. This is just a warning so, you might understand why he is snorting. That is his way he shows contempt. However, it also can mean he is laughing at you. I will leave it to you to decide which it might be. Come on, he is outside right now."

Morsian led the way out the door of the cabin. All three men stood as like statues at seeing a mastel for the first time. Finally, Branley let out a whistle. "He is beautiful! I heard rumors from our elders that such an animal existed. I thought it was only a myth until now."

Rydor shook his head up and down in agreement and mentally told Morsian, 'I like this one. He is smart.'

Morsian laughed and replied out loud, "Of course, you like Branley since he flattered you. You are such an egotistical mastel."

'Not true. I know that I am one impressive stallion. It is a fact that any fool can see my grand physique with their own eyes,' Rydor snorted.

When Morsian relayed Rydor's thought to the other men, all three laughed. Sturjen added uncharacteristically, "He has a point. If it is true, then it is not conceited to admit it. We may all be fools, but we can see for ourselves that Rydor is the most beautiful animal on this planet."

Rydor snorted in agreement, shaking his head up and down to accent to his snort. Suddenly, Rydor's snorted loudly and reared on his high legs, and the snort took on a different meaning that all could decipher. It was no longer a chuckle but an alarm.

"Back into the cabin. Rydor says there is a terrible storm heading this way," Morsian said, guiding the men back inside. Rydor turned on his paws and ran back to the herd, who had already telepathically received his command to head for the large mastel cave at the far end of the meadow.

Racing as fast as possible, the herd tore up the grass as their claws gripped the turf. A scream of pain and fear was heard as far away as the cabin and Morsian reached out to Rydor to make sure he was alright.

'It is one of my fillies that tripped over a log, and now her leg is crooked. She can't get to her feet. Bring prostheses quickly!' Rydor projected into Morsian's mind. 'Quick! The storm is approaching very fast.'

Morsian grabbed Sturjen, who was closest. "Grab your bed mat and follow me." Morsian ran to the corner of his cabin, where he set up a small lab and grab the last batch of polymer made last night.

The two ran quickly down the hill and made a beeline towards the mare who was struggling to get to her feet. Her desperation and pain were obvious. Rydor stood over her until he saw Morsian coming. Knowing the storm was approaching quicker than Morsian, and the other man could arrive, Rydor raced to them and allowed both to sit on his back. Sturjen sat in front, allowing Morsian to help stabilize him as Rydor raced breathtakingly fast to their destination. Reaching the filly, Morsian told Rydor to get to the safety of the cave, and he and Sturjen would keep the young mastel safe.

Not arguing, Rydor raced away with the storm only moments away. Sending a mental command for his daughter to lie there and not move. Rydor commanded that she not fight with Morsian and allow him and Sturjen to help.

Morsian told Sturjen to lay next to the filly's head as Morsian commanded the bed mat to expand large enough to cover the injured mastel, Sturjen, and himself. Under cover of the mat, Morsian plied his polymer between his hands and laid it on the fractured leg. The polymer extended over the limb, molding to the leg to correct the injury.

Sturjen lay upon the mastel's neck, stroking and comforting her as best as he could. Whispering calming words, Sturjen was surprised when he could feel the filly's pain and sudden relief when the polymer mended her leg.

"Morsian, I could really feel her pain, …and then it stopped. Am I crazy? I have never felt anyone else's pain before. Was it my imagination? Was it really my mind being empathetic with this poor mastel?" Sturjen asked quietly yet unnerved to feel his brain crackling and sparking with exhilaration.

Morsian was about to explain about bonding when Sturjen exclaimed, "Her name is Fonrah. My gosh! How do I know that? I am crazy, that has to be it!"

Morsian said, "Congratulations! Give your new bondmate a gentle pat on her shoulder. Fonrah has picked you. Welcome to my world. You are going to love it."

CHAPTER SEVENTEEN

Sturjen was reluctant to leave Fonrah's side once the storm passed, even to eat or sleep. He marveled at her beauty. Fonrah's stripes were more pronounced than some of the other female mastels since her predominant coloring was almost red, rather than strawberry. The contrast with the cream color base was dynamic. Like many mastels, Fonrah's eyes glittered emerald green. Sturjen learned Fonrah was quite young. She was too young to bear a foal. Being the daughter of Rydor, she would look elsewhere for a mate.

Sturjen became concerned. 'If you find a mate, will you join his herd and leave this one? How will I fit in the equation if that happens?'

'Look around, bondmate. Do you not see many young stallions? They are not all sons of Rydor. Many young stallions leave their herd and join another. Rydor welcomes them if they do not try to steal his mares. Mastels are peaceful animals unless provoked,' Fonrah said as she nuzzled her special human.

Sturjen received a message from Morsian indicating that dinner was prepared, and Sturjen should join himself, Kellyn and Branley. When Sturjen explained the interruption, Fonrah pushed Sturjen a few feet away with her muzzle. 'Go and eat. I need to find grass, as well. It is getting hot, and the grass is starting to dry. I know Rydor is becoming nervous. He does not want to leave the griswells, yet the herd will starve if we do not depart for the high pastures soon.'

Distressed by what Fonrah expressed, Sturjen walked back to the cabin with a heavy heart. Walking in and sitting down at the table, Sturjen declared that there was a problem.

"We know. Rydor already informed Morsian of the problem. We have been discussing how we can help. Kellyn suggested that we go back to the village, load the carts with as much hay as we can, and bring it back here for the mastels. That way, they will not need to leave the valley," Kellyn said, verbally finding it easier to use words for some things.

Morsian continued the discussion. "We feel that Branley should take phyrium to the village and show the people what can be made from this unique mineral. The villagers would probably be willing to provide hay for the mastels in exchange for phyrium once they can see the applications. Branley is quite good at making the polymer and has some expertise in building with the polymer bricks. He is already experimenting with other forms into which the polymers can be manipulated."

"I want to remain here," Sturjen announced. "I really don't want to leave Fonrah. She is very young. I feel that she needs me."

Kellyn laughed and then added, "You can stay. Branley and I can handle getting the carts of hay. We will bring back enough to nourish the mastels until we can get a regular trade going. We will need more phyrium than what we are getting at present if we intend to supply the villagers with the many items they will want. We need to figure out how to bypass the griswells."

"That is not going to happen. What we really need is to figure out how to mine with the griswells. From what I have observed, they are the only means of excavating the mineral since it is extremely fragile...our equipment would ruin it. Rydor also suggested that the mineral is not easily detected. The griswells have some innate ability to find it, even when it is deep within the walls of the cave. I think the griswells are here to stay," Morsian relayed. "We have some details to work out yet. First things first, tomorrow Branley and Kellyn will depart our company to get the hay. Everyone needs a good night's sleep—and that includes you, Sturjen. You are not going to sleep under the stars with Fonrah again."

"Don't tell me that you did not sleep with Rydor when you first bonded with him," Sturjen said defensively, crossing his arms tightly against his chest.

"I certainly did not!" Morsian said with emphasis and then added meekly, "Rydor would not stand for it."

The group laughed at Morsian's expense. They all knew that Rydor was a stallion, and he guarded the herd at night. There was no way he would allow a human to interfere with his duties.

The men talked a bit longer, and then one by one, they excused themselves for bed. Morsian explained to Rydor what the other humans would be doing to bring cut grass for the herd.

'Sounds terrible,' Rydor snorted a complaint. 'Dried grass will need to do, I suppose. It is better than leaving the griswells to fend for themselves again. They have become quite dependent upon us for meat, and we are as dependent upon them for phyrium. I need to be able to communicate with the whole herd at one time. It is good to be able to tell the herd to run for cover instead of having to nip at their heels. Life is better now. Thank the men for their travels to get the grass cuttings…even if I am certain it will taste terrible.'

'You realize that there will be some changes now that more men will come to your valley. They will want phyrium, too, and that means the mastels need to ask the griswells for much more phyrium allowing us to build here. There will be benefits to the herd, though,' Morsian added before Rydor could object.

'What benefits?' Rydor reached out to Morsians mind, quite curious.

'Well, we have modern medicine that can cure many ills and wounds when there are no berries growing or feigons available. I know the feigons burrow deep within the ground when it is cold,' Morsian said. He continued, 'Speaking of cold, we can build a huge barn out of a polymer that will house all the mastels when the weather becomes too cold or too hot to tolerate. We can also store all the hay that the herd will need. We have weapons that we can use to fight the horrible river monsters from a great distance away; that way, the monsters will never get close enough to kill one of the foals. If that is not enough, we will brush your coat, til it shines brighter than the sun. We will pull burrs and thorns from your fur. We will even clip your claws if they grow too long.'

Morsian took a breather as he thought about all the other things that humans did for the beasts of burden in their village. Carefully he guarded those mental pictures knowing Rydor would become incensed. Morsian was about to list several other things that came to his mind when Rydor stopped him.

'Enough. I am sure you have good intentions. Some things appeal to me. I like the idea of you picking out the burrs from my coat or between my paws. When I try, they get stuck in my mouth. That has always been an unpleasant task. We will make it work,' Rydor said in mental pictures.

Morsian laughed at the vision of Rydor, spitting out burrs from his mouth. He was enchanted with his bonded mastel. Brusque as Rydor could often be, he was also witty, charming, and fun. Morsian hoped their bond would last forever.

The griswells were completely a puzzlement for Morsian. He could not understand their hatred towards him, and the explanation that Morsian smelled like death to the griswells did not really seem feasible. However, Rydor did say their nasal passages were different than humans or mastels. Maybe humans really did smell bad. There was no realistic or safe experimentation that

Morsian could perform on the creatures to find out further answers--or none that he dared to try.

Another thing that concerned Morsian was how the mastels might persuade the griswells to toil harder to dig for extra phyrium. The incentive presently was to acquire daily portions of meat. The incentive for more meat would not work as the extra meat would only spoil. What could inspire the griswells to work that much harder when their extra toil would mainly benefit humans, whom they hated? The beast's needs were minimal—food and occasional medical attention. Those needs were all Morsian could decipher from communication with Rydor.

Rydor broke into Morsian's thoughts. Morsian not guarding his mind's output as he went through scenario after scenario, trying to find the one possible solution to motivating the griswells to dig for more phyrium. 'Flint has shown me one major concern the griswells are presenting...,' Morsian started to interrupt when Rydor sent a powerful mental bolt of disapproval for the interruption.

Rydor clearly felt it was his prerogative to interrupt Morsian's unfinished thought and was irritated when Morsian's mind intruded into his own. Afterall, Rydor is the king of the valley, and certain rights are his and his alone.

Rydor continued with a long mental sigh of frustration, 'Can you ever be patient and let me finish what I am trying to tell you? Now, let me finish.' Rydor feeling Morsian's resignation continued. 'As I was trying to convey, the griswells can dig into the existing cave walls to dig out the phyrium. However, the source is dwindling. The griswells need phyrium as much as we do, and they say there is more phyrium deeper down within the ground, but they cannot dig down through the layers of rock with their claws. If humans can dig new tunnels, the griswells agree to excavate the new veins of the mineral, as long as the humans stay away from their dens.'

Morsian was more than excited. He could not keep himself from shouting out loud. "That is perfect! Our miners have equipment that can drill down into the cave walls creating new tunnels and even new shafts much deeper down. I am sure we can work with the griswells, or at least, keep out of their dens. It will work, I am sure!"

Hearing Morsian shouting and talking to himself, Kellyn woke and came to Morsian's room. "What is all the shouting about?" Kellyn said, reverting to the spoken language.

"I am sorry I woke you. Rydor has come up with the solution to the problem that has been bothering me for weeks," Morsian said.

Kellyn, curious, replied with a question, "Which is what?"

"You know we will need lots of phyrium, and I could not think of anything that might motivate the griswells to dig more of the mineral. Rydor now informed me that the amount of mineral remaining in the present caves is diminishing quickly. If we could dig more tunnels and shafts to make caverns, the griswells will continue to excavate the phyrium, and we will all share the mineral. It is perfect."

"Except you said the griswells hate us; what is going to keep them from attacking us once we are down in the mines?" Kellyn said, reminding Morsian of the obvious other problem.

"That is where bonding comes into play. I have Rydor, who has bonded with Flint. Rydor can keep Flint calm enough for me to enter the cave. If every miner bonded with a mastel that was bonded with a griswell, we could go down and work in relative safety from the griswells. There are only a few renegade griswells, and we will need to decide what to do about them once the miners begin to arrive. In the meantime, I am feeling very optimistic about this venture." Morsian replied with a huge smile spreading across his face.

"If any of this is going to work, I guess I best get some sleep. Branley and I must start off in the morning. The earlier we get started, the sooner we can get back. I anticipate that it may take a few days to return to the village, buy and load the hay, talk with the people about the benefits of phyrium and get them excited enough to be on board, and then return with the hay," Kellyn said as he opened the door to leave Morsian's room.

Morsian stopped Kellyn with one last thought, 'I could possibly, and I do mean possibly, shorten your trip back by two days if Rydor can convince two mastels to allow you to ride on their backs. They would get you back to the village a bit after dark tomorrow. Any reason you would not be willing to hitch a ride?'

Gulping, Kellyn asked, 'You are sure that mastels only eat vegetation, and there is no way they might want a snack of meat, right?'

'Go to bed, you goof head. Mastels don't eat meat. You will be perfectly safe. In fact, you will be very safe if you remember those buds become weapons if anything should attack you on the way home. And have you seen those claws? Nothing is going to bother you while you ride one of them. Should I ask Rydor? I can't say for sure any mastel will allow you to ride without bonding. Lattee, however, carried me, and we weren't bonded,' Morsian said.

'Sure, go ahead and ask. I will see you in the morning, bright and early.' Kellyn closed his mind as well as the door and returned to the cozy polymer bed mat.

Lattee and another graceful mare were standing at the cabin door, waiting to carry Kellyn and Branley to the outskirts of the village. Sturjen was standing beside Fonrah, agreeing to accompany the two for several hours. He would go to translate anything the two mares may need to communicate with their riders. Rydor was the one to suggest that Fonrah and Sturjen go with the others for reassurance.

Feeling nervous about climbing onto the backs of the mastels, Sturjen gave each man suggestions. "Don't grab the mane! You can gently hold on if you need to do so. Try to use your legs by squeezing your knees inward, gently...do not, and I mean do not, grip them with your knees tightly, since that will hurt the mare's ribs. Be sensitive to their needs. They will go slowly at first until you get balanced. Then the mares will want to stretch out and run fast to get you to the village in good time. Come on, let us get this trip started. I will interpret for you for a few hours, and then you are on your own," Sturjen instructed.

Letting go of the manes for a few seconds, the two men waved goodbye to Morsian. Big smiles appeared on their faces when they realized they were riding on a mastel. Morsian wished he could convey how much more remarkable it would be if they were bonded.

While left alone, Morsian settled down to try another idea that formed in his mind several nights earlier. Looking at the magnetic rock he and Branley found close to the cabin, Morsian went about breaking it down into a fine powder. Adding it to a batch of polymer made with the resin of the jicerian tree and phyrium, Morsian prepared the new polymer over an open fire, boiling it while stirring the chemicals. The result was a diamagnetic polymer.

Thinking about ways he could use the diamagnetic polymer, Morsian made molds for a rotor that would be placed inside of the housing mold he also created. Morsian waited for the new polymer to cool before pouring the polymer into these waiting molds.

From the batch of diamagnetic polymer, Morsian created a Teleetheric switch that could respond to thought as well as the biofeedback needs of humans. This third part would allow Morsian to mentally communicate with the switch to turn the contraption on or off... Morsian hoped.

With the rotor turning rapidly within the housing and operating on thought command, Morsian went about making a polymer panel. Once the original polymer panel was attached to the spinning shaft of the rotor...the panel became as bright as the sun. Delighted when he found the panel lighting upon command or turning off completely with a thought command, Morsian decided with a few changes, the panel could be commanded to become hot or cold as well. A new thought crossed Morsian's mind that he could vary the intensity of the light and the room temperature by commanding the rotor to spin at varying speeds. With a little time, the switch would decipher the humans' needs and respond accordingly.

Startled by a piercing thought from Rydor, Morsian received a graphic picture of the herd fleeing from the terrifying screaming sounds coming from Morsian's cabin. Not realizing the generator was making that much racket, Morsian quickly commanded the generator to halt.

'I am very sorry, Rydor,' Morsian sent a mental picture down the hill and across the meadow to where Rydor was overlooking the panicked herd. 'Tell the herd it is safe. The noise they hear is only a few whining sounds from my newest invention. I will figure out a way to stifle the irritating noise, I promise.'

Relieved, the herd would be back to grazing once Rydor convinced them the noise would be muted; Morsian danced with glee at his invention. Thinking about how he could attach a generator to the walls on all the buildings created with a phyrium polymer, the problem of heat, cooling, and lighting would be eliminated.

When Sturjen returned from accompanying the other two men on mastel back, he found Morsian busy connecting his generator to the cabin walls. Morsian greeted him with a huge smile. Sturjen, seeing the contraption, hesitated to enter the cabin.

"Look what I created? Now I can heat or cool my cabin with my mind. I can also command the panel to light the cabin, or I can turn it off. My mind is whirling with all the possibilities! My diamagnetic polymer will revolutionize our energy requirements. I might even be able to create an oven that would respond to my mental command. Isn't it astounding?" Morsian continued to beam, waiting for Sturjen to show signs of excitement as well.

"It would be great if you could invent a vehicle that would go where you want it to go and not need to send men on mastel back to retrieve the hay. The cawwen, the bulky beasts of burden, are going to be too slow hauling the hay back. It is going to take a lot longer for the wagons of hay to arrive then it would if the mastels were pulling the wagons. I know the mastels won't agree to pull wagons. I already made the mistake of picturing it in my mind without guarding my thought to Fonrah. She was extremely haughty while scolding me for thinking she was a beast of burden. She almost bucked me off her back.... I was thinking it would be better not having any animals doing the work," Sturjen said, stating his opinion.

"You might have come up with an interesting idea. What if I attached smaller generators to all four wheels on a wagon or cart? I could make wheels out of phyrium polymer, make the smaller generators, and the rest would only need to be 'cerebral,' thinking the wagon where I wanted it to go. Well, maybe I would need to figure out how to communicate for one wheel to slow down and another to speed up to make a turn. Those are fine points to be worked out. I believe with time, the phyrium would make biofeedback adjustments as well. I probably would not need to make such specific directional thoughts in time. I need to figure out how to direct the wagon from place to place. Hopefully, Branley may have some suggestions, as well. He is a smart young lad," Morsian shared this thought with Sturjen verbally.

Slipping into thought communication, Sturjen reacted, 'Leave me out of the process. I am never going to understand how phyrium can do what it does. After all, it is only a mineral.'

Loudly, Morsian said, "Only a mineral! All minerals have incredible properties, but phyrium is the King of all minerals. It is not just a mineral. This mineral is going to turn your world upside-down."

"Alright, it is not just a mineral. It is amazing! Actually...I do like the fact that we can regulate the temperature in the cabin. This is nice. I will sleep well tonight on my phyrium bed with the walls nice and warm. Thanks. See you in the morning," Sturjen said as he went to his room to sleep, leaving Morsian drawing up plans for Sturjen's idea of a beast-less moving cart.

CHAPTER EIGHTEEN

The mastels left Kellyn and Branley to walk the last several k-rods, not wanting any contact with other humans. Even though the herd had come to trust the humans in their company, mainly due to Rydor and Fonrah being able to sense their sincerity and kindness, Morsian implied to Rydor that not all Aztarians are good. Rydor told the herd members that Morsian said some humans were sent away from the city and villages because they did bad things. These men were living in the wilds or badlands someplace and must be avoided at all costs.

The mares returned from carrying Kellyn and Branley, saying that they had no encounters with townsmen or villagers. Therefore, they could not say whether Aztarians are all good, wonderful people or not. Knowing that men would probably accompany the wagons with the cut grass, some of the mares wanted to run to the hills and hide until those men went away.

With descriptive pictures, Rydor conveyed these thoughts. 'There will only be a few Aztarians who are needed to drive the beasts to our valley. If I sense any danger, I will tell you to hide, so don't be rash. Planning will be necessary. I may ask Morsian to accompany me, and we will meet these wagons. If Morsian finds any of the Aztarian men to be suspicious, I will send word for the younger stallions to take you to a place where you can be concealed. Remember, we have obligations to the griswells. We can't all leave no matter what I feel about the men I encounter.'

Since Rydor was not guarding these thoughts, Morsian received the same mental pictures as the herd. In the middle of making molds for wheels and smaller rotors and housings to make the generators that would be used to move wagons, Morsian hid his own thoughts of annoyance that he might need to leave his precious work to calm some hysterical mares. The last thought was not concealed, as well as he thought.

Rydor responded quickly, 'My mares are not hysterical, whatever that means. They have foals, colts, or fillies to protect. We don't know if these men are as good as you, Branley, Kellyn, and Sturjen. I need you to come with me. I want to check them out for myself.'

'When?' Morsian sighed. 'I am right in the middle of another invention that could benefit the herd greatly. If I can make the diamagnetic polymer generators move and turn the wheels on the wagon with mental thought, we could have wagons, with no more than one man at the lead, going back and forth quickly to the village to gather more hay and other supplies. The wagons could go during any weather unless passable terrain was washed away by floods. Even the pelting lightning bolts would not stop the wagons. Think about that, Rydor!" Morsian let his thoughts flow rapidly from one picture to another.

Rydor snorted, 'It would be nice to get the cut grass here quickly and not have those filthy, stupid beasts of burden coming into my valley. Those beasts are only huge glemee and nothing more. I can't abide by them.'

'Won't it be good if I can get the wagons to move by themselves? No stupid huge glemee coming here!' Morsian thought with glee, knowing he was making a point that could possibly sway Rydor. He wanted nothing more than to remain working on his invention.

'That is in the future. I would like for you to come with me to meet the wagons,' Rydor said, causing Morsian to feel a bit let down. 'I need to personally see these other men. I want to make sure they are not bad men.'

Morsian sighed and resigned himself to the fact that his invention must wait. 'I am sure Kellyn and Branley would not allow bad men to come with them to the valley. If it puts your mind at ease, I will be glad to go with you. Do you need to see them close up and personal, or can we maybe look at them from afar?'

Morsian was relieved when Rydor agreed. If Morsian could tell him who the other humans are and assure him that they are very good men, he would not need to be close enough to smell them. Morsian wasn't sure that would really shorten the time away from his inventions. However, it was better than riding all the way to meet and greet with the drivers of the wagon.

'In three days, I think we should leave the herd and approach the arriving wagons,' Rydor decided.

'Oh, I have three days to work on my invention. That is wonderful. I thought you might want to leave tomorrow,' Morsian thought and went back to work on his small generators.

Rydor snorted in disbelief that his bondmate could get excited about anything that was not edible or harmful. Turning his attention back to the herd, he watched as his sons played fight-games, honing their skills for battle when the need might arise.

Teetawn and Frisky were together constantly. Neither seemed interested in playing with the other young mastels. All the other youngsters were half-siblings. They were older or younger than Teetawn and Frisky and not very interesting to them. Occasionally, Wildflower would want to join in their games, but the two would outrun her and leave her to complain to her mother that the boys were mean.

Rydor barely noticed when Wildflower decided she was not going to be left behind on this morning. Teetawn and Frisky headed for the forest. Often, the two would commune with Sunshine and Bog in the caves to see what the two young griswells were doing. Today, griswells resentful communication showed that they were awakened by the young mastel's thoughtless intrusion into their minds. Apologizing profusely to their bondmates, Teetawn turned his thoughts back to Frisky, suggesting that they go further into the forest.

Running merrily around trees, up into the branches, and leaping from limb to limb, the two young mastels were enjoying life and their nearly mastered skills in the trees. Looking to the edge of the forest, Frisky spotted some huge boulders that looked perfect for scaling. Frisky remembered how difficult it was when the herd was enroute to the high meadows. He pictured his fall and the ensuing break that gave him the name of Three Legs. Now, he wanted to prove to himself that he could leap from boulder to boulder to the top of the hill as Frisky.

Teetawn, always game for another challenge, encouraged the idea, and the two set off at a fast run to the bottom of the cliff. Not realizing that Wildflower was in pursuit, the two started their ascent without looking back.

Halfway up the hill, Frisky spotted Wildflower at the base. He sent a warning for the younger filly not to try to climb after them. It was then that Teetawn smelled a horrible stench that reminded him of the Orange River and the monsters that lived within that murky water. Scanning the horizon, Teetawn saw a flash of a spiked tail as it slipped into the shadows of a large jutting rock not too far away.

'Wildflower, climb now!' Teetawn mentally shouted at the little filly, showing the spiked tail in his communication.

Confused that Frisky said not to climb and now Teetawn was telling her to climb, Wildflower hesitated as she decided which course of action she should follow. Sniffing the air, the filly let

Teetawn's warning win. She sprang to the top of the lowest rock and frantically tried to decide which boulder she could leap to next.

The river monster appeared below her and reared up on its hind legs within an inch of the filly's legs. Stretching out its body is all that the monster would need to do to knock the filly off the rock.

'Climb!' snarled Teetawn as he watched the river monster's beady eyes lock onto the little female mastel.

Frisky screamed his fury at the monster and sent out a message to the herd for help. Knowing the herd could not come before the little filly would be killed, Frisky leaped back down the several large stones he had previously scaled. Teetawn followed.

Wildflower, while trying to figure out which boulder she might be able to leap upon, was caught off guard as the river monster leaped upwards and knocked her legs out from under her. Falling to the ground between the legs of the scaly monster, Wildflower screamed in fear but managed to scramble to her feet.

The river monster pinned the filly down by lowering his body and blocking her escape. Meowing noises escaped the frightened filly as the breath was slowly being pressed out of her lungs.

Teetawn and Frisky extended their small horns and lowered their heads for a charge at the armored beast. Spikes protruded from every part of the foul creature.

Teetawn showed Frisky the only vulnerable spot for the attack, and the two mastels spread out; each was on one side of the monster's head, searching for the vulnerable spot. 'Aim for the eyes!' visualized Teetawn.

Rushing in quickly, the two attacked simultaneously, aiming for the target. The monster lifted its head, high, to remove his eyes from danger and braced himself for the attack. His tail whipped around, aiming its blow at Teetawn, who quickly leaped to a rock above his head.

Frisky rushed again and managed to strike between two of the spikes causing the monster to bellow in pain. His beady eyes turned their entire attention towards the young colt.

The monster shifted his weight to launch an attack at Frisky. Teetawn saw an opening for Wildflower to escape when the monster moved to attack. Teetawn quickly communicated to Wildflower a way to get out from under the crushing weight of the monster. Seeing the safe opening in her mind, Wildflower, though exhausted, forced herself to move quickly to get free from under the bulky body.

Feeling his prey shifting her weight from under his body, the monster took his eyes off Frisky and turned his attention to the fleeing female mastel. Frisky lowered his head and charged as Teetawn jumped down and circled to the other side of the monster.

Wildflower's little buds erupted into small weapons and snorted her threats for the monster to back away from her. Spewing saliva, the river monster advanced the short distance that separated him from his next meal.

Teetawn and Frisky coordinated their attacks, and both plunged into the monster, trying to hit the eyes. Teetawn grazed one eye and was rewarded with blood spurting onto his body. Frisky's horns hit well below the eyeball, adding to the pain the monster was feeling.

Enraged by pain, the river monster whirled around to face Teetawn, knocking Wildflower from her feet and sending her rolling across the ground. When she did not get to her feet, Frisky rushed to stand between her and the monster.

Teetawn leaped upon a boulder an instant before the vicious monster charged full speed at him, causing the monster to hit the rock wall with a crushing force. Shaking his head, the monster backed slowly away. Looking up and seeing he could not reach his prey; the river monster turned his bulk to face Frisky.

Snorting and pawing the ground, the monster was preparing himself for a full charge at Frisky. Trumpeting could be heard in the forest as the entire herd of mastels charged into view with gleaming horns fully extended and ready for battle.

Realizing his only chance at a prey was now, the monster charged at Frisky and Wildflower, with the hopes of snagging one and running back to the safety of the river. Mouth wide open with long, sharp teeth visible, the monster charged with Frisky instantly making the decision to stand his ground and protect his sister.

Teetawn seeing his siblings in danger, leaped upon the monster's back with claws extended, causing the animal to swerve barely enough to miss the two mastels. Falling off the beast, Teetawn lay bleeding where spikes impaled his underbelly.

The mastel herd reached the youngsters and formed a circle to protect them from the monster. With adult mastels and their formidable weapons exposed, the river monster retreated with several stallions taking up the chase.

Rydor bent down to examine his fallen son. Blood flowed freely from the wounds. Geselle came forward and licked the wounds while Rydor reached out to Morsian to come quickly to the hilltop, where Rydor would meet him to carry him to the injured young mastel.

Several mares were given the task to find berries and feigons as quickly as possible as Rydor raced to retrieve his bondmate. Tearing up the grass, Rydor continued to communicate to Morsian what might be needed.

Morsian, with his first aid kit inside his backpack, raced down the hill to meet his beloved mastel. Knowing how much Rydor loved his son, Morsian felt a huge responsibility to save the strong-willed young animal.

Leaping upon the stallion's back, Morsian clung on while the mastel raced against time. Morsian ducked, seeing the terrain through Rydor's eyes, as Rydor swiveled around trees with low hanging branches. Even knowing Rydor was about to take to the treetops to shorten the distance between him and the injured colt, Morsian almost lost his seating. Rarely had Rydor leaped into branches with Morsian on his back, and Morsian was unprepared for Rydor's muscles knotting up for such maneuvers.

Coming into the clearing with mares in a circle to protect the young mastel, Morsian leaped from Rydor's back as he grabbed his backpack from his back and placing it in front of him. Before reaching Teetawn, Morsian had pulled his first aid kit out of the bag.

Kneeling by Teetawn's side, Morsian searched for a pulse and found it thready and shallow. Knowing the young mastel had lost too much blood, Morsian felt it was imperative to stop the bleeding. 'Would that measure be enough?' Morsian asked himself. Asking Rydor to place his large paw on the gauze covered wound to apply pressure to cease the bleeding, Morsian threaded his needle to begin suturing the wound together. As mares arrived with feigons, Morsian visually told Rydor which minor wounds to allow the insects to close. Chewing berries into juice, the mares let the fluid flow freely onto the minor injuries while Morsian worked to close the many layers of muscle injured by the monster's spikes.

The young mastel lay as if dead even after all the wounds were closed, and Morsian knew Teetawn needed to replace the lost blood as quickly as possible. Explaining to Rydor as clearly as he could with mental pictures, Morsian showed how he would take blood from the stallion and introduce it into the colt's own bloodstream.

Rydor's ear pricked forward, and a startled snort escaped his mouth. 'It is the only thing that will save the colt,' Morsian explained.

Rydor dropped to the ground and lay beside his son while Morsian gathered the instruments from his kit. Needing to be the physician often in his village, Morsian confessed to the stallion that he had only done this procedure once before in his life.

Rydor lay his head down, and his crystal-clear eyes swirled in his trust and love for his human. 'I know you will save my son even if you must take all my blood to save him.'

Morsian gathered his wits about him, and after applying a venous restriction band onto the stallion's upper foreleg, Morsian proceeded with making the initial cut into the stallion's vein. 'I will not lose you,' Morsian conveyed with desperation.

Once the procedure was completed, Morsian wiped the sweat from his eyes and a tear of joy that his beloved bondmate survived the procedure. He advised Rydor to go and drink plenty of water to help replace the blood he donated to his son. He and the mares would remain by Teetawn's side. The day was hot, and the colt needed water, too. Morsian took vitals on the colt and decided Teetawn was stable, and he could go and make some preparations for the young mastel to be transported to a safer place out of the sun to convalesce.

Morsian conveyed his intentions, and Rydor reached out to Lattee to once again carry Morsian back to the cabin. Having made a large platform of polymer, Morsian set about placing it upon the four generators already attached to the wheels. 'This experiment had better work,' Morsian said to himself. 'The colt's life is not out of danger yet. I need to get him to the mastel cave quickly.'

Once the platform was secured to the generators and wheels, Morsian using his mind thought forward motion, and the four wheels worked together to move ahead. Exhilarated, Morsian let his mind go blank to everything but the details he needed to direct each wheel as he practiced making turns to the left, right, and to back up.

Once Morsian could steer his new Morsian Lorry or Morry as Morsian fondly called his invention, Morsian drove his beast-free cart down the hill and across the meadow. Finding paths in the forest that would accommodate the width of the Morry, Morsian arrived where Teetawn lay, encouraged to see the colt's eyes open. Regrettably, the slow whirling of the eyes indicated Teetawn was in pain. One only needed to look at the little colt to see how weak he was.

Rydor returned from drinking his fill of water to stand beside Geselle and Teetawn. Seeing the Morry, Rydor vocalized his glee that Morsian completed his invention. Something between a whinny and howl escaped Rydor's mouth as he stomped, throwing his head up and down in excitement.

'Now you will see how it will be useful,' Morsian said pridefully. 'We need to get Teetawn up on the Morry. Rydor, see if Teetawn can get to his feet long enough to lie upon the platform?' Morsian instructed.

Rydor reached his son's mind and showed the colt what was expected of him and what he was to do. 'Get to your feet. I know it will be painful, but we will give support.'

Teetawn pulled his legs under his body to try to rise. The pain was excruciating; screaming, he fell back to his side, panting and whining.

'Get to your feet, son.' Rydor pushed again. Going to Teetawn's back, Rydor leaned his head against the colt's back and pushed as Teetawn struggled to his feet, whimpering sadly as he made an attempt. Geselle rushed in to lend her body as support, and the two adult mastels gently guided the colt from his knees to his feet.

Morsian moved the Morry as close as possible to Rydor, and Rydor slipped out from between his son and the Morry. Teetawn fell backward onto the Morry as Geselle supported the colt's legs to help position him onto the platform. The mat softly accommodated the colt's weight and curled slightly around his body to secure him to the platform.

Not wanting to move the Morry before Teetawn was comfortable, Morsian instructed the platform to soften any bouncing that may occur as the Morry hit rocks, dips, or uneven ground along the way to the cave where the mastels took refuge during storms. Small adjustments could be seen visibly as the polymer platform responded to Morsian's thoughts.

Moving slowly and methodically through the forest and adjacent meadow, the Morry continued its forward movement until the cave was reached. Not wanting to make the colt move to his feet again, Morsian suggested leaving the colt on the platform until he was in less pain.

'The platform will be more comfortable than the hard ground of the mastel cave anyway,' Morsian suggested to Rydor.

Looking to Teetawn, Rydor could see that Morsian was right. The colt seemed comfortable now that the Morry was not moving.

Days passed, and Teetawn wanted to get to his feet to graze. The sutures were holding, and the feigons remained clamped down with their sizeable mandibles. From time to time, Teetawn needed to be reminded not to scratch at the healing incisions. Geselle used her muzzle to press him back down on the platform making it clear he was not to rise yet. Geselle would continue to bring him mouthfuls of grass she could find. Morsian contributed by bringing in a large wood trough to hold water. While recuperating, Teetawn barely needed to move to reach the water and food.

Rydor felt comfortable enough with the colt's progress that he reached out to Morsian. 'Time to ride out and meet the wagons coming in this direction. I want to make sure you know the men coming with Kellyn and Branley.'

Morsian was already working on another project. He knew how much the bumping along the uneven ground pained the young colt even with the cushioning of the platform on the ride to the mastel's cave. Morsian thought it might be beneficial to figure out how to make the Morry move without wheels. If it could hover over the ground, the ride would be smoother, and terrain would be less of a factor.

'You can think about it as we ride,' Rydor conveyed his impatience to Morsian.

Morsian knew he would give in and meet Rydor at the cabin door and said as much. When he walked out, Morsian found Rydor waiting. Morsian wondered whether Rydor was there all along.

'Let's get going before it gets hot,' Morsian indicated the level of the sun with a glance at the horizon.

Morsian carefully climbed onto Rydor's back. Rydor allowed Morsian to leap upon his back when Teetawn was injured; now, it was a different circumstance, and Rydor expected Morsian to be considerate. Lowering his body, allowing Morsian to settle comfortably before Rydor leaped into a graceful lope, the two were off and gone in moments. Only a few mares even bothered to watch as they moved out of sight.

Climbing to the top of a hill, Morsian saw the wagons moving slowly along below. They were not close enough for Morsian to distinguish individual faces. He told Rydor they must get closer. Moving down the hill, Morsian kept his eyes trained on the people in the wagons. Halfway down the hill, Morsian could make out Branley and Sturjen.

'Oh, that third man is Tyleed. He is kind. Notice he does not use his whip on the beasts at all. The man driving the third wagon I recognize as Kobart. He is a good man, too. I can't tell who is driving the middle wagon yet. His hat is hiding his face. We either will need to get closer or stay a bit longer until the wagons draw nearer,' Morsian told the stallion.

Rydor responded with pictures of the blazing hot sun and not wanting to exert any more energy than needed. 'We already need to go back up the hill. I don't want to go down any further. We will wait until they get closer.'

Morsian chided himself, as well as Rydor, 'How stupid we are. We didn't need to come at all since Branley and Kellyn have been consuming phyrium for quite some time now. In fact, the others have been consuming the mineral since...well, before leaving the village. I could have reached out to one or both and asked who was coming along on the wagons. How stupid of me.'

Morsian let the rest of his thought become guarded as he thought that Rydor should have supposed that as well. After all, Rydor communicated with his herd far longer than Morsian communicated with the other three Aztarian men.

Rydor snorted. 'You are correct. You should have thought of that before I needed to carry you all this way for nothing.'

Morsian almost reprimanded the stallion. Thinking better of that decision, Morsian thought of how far he would need to walk back if he offended him. He decided to hold his tongue.

'Well...reach out to Branley or Kellyn and find out who the man with the hat might be,' pushed Rydor's thought into Morsian's mind.

"Oh yes, that is what I need to do," Morsian said out loud to cover the annoyance he was trying to hide from Rydor.

Reaching out to Branley, Morsian told him about his invention of the Morry and how he used it to transport Teetawn to the mastel's cave. He was conveying these thoughts when Rydor interrupted him.

'How long does it take to find out who one man is? I want to get back to the herd,' Rydor's thoughts flowed with impatience. 'You can tell him about the Morry when he arrives.'

Morsian immediately changed the subject and questioned Branley as to the name of the other driver. Breckon was named as the man who Morsian could not see from a distance. Thanking Branley for the information, Morsian turned his thoughts back to Rydor.

'All three are good men. I especially like Tyleed. As I said, he is very kind. If anyone would bond quickly with a mastel, it will be him. He is an animal doctor. Isn't that great? He can check Teetawn to make sure he is healing well,' Morsian said to try to keep Rydor from being annoyed that he needed to carry Morsian all the way back.

Returning to the valley, Morsian's mind was preoccupied with the different methods he might try to levitate and propel a Morry without wheels. Rydor's thought, however, was on changes that men would bring to his herd and whether the changes would be for better or worse. It was ultimately his decision whether he would allow new interdependent relationships to proceed and flourish.

CHAPTER NINETEEN

The wagons loaded with hay were greeted both with excitement and suspicion. Nearing the end of the growing season, the purple grass in the mastel valley was no longer a vivid color. The blades were muted, almost gray, as it dried to little nutritional value as the season declined. Spreading the cut grass, from the village, onto the valley floor, mastels cautiously approached and sniffed the cuttings. Brave mastels took a mouthful of the hay and chewed it contentedly. The consensus was that it was not as good as fresh grass. It was almost palatable, and the mastels were grateful to have food and not need to make the dangerous trek to the high meadows.

Until a building could be erected, the mastel cave would house the load of hay brought in on the three wagons. Branley was anxious to go to the cave to see the Morry invented in his absence. Morsian asked the drivers of the three wagons to head the cawwen towards the mastel cave to unload.

Once the wagons and men arrived in the cave, Tyleed climbed down from the wagon. "Tyleed, would you mind grabbing your medical bag and come look at this injured colt. I am thinking he is well enough to allow him to rejoin the herd, however, having your professional opinion would make me feel better." Morsian requested, imposing on the Tyleed's judgment.

Rivetted with the mastels, as were the other two men, Tyleed's fascination went far beyond the obvious beauty and grace of the animal. Having heard stories of the mystical, magical creatures most of his younger life, Tyleed wanted nothing more than to inspect one closely to see if the folklore was correct about these creatures. Here was his chance to do just that with the injured colt.

Moving slowly and quietly towards the colt, Tyleed spoke softly and reassuringly. Rydor stood by to comfort his son and make sure he was not injured by this new man to the valley.

Teetawn lay without moving. His breathing became rapid at the touch of an unfamiliar hand. With comforting words, Tyleed inspected each wound, paying close attention to the major one Morsian sutured.

"Very nice job, Morsian. You said you also transfused blood from the stallion to this colt? I am impressed. I know you did some work as an associate doctor in the village when our own physician was absent. I never guessed that your skill was as remarkable as it is. I am really impressed. I am intrigued and fascinated by those insects. Did you place them on the minor wounds? They have almost healed already. What will happen to the insects when they have done their job.? Do they die or what?' Tyleed fired question after question.

Morsian informed him how Rydor had shown him how certain berries held healing powers as well as the use of feigons to close wounds. Morsian went on to say that the insects would release their hold on the skin when the wound was closed completely. As he was giving the explanation, several feigons dropped to the ground and scurried away to find shelter under rocks.

"Wow! Just like that, they are gone and look at the wound. It is healed perfectly. I need to get a whole swarm of feigons for my practice. Amazing!" Tyleed exclaimed.

Patting the colt on his long neck, Tyleed turned to Morsian to ask if the colt had a name. Before he could finish the sentence, Teetawn popped into his thoughts.

Puzzled, Tyleed asked, "Did you say the name Teetawn, or am I crazy?"

"I didn't say a word," answered Morsian. "If you heard the name Teetawn, then I would say the colt told you himself."

Tyleed scratched his head and looked at the colt. The colt's green eyes whirled a response and generated pure love and devotion. Looking into the colt's eyes, Tyleed stood transfixed. His heart melted, and he couldn't take his eyes off the colt.

"Teetawn? Is that your name?" Tyleed asked out loud.

In his mind, Tyleed saw Geselle, and the word mother affixed to the mare. The great red stallion with a dazzling gold mane came next to his mind with the word father attached.

Tyleed looked to the stallion standing next to Morsian, who shook his head up and down as if he was saying 'yes.' Tyleed looked again at Morsian for confirmation that he was not a lunatic.

"You aren't crazy or foolish. You have bonded with Teetawn this very moment. For some reason, he has picked you to be his bondmate. You should feel very privileged. Of course, you will need to set up your practice here in the valley now. I would suggest that we build a cabin for you and your spouse quickly; that way, you can return to fetch her."

Tyleed was overwhelmed and forgot to tell Morsian that he would be bringing Lalaya, Morsian's wife, as well. Since Lalaya found out she was pregnant, all she wanted was to be with her husband when the birthing event took place. Instead of telling Morsian the news, all Tyleed could dwell upon was his new friendship with the young colt.

"Friendship is not the right word, is it?" asked Tyleed.

"We say bonded. Teetawn is your bondmate. It is for life, and it will be a relationship that is as important as the bond you have with your wife, if not even more so." Morsian said, reaching out his hand to stroke Rydor.

Rydor snorted his chuckle snort, 'Maybe for you, Morsian, but I have a whole herd of mares for which to account. You only have one woman. I am not sure it is the same."

Morsian knew the stallion was bragging. Rydor, himself, visualized that he would die if Morsian died. He never showed him dying if one of his mares died. Morsian knew he was all-important to Rydor no matter how cavalier the stallion might act. Each night Rydor's last thought before he slept was of Morsian…of his comfort and his well-being. Morsian knew he was loved by the stallion as much as he adored the mastel. Tyleed would now join the ranks along with Sturjen of bonded Aztarian men who would build the new community here at the mastel valley.

Leaving the other men to unload hay, Morsian directed them to come to the cabin for food, drink, and the surprise of their lives when they were finished with the job at hand. Breckon and Kobart didn't know what to expect, seeing how Tyleed was now acting.

Kellyn and Branley already witnessed Sturjen's bonding with Fonrah. They were not surprised when a man who devoted his whole life to the care of animals managed to bond before themselves. Kobart and Breckon were both in the dark and needed an explanation as they stacked the hay in the cave. Kellyn supplied them with the answers they requested as they worked side by side.

Breckon looked out to the herd and exclaimed, "You mean someday I might bond with one of those amazing creatures? That would be glorious. I don't even understand telepathy, but I am ready for it to happen to me. How much more phyrium do I need to eat?"

Branley shrugged off Breckon's question as he was not bonded either and really didn't know. Branley moved to the Morry and called out to Morsian before he got too far away. "Morsian, how does this operate?"

Passing his thoughts to Branley, Morsian showed him how he commanded the Morry with his mind. 'Try it. In fact, bring the Morry back to the cabin. Tell the others to bring the wagons to the cabin as well. Rydor said he wants those stinky beasts out of his cave!' Laughing at Rydor's arrogance, Morsian continued to walk back to the cabin. He must admit there was no comparison between a mastel and the cawwen.

CHAPTER TWENTY

The mastels were pleased to have the hay to eat. It allowed them to continue to hunt for the griswells and obtain the much-coveted phyrium. The men worked daily to construct buildings made with the phyrium polymer, which Morsian and Branley continued to make with the dwindling supply of mineral. The griswells did not want any humans in their caves. With the fact that the phyrium was becoming harder to find in the existing tunnels, the griswells were starting to become more accepting of the idea of miners descending below in their dwelling place.

'It would be too dangerous to go down into the cave without each of the men bonded to a mastel, and even at that, there would be several renegade griswells running loose. I hate to suggest trickery and somehow contain those griswells...I don't know what else to do. For some reason, the renegade griswells have resisted bonding with a mastel. Of course, Rydor hasn't really put pressure on the younger mastels to try to bond with them yet either. I am not sure if he feels the youngsters are too immature, and they would never have the attention span to keep the griswells focused or what,' Morsian thought as he and Branley worked side by side.

Out loud, Branley said, "We will need a lot more men to dig a mine than you, Sturjen and Tyleed. Once we get more buildings built, we will need for the men who decide to join us, to bond with a mastel. That includes me. How do I go about bonding with a mastel?"

"I have no idea. So far, each of us has been there when our mastel was injured and needed help. I can't imagine the horror if each man needed to wait until a mastel is sick or injured. That would be a catastrophe if that happened. I will ask Rydor and see if he has any ideas. I know that the mastels bonded to griswells met a need, and that is why they were able to bond. Maybe something as normal as grooming a mastel could solicit a bond. It is worth a try. Why don't you go out and brush a mastel and see what happens?" Morsian said.

"Worth a try, I suppose, if one would allow me to approach. Where is a brush? Once I get a brush, do I walk up to a mastel and start brushing? I keep forgetting those buds can become huge, sharp, spiraling horns in seconds. What if the mastel does not want to be brushed?" Branley said, getting cold feet.

Outside, the two could hear Kobart yelling, "Hey, stop that! I need that tool; bring it back!" Laughter could be heard from the other men, and Morsian's curiosity was getting the best of him. He opened the door and walked out to see what was going on with Branley on his heels.

Morsian observed a young mastel running in circles around Kobart with a tool in her mouth. It was obvious to all concerned, except maybe Kobart, that the mastel was having fun at the human's expense.

Frustrated and turning red, Kobart was not enjoying being made the brunt of the joke by an animal, no less. After realizing how stupid he looked to the other men when he was chasing the young mastel, Kobart stopped in his tracks and pleaded with Morsian to make the mastel drop the tool.

"I am not bonded with that mastel. I am afraid I have no control over it at all. I don't think Rydor will be of any help either since he is sending me a mental chuckle. You are on your own. I suggest you find something with which to barter and maybe...just maybe, she will give you the tool. Mastels have a sweet tooth. That is all the advice I can give you." Morsian laughed, turn, and walked back into his cabin.

Branley followed Morsian into the cabin. He didn't go back to work, as was expected. Instead, he went to the cabinet and looked to see if there was anything sweet inside. Seeing a biscuit, Branley grabbed several and went back outside.

Morsian, intrigued, went to the window to watch and see what Branley was going to do. With a biscuit in his hand, Branley walked up to the female mastel and held his hand out to offer her the sweet biscuit.

Sniffing, the mastel dropped the tool, reached out her tongue, and pulled the biscuit into her mouth. Chewing it, she immediately stepped forward and pushed against Branley, demanding more. Branley reached into his pocket and took out another biscuit. The mastel greedily snatched it from his hand and chomped it down quickly.

Branley realizing he only had one more biscuit, sent a message to Morsian to bring him several more biscuits. Morsian did as asked. Branley reached around the mastel and patted her as she took biscuit after biscuit from his hand.

"I am afraid that was the last biscuit. Your experiment failed unless the young mastel has offered a name," Morsian said softly, feeling sorry for Branley, but admiring his attempt to bond.

"That is all there is, pretty little filly," Branley said to the mastel as she nuzzled him, looking for more treats. "Well, the experiment was not a complete failure. Kobart, you got your tool back while she was preoccupied with the treats."

Giving the mastel one last pat before going back to the cabin, Branley felt disappointed. Realistic to the failed attempt, he compensated his emotion with a pragmatic thought. 'It was worth a try. I am not giving up. I will think of another option.'

'I will expect you to make more treats. I like these sweet things. What do you call them?' came a thought into Branley's mind.

Reflectively, Branley answered, "We call them biscuits, but I suppose we could call them cookies, too," Stopping suddenly, Branley turned around and looked at the men who were all busy at work.

'Which one of you is teasing me and pretending to be the mastel,' Branley sent out to the other men. Looking up from their jobs puzzled at such a ridiculous statement, each man denied sending any message to the young scientist.

'Morsian, are you messing with me?' Branley asked his mentor.

'Not me!' Morsian replied and went about his work. 'Maybe you should ask the mastel her name.'

Branley looked into the dazzling golden eyes of the female mastel and reached out with his mind. 'What do they call you, little one?'

Prancing in place, the filly suggested a picture of herself leaping gracefully over boulders. 'That doesn't help me very much. I can't imagine the herd calls you Leaping Gracefully over Boulders.'

Feeling like a bolt of lightning had struck him between the eyes, Branley realized he was conversing with the mastel. 'Are we bonded?'

Walking up to Branley, the filly licked his hand. "I know you want more biscuits. Be patient. I must make more before you can have more." Realizing he was talking out loud, Branley felt rather embarrassed. "I guess I am silly. Of course, we have not bonded, or I would know your name, or at least, that is what Morsian said." Hesitating, Branley added, "Maybe you don't have a name. Maybe your mother thinks the word 'come,' and you obey. Is that it? You don't have a name?"

Popping into his head was the word, 'Biscuit!'

'I know, you want more biscuits,' Branley let his thoughts flow to the filly.

Morsian walked to the doorway. "Branley, if you can communicate telepathically with the filly, you are bonded. I don't think she is asking for more biscuits. I think she wants you to call her Biscuit."

"How do you know we are talking about biscuits?" Branley asked Morsian. "Can you hear her thoughts in your head?

"No, I can hear your thoughts in my head, and you keep saying biscuits over and over. It is only natural for me to surmise that she wants you to call her Biscuit. Call her Biscuit and see if she responds," Morsian said and returned to the cabin, shutting the door behind him somewhat annoyed by all the prattle.

'Biscuit? Is that your name now?' Branley strained to press the thought into the filly's head.

'You don't need to try so hard. You are shouting in my mind. I like the name Biscuit. The treat is sweet, and it gives me pleasure. You can call me Biscuit if you would like. I know Leaping Gracefully over Boulders is a rather long name. My mother can picture it quickly when she wants my attention. I think that might be hard for you,' Biscuit said with her vivid golden eyes twirling and glittering in the sunlight.

'Oh, my mother wants me. I will see you tomorrow. I sure hope you have more biscuits for me by then,' Biscuit conveyed and was running back to the herd, leaping gracefully over boulders.

Branley stood watching the dazzling cream-colored filly as she ran out of sight. He thought she was the most beautiful mastel he ever saw with her golden mane and tail and golden eyes. If she had any stripes, Branley could not see a hint of them. She seemed solid cream-colored to him and wondered if striping would happen as she became older.

'No, she is the color she will be forever. Foals are the same color at birth. As they reach maturity, the colts coat changes. What you see with a filly is what you get,' Morsian reached out to Branley. 'Would you mind coming back inside and helping me. I know you are in a state of enchantment right now. Snap out of it! I have things for you to do. Besides, you will need to make biscuits later anyway.' Chuckling, Morsian returned to his own job.

Branley walked back inside the cabin, feeling euphoric. Questions filled his mind 'Were the biscuits made with phyrium? Why does phyrium enable telepathy? I really don't understand the properties of this mineral. It is beyond my understanding, and I think of myself as an intelligent person. Obviously, I am not as smart as I think I am.'

Morsian receiving his thoughts, answered. 'I don't know either. I am learning about phyrium myself. You are right, though, that it is an enabling technology that enhances what must be the 'Telepathy Gene' in Aztarians and creatures. Phyrium appears to enable telepathic communications between Aztarians, creatures, building structures, and machinery that has either absorbed or is made of the mineral. Beyond that, I don't know why it works. Maybe together, we will be able to find the answers.

'Right now, we need more polymer. Sturjen said they are almost out of panels to complete the building. I love the fact that the polymer can expand. We don't need as much phyrium to complete a building project because of that property.'

The group of men continued to build for the next several days. Morsian and Branley also completed two more Morries. It was decided that when Kobart, Breckon, and Kellyn returned to fetch more hay and some of the wives, the men bonded with mastels would remain to start the process of exploring the caves to see what mining equipment would be necessary.

Lattee would often follow Biscuit when she came to the buildings where Branley continued to work or experiment with phyrium. Biscuit demanded more treats, and now she was bringing her favorite playmate, Lattee, as well for the snacks.

'I can barely keep up with your demands, and now you want me to make extra biscuits so Lattee can have some as well? When do you think I have all this extra time to be baking only for your pleasure?' Branley joked with his young mastel.

Walking out to hand feed, Branley found Lattee to be bold. She was used to giving Morsian rides when Rydor was busy. She felt she deserved the treats for all the favors extended to Morsian. When Biscuit revealed what Lattee was thinking, Branley laughed and shouted out to Morsian. "It seems you will need to take a turn at making biscuits for these two. Lattee seems to think you owe her.'

Morsian came outside and patted Lattee on her neck. "She is right. She extended a favor or two for me to let me ride on her when I needed some extra help. I will be glad to make a batch or two to thank her. You can convey my message to Biscuit, and I am sure she will let Lattee know to come back tomorrow for fresh treats."

Kellyn watched the exchange with envy. He was the only man from the original team who was not bonded. He wondered if he was the one to make the treats, whether that could help the process and asked Morsian.

"If I make the treats, is there a chance I might bond with Lattee? I will even make the treats out of berries the color of her coat if it would help. I think she is the most beautiful mastel in the herd," Kellyn looked at Lattee as he spoke to Morsian.

"It couldn't hurt," Morsian replied. "However, I am not an expert on bonding. I would think kindness could play a hand in the bonding process. Making special treats is an act of kindness. It worked for Branley."

Looking over at Lattee, Morsian continued his conversation with Kellyn. "I suspect Branley has told Biscuit of your offer and your compliment towards her best friend. At least, I believe from the way Lattee is puffing with pride that she knows you think she is the most beautiful mastel in the herd. Mastels are vain creatures. Your praise of her beauty may go further than the treats for her affection."

Lattee came towards Kellyn and put her muzzle on his shoulder. Kellyn felt a warm sensation deep within his soul that he had never felt before. He wanted more than anything to bond with this magical creature. He let his thoughts flow from his heart, and before long, he could hear an answer in his mind. Lattee agreed to be his special bondmate. However, being practical, Lattee said she would expect the berry treats tomorrow.

Reaching out to Branley and Morsian, Kellyn insisted he must remain with Lattee, and he would not be able to drive one of the wagons back to the town. Both bonded men understood completely. Breckon and Kobart, however, could not drive three wagons by themselves. Morsian's thoughts betrayed his positive mindset. Totally unsure how he was going to solve this problem, he continued to act confident and assured the bonded men that he would think long and hard to come up with a solution, knowing how much he dreaded ever being away from Rydor.

Morsian let his thoughts reach Rydor, as he and the other mastels who were bonded with griswells, were heading out for the evening hunt. Rydor let thoughts stream out and pictured possible scenarios that might work. One was that Morsian would need to mentally direct the commands to the Morries, sending them down the road to and from the village. That would mean he would be away from the valley for a week or more. One man could drive one wagon while leading the extra cawwen behind. Kobart and Breckon would each have a wagon, and one wagon would be left behind or towed behind one of the other wagons.

Morsian asked Rydor why the team of cawwen could not remain behind to be used later to pull the remaining wagon, and Rydor immediately replied to Morsian's thoughts that the animals stink, and he does not want the ignorant beasts around any longer than necessary.

Rydor asked why it must be Morsian who leaves and not Branley since Morsian is the man who knows how to make everything. Morsian could tell Rydor did not want him to leave any more than Morsian wanted to be separated from his mastel stallion.

'I am the only one who knows how to communicate with the Morries for a long trip. Even though Branley demonstrated he could command one for a short distance, I don't think he is ready to control three Morries. It will be exhausting mentally to be able to keep three Morries on the road,' Morsian explained as best as he could.

'Oh, so you are so much smarter than Branley that the poor young incompetent fool could not be trusted with the task,' Rydor's sarcastic retort was felt like a thumping headache.

'I apologize, my bondmate. I don't want you to go. I know you are the likely choice. I will stay in contact with you over the many k-rods. I will be here when you return,' Rydor contritely conveyed.

Morsian's headache stopped immediately with the love that filled his heart and soul. Rydor could be proud, arrogant, and direct, but he was also pragmatic and wise. All these traits endeared him to Morsian as well as to the herd, who needed his leadership. Morsian knew it was difficult for Rydor to admit that he needed him.

Morsian understood the stallion since Morsian, too, was proud and arrogant and depended on no one, not even his wife, Lalaya, in the same way, he now depended on Rydor.

It was decided. Morsian would return to the town with Kobart and Breckon to retrieve needed mining equipment, lab supplies, and more hay. Morsian was also the only one who could make the villagers understand the significance of the need to mine phyrium and why many of the villagers should consider moving to the mastels' valley. Starting a whole new village this far from the other civilizations would take men of adventure and women who were willing to rough it. Eventually, the mining town would be in contact with all the other cities, towns, and villages across Aztara. In its infancy, there would be difficulties. Only the brave of heart would flourish in this new environment. It would take a special kind of man to bond with the mastels. That would be the most essential problem to overcome immediately. No one would be allowed to mine without a mastel to keep him safe. Morsian felt he was a good judge of mankind. He would need to screen the applicants himself.

CHAPTER TWENTY-ONE

The trip was taxing. Seeing Lalaya made Morsian overjoyed and lifted his spirits out of exhaustion. Morsian noticed that Lalaya gained a bit of weight. He gave his wife a hug and a long lingering kiss and told her that she would soon be moving to their new home. Lalaya wanted to pack and go with Morsian on this return trip. Morsian said he would be back for her shortly. He needed to arrange for new men to move to the valley to mine phyrium. Lalaya was full of questions. Morsian needed to cut his answers and his entire visit short of accomplishing all that must be done before returning to the valley. He knew he was unfair to his wife. She was tolerant of his eccentric behaviors, and he loved her for her patience and understanding nature as well as tolerating his neglect towards her. He told himself that he was thinking of her comfort and safety first.

"Did Tyleed, by any chance, give you my news?" Lalaya asked her husband.

"I don't recall Tyleed telling me anything. What is your news, my dear?"

Lalaya took Morsian's hand and placed it on the swelling below her stomach. "We are going to have a baby," Lalaya said with a bright grin spreading across her face.

Morsian stood dumbfounded and finally finding his tongue, he said, "And I thought you had been eating too well since I left."

Morsian suddenly felt giddy, and he grabbed his wife in a bear hug while dancing her around the floor.

"Okay, I believe you are happy! Maybe... relax your hug a bit. I don't know that our son is enjoying being squeezed in a vice," Lalaya said while wiggling a bit to get her husband to loosen his grip.

Morsian didn't think he could smile any larger than he was. At the mention of the word son, he felt his face would crack from the pressure of his lips straining against his earlobes. "How do you know it will be a son?"

Lalaya continued to smile into her husband's face. "We women have our ways. You men aren't the only ones who know science."

Morsian allowed her vague answer. He was truly delighted; he did not care why or how she knew the child would be a boy. He was too excited by her surprise that he would be a father and immediately wanted to share the news with Rydor.

"We will need more rooms for our baby boy and maybe even another child someday," Morsian said with a wink.

"I think having two or three children would be very nice. Let's start with the first, though. How long before I can see our new home? I want to be settled before our baby is born," Lalaya asked.

Morsian became more serious, "Let's see. I have the equipment, men and hay to take on this trip. You pack whatever you want to bring, and I will return with a Morry to carry our belongings back to the valley. I think in another moon's time, I could return. You will be fine here until then, correct?"

"I have plenty to do to get ready. I feel fine, and the baby is healthy. There is no reason why I need you around at present. You would just be under my feet and in the way. Get the things done that you need to do, and I will be ready when you return," Lalaya said, knowing how preoccupied Morsian gets with new projects. There would be plenty of time for him to explain all that he was doing these past months. At present, Lalaya only had two things on her mind—the baby and the move.

Wishing he could stay longer, consequently, that is what he told his wife, as his thoughts returned to Rydor, Morsian went about his business. There was much to do yet this day, and he wanted to be able to leave as soon as possible to return to the valley, which occupied a special place in his heart. He no longer thought of the factory town as his home. His home was where Rydor dwelled.

Missing Morsian was not as horrible as Rydor thought it might be since they stayed in close mental communication. Rydor revealed much to Morsian of the daily events and how the Aztarian men were progressing with the building. Rydor also showed Morsian that the griswells were not able to bring as much phyrium out of the tunnels of the cave as before, spurring Morsian to engage many villagers in finding new miners.

Morsian set up his lab as a make-shift human resources department, taking applications from young men who wanted to start a career away from the prying eyes of aunts, uncles, and parents. Morsian did not turn any of these young men away. He felt, however, that he needed to be honest about how hard and dangerous the work may be in the mines. Most of the young men were excited more than put off by his description of griswells and the importance of bonding with a mastel.

Hay was loaded on one of the Morries, and the other two were piled high with equipment for mining and lab supplies. A mental shout came from Rydor telling Morsian to hurry and to bring weapons. Suddenly afraid by Rydor's request, Morsian pressed for why weapons were needed.

A mental picture that horrified Morsian popped vividly into his mind. What he saw were huge beasts with thick bodies and legs. The mouths held savage, razor-sharp teeth, and two sets of tusks on either side of the jowls. The feet were cloven, and the hooves could separate like scissors to cut viciously into its prey.

'Why are you showing me this horrible creature?' Morsian asked.

'The griswells say they will be arriving very soon. It comes through the valley each year on its migration from the west to the east,' Rydor explained.

'Why have you never told me about these beasts before this?' Morsian asked.

'We are never here at this time of the year. We always left the valley by now to find the lush grass in the mountains. This is the first year the herd has stayed in the valley for the summer. We never had the duty of supplying food to the griswells before now either,' Rydor continued his explanation.

'How soon will they be coming through the valley? What are they called?' Morsian asked.

'What is it with you humans and names? We picture things in our minds. We don't often put names to them. I will ask the griswells and tell you later. Right now, get weapons and get back here quickly. The beasts are coming soon!'

Running to the forge and carpentry shop, Morsian burst through the doors and hollered for Diviak. "Diviak, where are you? I need some weapons quickly!"

Coming through the door from the storeroom, Diviak greeted Morsian with a grin. "Where have you been for all this time? You have been gone forever."

"I would love to tell you all about my travels, but I got word from the valley that some horrible creatures are about to descend on the

177

herd of mastels. I need weapons to take back as quickly as possible. What do you have in the storeroom?" Morsian said abruptly.

"What kind of creatures will you be fighting? That will make a difference in what I drag out here to show you," Diviak said in a slow, calm voice, trying to settle Morsian.

"The best I can describe is a strong, massive beast with sharp teeth and two sets of tusks on either side of his jowls," Morsian said impatiently.

Rubbing his chin, Diviak shook his head up and down as if knowing what the animal might be. He declared, "Oh, you are describing grorachs. They are a nasty beast and difficult to kill. You don't want one of them to get close, or they will tear you to pieces. From the stories my grandpa told me, they will gore you, tear you apart with their teeth, or cut you open with their hooves. Awful beasts, horrible...."

"That sounds like the creature," Morsian said nervously, cutting Diviak off. What weapons do you suggest?"

Walking back into the storeroom, Diviak signaled for Morsian to follow him. Lining the walls for display were several different weapons. On shelves, running in rows parallel to the walls were crates and crates of boxed weapons.

"That one on the far wall would be your best bet. It is called a Crossfire. I love that it can fire multiple arrows at once. It has two triggers. You can pull either trigger individually or at the same time to the first detent, and the upper arrows will fire. You can pull both or either trigger again to the second detent, and the bottom arrows will fire. If you are clever enough, you can get four targets in your sights and pull both triggers all the way back at the same time, and all four arrows will fire. As I said, you don't want even one of those creatures to get close to you."

Morsian asked, "How long will it take to reload?"

Chuckling, Diviak said, "Shouldn't be a problem. There are twelve more arrows in a magazine that will automatically reload. You will have sixteen total shots, and you can do a lot of damage with sixteen shots."

As Morsian took the weapon from the wall, Diviak went to another weapon. "This one is called a Piercer. If a grorach gets past the Crossfire, you will need one of these weapons close by. The long shaft is connected to an equally long, pointed, double-edged, serrated blade that will kill while keeping the beast far away from your body.

Another weapon that could be helpful is a throwing stick named the Jounce. Don't let its simplicity fool you. You will aim it at the target, and if it misses, it will return to you for another try. Notice the unusual airfoil shape, it is like a bird of prey's wing. It takes a little practice to throw it correctly. When it is thrown correctly, it is deadly, as you might surmise by the razor-thin center cutting edge on the outside. Don't ever try to catch a Jounce in the middle of the airfoil. It will take your hand off, and they will be calling you Stumpy. Make sure you catch it on either end."

Morsian found himself fascinated by the weapons. He immediately started thinking about how he could enhance each one with phyrium. His mind was mega-rods away, calculating how much phyrium would be needed for any changes when Diviak spoke again. "So, how many crates of each will you need?"

Morsian startled out of his thoughts, realized he was wasting time with problem-solving and needed to get back to the real world. "I will need several crates of each," Morsian said. "I will need them loaded immediately. I will start my trip back to the valley this very day." With a handshake, Diviak told Morsian it would be done promptly.

"Will your men mind unloading a half of the hay from one of the Morries? I will pick that hay up and more the next time I am in town, and that will leave room for the crates of weapons."

Diviak agreed to Morsian's request and called for several young men to come and do his bidding. As Morsian left the forge, he wished all the applicants had access to phyrium previously. In that way, he could contact each mentally at the same time to tell them to meet him at the Morries right now so they could leave. Instead, he would need to hire runners to find the applicants and give them the message to come to the village square, packed and ready to leave. It was all time wasted, and Morsian was getting anxious. His mastel could be in grave danger before he arrived with men and weapons.

Morsian was finding telepathy to be difficult as he juggled the many interruptions from Kellyn, Branley, Sturjen, Tyleed, as well as his stallion giving updates. Each man saw the horrible creature visualized from their mastels as their bonded griswells imprinted the vision deep within the mastels' heads. The thought of fighting such creatures, even with their spiraling horns, was terrifying. Protecting the newborn foals as well as the younger mastels, would be difficult.

Morsian suggested the mares and young mastels head for the cave where the hay was being stored. He then showed Branley how easy it would be to make several troughs to hold water for the mastels who would be staying within the cave. Morsian visualized all three of the weapons that he would be bringing with hopes that each man was adept at using the weapons.

Tyleed immediately replied that he never intentionally injured animals since his calling was to mend and protect them. Knowing the necessity of protecting the mastels, especially Teetawn, he would be a quick study once the weapons arrived. Kellyn and Sturjen, both claimed to be experts with the crossfire. Sturjen even projected his image as skilled with the jounce. Kellyn mentally laughed when he showed his actual experience hunting with Sturjen and how Sturjen was not as skilled with the jounce as he thought he was.

Morsian asked not to be included in the telepathic communications for several hours, as he needed time to coordinate the departure of the Morries with the new young men who hired on to be trained as miners. Morsian felt it was his duty to let the young men know of the possible, if not probable, dangers that they may encounter aside from the griswells.

As the young men gathered with satchels containing changes of clothing and not much else, Morsian explained that he received word that the valley was expecting a large pack of very dangerous animals called grorachs. Showing the young men, the weapons acquired to fight the beasts, Morsian asked if any of them were willing to travel to the valley under the new circumstances. When not, a single young man left the group, Morsian's next question was whether any of them could use the weapons.

Ten of the twelve men raised their hands and said they used at least one of the weapons before this day. Morsian let out a visible sigh of relief. "I hope most of you can use the crossfire. I think it will give us the greatest advantage over the pack of animals expected to cross the valley," Morsian said.

One young man that Morsian recognized as Aloftin claimed to be an expert with the jounce. "My father invented the weapon, and he schooled me in its use from toddler until now. I can show all the rest of these men how to use it if we have time to train once getting to the valley."

There were murmurs and nods of heads as several of the men admitted they had seen Aloftin use the weapon, and he was as good as he said he was. Timrick, a head taller than the rest, and as broad as a young cawwen, told Morsian that he saw Aloftin cut the head off a glemee while it was running at full speed.

"I would say that we are fortunate to have Aloftin in our presence. I will be very thankful if we have several days to prepare and train once we arrive. If you are ready to leave, jump onto whatever Morry has space," Morsian said while directing the young men to the loaded and waiting vehicles.

'There are no cawwen! How are we going to get these wagons moving without them?" Junyn asked.

"Oh, I forgot to explain how phyrium can be used. Once you have eaten a diet of it for a few days, you will be able to connect with my mind and see how everything works. Take my word for it...it is amazing! I don't have time to explain things now. Be aware that you are going to love your new lifestyle. Quickly, I will tell you that I will operate these Morries with my mind. Trust me that it works, and it is safe and hop aboard," Morsian said as he took a seat on one of the Morries.

All twelve men leaped aboard, with some reservations, and found spots between crates or sitting on top of the hay. Looking to make sure that each man was in a comfortable place, Morsian's mind gave the command to move forward, and the Morries moved in unison as the young men cheered.

"Feel free to sleep whenever you want. I know the road well. I plan to travel all night long to make good time. In the future, I will be able to direct the Morries to move from the village to the mastel valley on their own with just a couple commands. Of course, I have not tried that yet. I am not completely sure it will work..." Morsian said out loud but not really expecting any of the young man to be listening.

"Geez, Morsian, you will be able to do that someday? I mean, you really think you will be able to send a Morry to the village and have people there load it up and then have it come back? That is absolutely incredible! If I desire something from the village, I will be able to ask you to send a Morry to fetch it? I love it! This is going to be so much fun living around you."

Morsian was not sure which young man from the back of the Morry had made the statement. It gave him a feeling of satisfaction. That young man was right! He would be able to do that someday, and he felt flattered that the young man thought he was fun. No one ever accused him of being fun.

As the men fell asleep, one after another, Morsian wanted to connect with Rydor. He felt he needed all his attention on the Morries, although. The terrain was hilly during this part of the journey, and it would not do for Morsian to allow a runaway vehicle with men and supplies to be overturned. Staying focused was going to be a bit more difficult as the night wore on, and Morsian started to feel fatigued.

"I will stay awake with you, Morsian. I know you don't want me to talk since you are concentrating on the road, but I can nudge you if you start to get sleepy if that is alright with you?" a voice came from directly behind him.

Morsian asked a quick question, "I appreciate your offer very much. Who may I ask is my new apprentice?"

"They call me B'hant for short. My full name is B'hantalion. You can see why my friends shorten it. I will be quiet now and help watch the road. I have very good night vision."

Morsian softly said thank you and returned to his duties of operating the Morries around curves and up and downhills. Adjusting the speed with his mind was not as difficult as he thought it might be with the Morries heavy with supplies. Again, he marveled at the properties of phyrium and thanked his God for sending him to the valley of the mastels.

CHAPTER TWENTY-TWO

The men were busy preparing for the arrival of the pack of grorachs. Before Morsian became totally immersed in guiding the Morries away from the factory village, he gave his crew instructions. Rydor, too, was making plans as he sent young stallions in pairs to scout the land west to see if they saw the approach of the grorachs, as the griswells made it clear that the path of migration always went through the valley now occupied by the mastels. The little Jade Harbinger scouted from above.

Morsian's mental outreach to Rydor during a short break from guiding the Morries down a long straight stretch of the road asked whether it would be possible for the herd of mastels to leave the valley to avoid a confrontation. Rydor's response was the newborns could not manage a trip, and the griswells needed meat. He also showed Morsian the griswells' past experiences when the pack stayed in the valley for several weeks. Many griswells died while hunting for food during the grorachs' migration. It seems the grorachs hunt both in the daytime and at night.

Stewing over the possible loss of life of men and mastels, Morsian's thoughts became distracted when he should have been navigating the remaining part of the road home. Morsian was both surprised and relieved when he discovered the Morries were on course and heading for home without Morsian's guidance. Exhilarated to know that the phyrium seemed to have memory, Morsian allowed himself the luxury of relaxation to ponder strategies to keep the mastels safe instead of watching the road.

Starting to feel the effects of exhaustion, Morsian was relieved to see the buildings coming into view. Rounding the last bend, Morsian stopped the Morries and all aboard scampered to the ground.

Coming out of buildings, Kellyn, Branley, and Sturjen raced to meet the new young men who would now join their ranks as well as welcoming back Breckon and Kobart. Introductions were made even though some of the men knew each other from working side by side in the factory.

"We need to unload the hay in the cave and unpack the weapons and the mining equipment. First, Branley, will you show these young men to their barracks. I am assuming you have completed the structure in my absence, and it is ready to be occupied. I am also sure that our new members would like to see where they will be dwelling until they each decide to build a cabin of their own. No rush on that one. When time permits, we will all join in and help. Once you have your items stored, please come back here to help unload," instructed Morsian.

Branley led the way, joking with Timrick and Junyn, whom he had known since childhood. B'hant remained behind and stood next to Morsian.

"What will be my new duties as your apprentice, sir?" B'hant asked with enthusiasm.

Morsian had all but forgotten that he called B'hant his new apprentice while on the road. Pleased that the young man really was taking his comment to heart, Morsian decided he would, indeed, take this young man under his wings and teach him the same as he taught Branley.

"After you settle into the barracks, I will need to teach you all about phyrium. You will be using it in every aspect of your daily life. You must learn quickly to be able to function here. You seem quite intelligent. Therefore, I will not be surprised when you discover another property of the mineral that Branley and I have overlooked. Scurry along and get yourself a bed. Report back to me afterward," Morsian said, pleased to have another eager young man to mentor.

Rydor appeared in front of Morsian, almost as a phantom, since Morsian did not hear his approach. Wrapping his arms around the stallion's neck, Morsian sent visions of love and satisfaction to be back beside the mastel.

'I missed you, too,' Rydor said while shaking his body to unwrap the strangle-hold Morsian had on his neck. 'Right now, we have work to do. I have received an image from the Jade Harbinger. The pack is closer than I thought. They have not reached the forest east of the Orange River yet. My little friend says they are traveling fast and killing almost everything in their path. I recalled all the young stallions who were scouting. I would not like them to encounter the grorachs alone. What did you bring to fight those horrible killers?" Rydor asked.

Morsian let go of the stallion's neck and moved to the Morries. Climbing onto the platform, he pried open one of the crates. Taking a weapon from the top of the pile, Morsian held it out for Rydor's inspection.

'This is a crossfire. Once the men become familiar with this weapon, it will be a deciding factor in the battle. It can fire multiple arrows at once.' Morsian moved to another crate and opened it to reveal stacks of piercers.

'Now this one will be used on any of the ones who get past the arrows. It is called a piercer, and I would say it works similarly to your spiraling horns. The only advantage we have would be some distance. You notice the shaft is a bit longer than your horn. For the mastels to fight grorachs, the beast will be way too close to the bodies of the mastels. I fear that too many injuries could occur. That is why we will depend on the crossfire and the jounce.'

Not blocking his mind, Morsian became aware that all the young men now gathered behind him. The men who already lived in the valley immediately went to work to unload and uncrate the weapons. The new men stood with mouths open and eyes staring at the incredible animal standing before them.

Morsian turned and noticed the awe and respect being shown to his bondmate. "This is Rydor. He is my bondmate," Morsian said proudly. "I hope that each of you will bond with a mastel in the future. In fact, if you don't bond with one, you won't be able to go down into the mines. That is a problem to be figured out later. Right now, you all need to help unload the weapons. Aloftin, we will depend on your skills with the jounce to instruct the use of the weapon. We have very little time to learn how to use it. Everyone needs to make a great effort to learn since I feel this weapon will be vital to the success of this operation. Now, get busy."

All the young men moved cautiously around the blazing red stallion who stood his ground. Morsian laughed at the intimidation tactics Rydor was purposely imposing.

'Rydor, could you kindly move to allow the men to do what they need to do quickly. You have proven your point. None of these young men will ever take you for granted. You have their full respect,' Morsian showed in a mind-meld.

Rydor snorted, causing the young men to jump, and Morsian laughed out loud. Moving to the stallion's side, he gave him one more embrace and then sat upon the Morry filled with hay.

"B'hant, Timrick, and Junyn jump aboard. We will unload the hay as quickly as possible and then return. The rest of you continue unpacking the weapons on the other Morries and then pay attention to Aloftin as he starts your instructions in the use of the jounce."

Morsian knew he did not need to go with the Morry to the cave where the hay would be unloaded since the Morry could react to long-distance commands now. He also knew the two young men would be afraid to enter the cave with mastels milling within, without him there to give them assurance. Sitting upon the Morry, the two men talked quietly to each other.

"Can you believe how beautiful that mastel was? I can't wait to be able to bond with one. It must be unbelievable. I guess we will need to eat a bunch more phyrium than we have in the last day to make that happen," Junyn said to B'hant.

"I intend to eat nothing but phyrium if it speeds up the process," B'hant remarked good-naturedly.

Morsian watched the two young men for their reactions as they topped the hill, and the entire herd could be seen below. The mares, in hues of strawberry, red, beige, and stripes, grazed nervously on the hay that Kellyn and Sturjen had strewn about the meadow where once lush purple grass grew abundantly.

"That is the most beautiful sight I have ever seen," remarked Junyn. 'What graceful creatures. I never really believed they existed. There is no denying my eyes. Are they all females?"

Morsian knew Junyn was directing the question to him. "Below are females and youngsters. You will notice some vivid red foals in the mix. Those foals will be stallions someday. Some will leave to find their own harem, and some will stay and be content to be guardians of the herd. Rydor allows mares from other herds to enter his herd if a young stallion returns with new females. Rydor never tries to compete for another stallion's mares. Basically, mastels are peaceful creatures."

Getting closer to the cave, B'hant asked about the golden buds on each mastel's head. Again, Morsian knew the question was his to answer.

"You will be quite astounded when you see those buds grow quickly into long, spiraling horns for the first time. The mastels are not defenseless animals. Between their horns and claws, they are quite formidable. They are also fast and agile and can spring to the trees and boulders in great bursts of speed. I am hoping you will not need to see them fight. I fear you will sooner than any of us want."

Morsian became a bit sullen at the thought of any of the mastels being injured or dying. He grew to love them all and recognized each as an individual. Sensing Morsian's mood, the two young men stopped asking questions and watched the herd in wonderment.

As the Morry pulled into the cave, mares put themselves between the new arrivals and their newborn foals. Seeing Morsian, the mares relaxed and knew their babies were safe. Timrick noted one young mastel having difficulty getting to its feet.

"What is wrong with that baby?" he asked Morsian.

"I don't know. Let's go over and see," Morsian said, leading the way to where the foal was stranded on its back. The little filly was caught in a dip between a boulder and a swelling in the cave floor.

"Oh, it is stuck. Timrick, you look as strong as a cawwen; why don't you see if you can give the little tyke a hand," Morsian directed.

Timrick cautiously moved towards the foal, keeping an eye on its mother, fearing her buds would become the sharp horns Morsian described. Morsian saw his distress and moved towards the mare to pat and calm her.

"It is alright, Timrick. She won't hurt you. She knows you are trying to help," Morsian encouraged.

Timrick moved to the bawling foal and squatted down, he put both hands under the body of the young mastel. Even though newborns, the foal weighed more than most full-grown men. Timrick kept his back straight and lifted with his legs, groaning with the effort. With the count of three, Timrick stood, holding the foal in his arms while it kicked and cried for its mother. Setting the little animal on its feet, Timrick moved out of the path allowing the little creature to join its mother.

As the foal raced to her mother's side, the mare walked quietly towards Timrick. Putting her head down for him to pat, she showed her appreciation to the large man.

"Go ahead and pat her. She is trying to thank you for your efforts in helping her little filly. She is a pretty thing, isn't she?" Morsian said.

"Pretty does not go far enough in describing her. She is gorgeous. I thought mares were supposed to be strawberry. This one is almost white as sea foam," Timrick said as he gently stroked the mare.

"Sea Foam. I like that. I have never known her name. I think we shall call her Sea Foam," Morsian said, acknowledging the name given to her by Timrick. "I suspect that you might bond with her soon. All you need is a bit more phyrium in your diet, and who knows..."

As the Morry was unloaded by the three men, Sea Foam remained by Timrick's side, often demanding another pat. Her foal calmly nursed and seemed completely unphased by what happened earlier.

Timrick was dragging his feet when it was time to leave the cave. He wanted to stay with Sea Foam. Morsian reminded him that weapons training was in process, and even though he used the jounce on occasion while hunting with Aloftin, it would be in Sea Foam's best interest if he practiced a bit more.

Realizing that Sea Foam might be in danger at any time, Timrick picked up his pace and jumped aboard the Morry with longing glances at the mastel mare. He hoped Morsian was correct, and all it would take would be a bit more phyrium in his diet and this lovely mare, and he would be a team working the phyrium mines.

"Morsian, is Sea Foam bonded with a griswell?" Timrick asked, starting to understand how the relationship would work if he were to go down into the mines.

"Why yes, she is. Presently, the other mastels supply meat to her griswell since she is not allowed to hunt due to her newborn foal. In a few months, she will be back with the hunters that leave each evening. I sure hope we have the grorachs dispatched by then, or we must abandon our whole plan to live here."

The two men pulled away from the cave with Sea Foam and her foal staring after them. Timrick continued to sit sideways to watch the mastels until they were out of sight. His attention turned to the men in groups practicing the three different weapons. The reality of the situation hit him hard as he realized what would happen if he and the nineteen men could not fight the grorachs. The mastel stallions and mares would fight to the death to save their young, and Timrick had little doubts that the casualties would be many, despite the horns and claws the mastels sported. The mastels, as a herd, could overcome a single river monster by sheer numbers. However, this was a different set of circumstances. Now, the grorachs would outnumber the mastels by more than two to one.

Joining the group of men who were practicing with the crossfire, Timrick let all his attention concentrate on the targets for the duration of the time allotted to practicing each weapon. By evening, Morsian asked the men to bring their plate of food and for them to meet him outside to discuss the plan for the following day. The Jade

Harbinger relayed to Rydor that the grorachs could possibly be in the valley by the middle of the next day. That left very little time to complete what needed to be done.

As the men ate, Morsian explained his plan of action. Rydor, present in mind, relayed what needed to be done to the mastels. With the cartons unpacked and the weapons in view, Morsian began his conversation.

"Men, we don't have much time. We have over three hundred piercers. These weapons are difficult to master due to the size and weight of the long handles. I am suggesting that we use them as a barricade surrounding our men, the mastels, and to protect the foals in the cave. If we place them in a semi-circle with the tips of the spears at an angle pointing outwards, it should stop the advance of many of the grorachs," Morsian detailed on board as a visual to the men.

"How will we keep the piercers in place?" one young lad asked.

"The mastels are busy digging holes all around the entrance of the cave where we will place the piercers. The mastels will then cover the bottom of the shaft to stabilize them in place. Before that can be done, I will move the three Morries inside the circle to give the archers an elevated platform from which to shoot," Morsian explained.

"Will the mastels be inside the circle with the men or outside fighting on their own?" Branley asked with concern in his voice.

"The mastels will be inside the circle with us. At this point, we will have some of the mastels standing over some of the piercers to act as bait to pull the grorach into the sharp tips of the piercers. They will retreat backward as the grorach charge to allow the beasts to run head-on into the pikes. All of you men who have bonded with a mastel will be on your mastel's back with crossfire and replacement arrows ready to reload. Aloftin, I have a special job for you," Morsian continued with his plan.

Aloftin rubbed his chin, "And what might that be, Morsian?"

"You are by far the best marksman with the jounce. In fact, you are the only one here who has mastered the weapon. I am asking a lot from you."

"I am listening, Morsian. What do you want me to do?" Aloftin asked, listening intently.

"Do you see that large tree yonder?" Morsian said, pointing at the biggest tree at the edge of the meadow.

"I see it, Morsian. What are you asking me to do—chop it down with my jounce to prove my abilities?"

Laughing, Morsian said, "No. Just the opposite. I want you to be at the very top or as high up as you can go and yet be balanced enough to use your jounce. You will be our sniper. I want you to target the leaders in the pack and take them out. I hope the rest of the pack will become dispirited and run for the hills. It is a long shot, but I think it could help our cause."

"How am I going to get up there? I am not exactly the best climber on Aztara. It could take me all morning to reach the top."

Morsian stood transfixed, and finally, a smile crossed his lips. "Rydor has a solution to your problem. Frisky will carry you to a position where you can target your attack. Yes, that is a great idea!" Morsian said more to Rydor than to Aloftin.

"Wait…. What? You want me to sit on the back of a mastel while it jumps upwards from branch to branch? I don't think so," Aloftin said, shaking his head back and forth to the negative.

"You will be fine. Hold on and close your eyes," joked Morsian.

The rest of the evening was questions and answers, as well as changes in the plans as one man or another came up with a suggestion that was better than Morsian's idea.

"I suggest everyone try to sleep. If you are having some trouble falling to sleep, I have added some new properties to your sleeping mats that may help. Think of something that relaxes you, and your mat will take it from there," Morsian said.

"Like what? Kobart asked.

"Use your imagination, or if that fails, try remembering a lullaby your mother sang to you. I don't know. Think of gently falling rain, or a babbling brook or a favorite bird's song. It will be different for each of you. I invite you to try different ideas. Now go, get some needed sleep."

Morsian sat in the darkness alone for several more minutes, reaching out to Rydor. 'What do you think? Will this work?'

'You are asking me,' Rydor's thought immediately returned to Morsian. 'I have never seen a grorach. I only have the griswell's impressions of the creature. I hope your plan works since I don't want to lose one of my herd to their tusks, teeth, or slicing hooves. The fact that they will eat anything does not bode well for mastel or man. Let's hope your plan works. Otherwise, I fear I will not see the end of the day tomorrow. I will fight to the death to protect what is mine.'

Picturing his beloved stallion on the ground, breathing his last breath gave Morsian more determination than he ever had for anything in his life. He hated the thought of leaving his unborn son fatherless, but he knew he would not live if Rydor died. He also knew he would fight to the death beside his mastel. It was not going to be easy to go to bed and think of anything relaxing to help him fall asleep as he instructed his young apprentices to do. He needed to have his wits about him tomorrow, and sleep would help. Sleep would claim him eventually.

CHAPTER TWENTY-THREE

The little Jade Harbinger sat in the treetop, watching the grorachs as they divided into two groups. One group settled down under his tree and slept while the second group ran off into the woods to hunt. The little bird didn't like flying at night as the sunlight was starting into its glorious kaleidoscope display of colors preceding darkness. In just a matter of time, the sun would set, and the night sky would be totally dark. Flying into an eight eyed reclusa's web set between trees was always a possibility, and the little bird did not fancy itself as a meal trapped in the sticky fibers. The time factor was desperate for his mastel friend. That made it desperate for the bird as well.

Ignoring the risks, the green feathered bird flittered out into a defensive flight pattern into the darkening sky, following the large band of grorachs as they devoured anything they could catch. When the small bird realized the grorachs were closing in on the valley, the little bird sent out a warning vision of the two groups of grorachs to Rydor.

Rydor's mastels were digging holes frantically in a large circle around the cave while the mothers of the newborn mastels were inside the cave, settling the foals. The young mastels under the age of one season were also inside the cave without their mothers as they were needed for the battle. That left the mares of the newborns to watch and protect all the young mastels as well as their own.

When Rydor received the vision of the two parties of grorachs, one sleeping, and the other hunting, the stallion knew instinctively that the sleeping grorachs would be hunting in the valley the very next day. The Jade Harbinger would stay with the group hunting now as best as he could and give a warning if the band should move faster than anticipated.

Morsian woke from his restless sleep with stirring dreams in his mind that the grorachs would reach the valley sooner than anticipated. Morsian knew this was not a dream when he awoke. It was Rydor pounding into his mind, frantically telling Morsian to wake the men.

Once dressed and assembled, Morsian told the men to climb aboard the Morries. "As soon as we arrive in the valley, we must start placing the piercers into the holes the mastels have been digging all night. They will help to fill in the holes and hopefully make short work of placing all three hundred into the ground at the correct angle. You men who have bonded with a mastel will shout out instructions to the rest of the men. We will need to work quickly at unloading and stacking the piercers around the circle. Once the piercers are in place, it will be necessary to make sure that arrows are loaded in all the crossfire magazines. There will be no delays firing as many arrows as possible if that is done correctly. As soon as I receive word that the grorachs are coming close, Aloftin and Frisky will make for the highest tree in preparation to target the lead grorachs. Are there any questions, and do each of you know the part you will play in the battle?"

Murmurs and head-shaking indicated that the men understood what was expected of each of them. Jumping onto the Morries, Morsian guided the vehicles down the hill, making sure that none of the three vehicles hit any holes along their path.

In the dark, the colors of the mastels could not be discerned. Each mastels was a mere shadow. As their eyes adjusted, the men and animals were working as a coordinated team. Once the mastels dug the holes with their claws, the men lifted the piercers into the holes and laid them at the appropriate angle. The mastels used their paws again and filled the holes in with the dirt. Once the dirt was tamped down firmly, the sharpened spear glinted in the starlight at an ominous angle. The men continued working quietly through the remainder of the night until a circular wall of polished spikes gave the Aztarian men a sense of security that Morsian hoped would not fail them.

With a few more hours of darkness and no word from the little green spy, the men laid on or under the Morries to catch a bit more sleep knowing rest would play an important part in the battle. Fatigue could turn the tide in the grorachs' favor. Being rested and alert was necessary for the men to battle the beasts since the grorachs are cunning and vicious.

Morsian stood beside Rydor in unified mental communication. Playing out Morsian's strategy in his mind, Rydor tossed his head with the brilliant gold mane flaring to the sky, indicating he would convey to the herd what would be needed from each of them. The mastels stood transfixed as they received the mental pictures from their stallion and leader.

The darkness was barely giving way to the much-dreaded breaking of dawn. The red and gold colors of the stallions were not yet apparent in the dim gray light of the earliest part of the day. Morsian noted he could see the outline of the trees in the distance and, with his increased vision, knew the time was drawing near. Soon the morning light would show the approach of the hordes of beasts swarming into the mastels' valley. His stomach was in knots, and he wished he thought to bring food and medicine.

'Rydor, you have not heard from your little bird friend yet. Do you think we have time to make a fast trek back to the cabins? I need to retrieve some supplies I forgot.' Morsian quickly pictured the items he needed.

Rydor indicated that Morsian should mount upon his back and before Morsian was settled properly, the mastel bounded over the piercers and raced up the hill. Morsian gripped tightly and held his breath as the cool morning dew settled into his burning lungs.

Reaching their destination, Morsian slipped off Rydor's back and quickly ran into the cabin. Finding satchels, he stuffed them full of items, including bandages, suturing materials, healing berries, and food. His frantic pace was interrupted by Rydor, who quickly showed the picture of the sleeping grorachs now waking and ready to hunt. The night hunters were within an easy travel distance from the valley. Since the night hunters killed most everything caught out in the open on the ground in their path, the day hunters would not hunt until they reached the valley. That meant, the pack of grorachs would not stop running until they reached the mastel herd. Rydor was impatient to get back to his herd, and Morsian knew he needed to grab the satchels and return to the stallion before Rydor left without him.

Returning as quickly as they left, Morsian became alarmed when he saw clearly the sparkle of the spear tips in the brightening sky. He feared for Rydor's life as the stallion leaped onto a boulder at the last second and barely cleared the piercers in two bounds. 'What if the grorachs are equally as athletic as the mastels? Could they clear the piercers in the same manner?' Morsian wondered.

Looking to see how many boulders were within easy access, Morsian revised his plan. Timrick and Sea Foam would need to be re-stationed to guard the cave entrance from any grorachs that may scale the cave from behind. They could prevent any grorach from leaping past the defenses of the four men positioned on top of the cave. There were only two other boulders that might be scaled easily, as Rydor demonstrated. Placing a man on mastel on each boulder with crossfires should keep any grorachs from jumping over the piercers by that method.

Morsian continued to rethink his battle strategies. He wondered whether his plan had too many flaws. He believed the men mounted on the three Morries inside the circle with crossfires to defend the mastels was a failsafe. He questioned whether more men needed to be positioned outside the circle with jounces as well as crossfires, or would being outside the protective circle put them in grave danger? Morsian's head began to spin from the stress of planning the defense and the fear that he would be responsible for the loss of life if his plan failed.

'You need to eat. Your mind is not clear,' came a thought into Morsian's head, and the inventor knew it was Rydor reminding him that he had not eaten and neither had his men. Looking around, Morsian saw the mastels grazing on bales of hay that were brought into the circle and knew Rydor was correct. He totally forgot about the satchels packed with food.

Reaching out to the men who could receive his thoughts, he directed them to the satchels of food and asked them to make sure everyone had eaten. Water would need to be shared with the mastels since he did not expect Rydor to carry water as well as the satchels filled with supplies. Watching as the men gathered to divide up the food, Morsian received a shove from behind to move him towards the men who were already eating.

'I know, I know. I am going to eat, too. By the way, pushy stallion, I don't believe I have seen you eat your share of the hay either,' Morsian conveyed to his mastel as he moved towards the men. Having barely eaten a biscuit when a flurry of green flew past him and onto the back of Rydor, Morsian knew the grorachs were now entering the valley.

"To your places, men!" Morsian shouted as a flurry of color whirled around him as mastels came towards the men who would be on their backs. Morsian saw Aloftin on Frisky sprinting towards the tree, and Morsian hoped Aloftin would not fall as Frisky bounded from limb to limb to the highest perch. Distracted by all the commotion around him, Morsian did not see if Aloftin and Frisky were in place.

Men scrambled to the Morries and gathered crossfires. Mastels moved to stand over the designated piercers to block the spears from the view of the grorachs. The four selected men climbed to the top of the cave with crossfires and jounces ready.

Morsian strained his eyes to see if Aloftin and Frisky were in place to pick off the leaders of the pack. He could not see a hint of them through the foliage. Moving his eyes to the trees from where the grorachs would first appear, Morsian made himself breathe slow and steady. It was at this point that Morsian realized he did not have a weapon of his own. Racing to the Morries, Morsian heaved himself up onto the closest one and gathered a weapon. Rydor did not need him on his back as he circled his mastels to make sure each was ready to battle.

When the first grorachs came into view, Morsian gaped in amazement. The beasts were three times larger than he thought they would be, and their numbers were unbelievable. Each beast was naturally equipped with enough weapons to take on an army. Morsian started to feel miserable and defeated. Immediately reprimanding himself for his negative thoughts, he looked at the young men who depended on his leadership. Seeing fear on each of his men's faces, Morsian gathered his spirit and called out words of reassurance.

"Remember men, your crossfires can take out four targets at once if you lock onto the beasts. I have made some modifications to the arrow tips with phyrium. I believe that most of you will be able to direct the arrows with pinpoint accuracy with your thoughts. The ones who have not eaten enough phyrium to connect telepathically will need to use your acquired skills. I have great faith that you will all do well. Only a few jounces have been modified, and Aloftin has several of them. Relax and make each shot count."

Morsian realized he forgot to tell Aloftin of the modifications made to his jounces. Reaching Rydor with some effort, Morsian was about to ask the stallion to convey the message to Frisky when he realized Aloftin and Frisky were not bonded. Quickly giving Rydor his love, Morsian dismissed his original reason to contact the stallion.

The grorachs sniffed the air and caught the scent of the mastels and men. Savage squeals and barks were heard as the pack of grorachs moved in a mass towards the circle. Aiming at the head beasts, the men were surprised when the pack split into three groups, and it became obvious that the creatures planned to surround them and attack from multiple angles instead of a single head-on charge.

The mastels standing over the piercers held their ground, knowing that timing was essential to catch the grorachs unprepared for the shock that would meet them when the mastels leaped away. The front line of grorachs headed full speed into the tip of the piercers as the mastels backed quickly away, leaving the spearhead visible at the very last moment. The grorachs immediately behind the impaled beasts used the bodies of their fallen pack members to scramble over the clogged spears and into the circle.

Men on the Morries fired rapidly at the grorachs who managed to penetrate the circle. Squealing and yelps were heard as arrows struck the targets killing or injuring the many who got through the circle of spearheads. The mounted lead mastels horns appeared like blazing swords, and each lowered their horns to prepare for one on one battle with advancing grorachs.

Rydor called for the secondary mastels to retreat to the Morries, where additional men were waiting to mount onto their backs. With jounce and crossfires in hand and horns erected to full size, grorachs found themselves riddled with arrows before they could reach and gore any mastels.

Unaccustomed to riding mastels, many men found themselves unseated and on the ground with lunging grorachs coming at full speed towards them. Grorach's gnashing their teeth and focusing on the fallen men were taken unprepared by the mastels when their spiraling horns tore into the grorach's bodies. Quickly retracting their horns, the proud mastels left the beasts to die. Getting to their feet, the men bounded into action on the mastels backs who just saved their lives.

Aloftin from the trees carefully picked his targets, watching to see which grorach seemed to be the pack leaders. With Frisky holding Aloftin's tunic in his teeth to help steady the man in the treetop, Aloftin sent his jounce in a flashing arc to slice one grorach as it tore up the dried grass looking for prey. Falling to the ground in two pieces, the grorach never knew what hit it. The jounce returned as gracefully as a bird of prey to the waiting hand of Aloftin. Picking another target, Aloftin sent the jounce on its deadly mission time and time again.

As men continued to pick targets and let their arrows fly, other men with piercers found themselves in one-on-one duels with the grorach's rasping teeth and glinting tusks. Mastels, ever by their side, impaled any of the grorach's that found their way past the piercers.

Sweat covered both men and mastels as they raced inside the circle to block any grorach that broke through the defenses. Timrick and Sea Foam saw more action than they bargained for as several grorachs attacked head-on smelling the newborn foals inside the cave opening. With arrows flying from over their heads, Timrick was thankful for the men stationed on top of the cave. Before long, those men were forced to engaged the grorachs that maneuvered around from the back and scaled the top of the cave. Squealing and growls could be heard from above, and Timrick knew he and Sea Foam were on their own to protect the entrance to the cave.

With an onrush from one huge hairy boar, Timrick let loose his jounce as Sea Form lowered her head to meet the advance. Sliding to a stop, the beast lay dead at the feet of the white mastel, and Timrick stood with his jounce back in his hand. Sea Foam snorted her disapproval of the smell, assaulting her nostrils and turned her gleaming golden eyes with admiration to the man who saved her and her filly.

'Thank you, Timrick,' came a clear projection into the man's mind, and he knew without a shadow of a doubt that Sea Foam was now linked to him forever. Wanting to savor the moment, Timrick allowing himself to be distracted, turned to see a charging beast heading directly towards him. Not having time to let loose his jounce, Timrick knew this was the end when Sea Form leaped upon the grorach with claws piercing into the spinal cord, paralyzing the creature immediately. The creature still alive and without defense, Sea Foam easily finished the beast with a downward thrust of her horns, ending the animal's misery.

'Now it is my turn to thank you!' Timrick signaled with his eyes gleaming with love and pride. The moment lasted for only a second as another grorach came barreling into their view. Each knew the other would protect each other's back, as the wave of new grorachs headed toward them.

Becoming more confident in the treetop, Aloftin took risks to fire several jounces at one time, amazed that each was hitting the targets easily. Balancing on a limb too thin to support his weight, Aloftin slipped as the limb gave way, falling headfirst from the treetop. Before hitting the bottom limb, Aloftin's freefall stopped abruptly as Frisky grabbed Aloftin's trouser leg in his claws. Dangling, Aloftin became aware of a grorach that noticed his descent and was hurrying to snatch the human in his vicious teeth.

Frisky, tugging at Aloftin's trousers, pulled the man rod by rod length back up the tree with the grorach howling in frustration at barely missing his prey. Once on a sturdy limb, Aloftin hugged the bough for dear life, realizing he was almost dead meat. Frisky mewed his relief that Aloftin was safe. Shaking and fearful, Aloftin refused to release his grasp on the branch until Frisky licked his face and offered his body for support.

Aloftin realized all his jounces now lay on the ground under the tree. He feared to descend from his perch to retrieve them. In a flash of insight, Frisky read Aloftin's mind and jumped to the ground to gather the jounces in his mouth. Not seeing several grorachs heading his direction, Aloftin was about to scream for Frisky to retreat to the tree, when Frisky sprung frantically to the limb beside him.

"You could read my mind," Aloftin said out loud. "You needed to have read my mind since I couldn't get the words out fast enough!"

Without words, Frisky responded with licks and purrs, and Aloftin could easily see everything that Frisky was sending to him in vivid mental pictures. A sensation of pure ecstasy filled Aloftin. The emotion was checked quickly as Frisky showed the grorachs, without success, frenziedly cutting the bark away from the bottom of the massive tree with their scissor hooves. Climbing now on each other's backs, the grorachs were determined to reach the newly formed team.

Taking all three jounces that Frisky laid on the broad limb, Aloftin mentally pictured each grorach being sliced through with his next throw. All three jounces flew into action and decimated the snarling beasts as they struggled to climb the tree.

Looking back at the battle, Aloftin knew he needed to have a higher perch once again. Climbing on Frisky's back, the team headed to a higher branch where Aloftin could pick out the next targets.

Teetawn was beside Tyleed's side on the Morry. His job was to track the battle and send encompassing images to Tyleed as to where any grorachs were penetrating defenses. Tyleed allowed Teetawn's vision to direct his crossfire and beast after beast fell under his arrows.

Geselle, refusing to be far from her colt's side, remained near the Morry where Tyleed and Teetawn fought side by side. With her horns ready in case any grorach should threaten her offspring, Geselle put herself at risk as several grorachs broke through the circular defense.

Teetawn, seeing his mother's imminent peril, guided Tyleed's arrows at the deadly grorachs. More arrows followed rapidly to the targets of the advancing beasts. As fast as Tyleed released his arrows, more and more beasts attacked.

Rydor feeling his favorite mare's fears, bellowed a challenge and charged into the mass of grorachs with his horns piercing and claws striking to protect Geselle. Tyleed continued his salvo of arrows knocking down as many grorachs as possible.

Sensing Rydor's danger, Morsian focused his sight on the grorachs who were about to reach his stallion and sent a flurry of jounces into the mix. Slicing and maiming one after another, the dead and dying beasts littered the ground near Rydor and Geselle. Exhausted but relieved, Morsian jumped from the Morry and raced to Rydor, who was nuzzling Geselle. Wrapping his arms around both mastels, Morsian found himself in tears of relief and exhaustion.

With the smell of many dead grorachs lingering in the air, the remaining grorachs reacted to the scene and ran into the eastern forest. Fearful that they may regroup, Morsian mounted Rydor and called to all mounted mastels to pursue the creatures and run them out of the valley and into the badlands for generations to come.

CHAPTER TWENTY-FOUR

As the sun settled over the top of the nearest mountains casting shadows in the valley below, the returning mastels and riders made their appearance back to the barricade. Cheers could be heard from the men who remained behind to help guard the newborns, young mastels, and new mothers. Littered throughout the meadows were the bodies of grorachs, numbering almost one hundred.

"We are going to need to remove these bodies before they spoil and stink up the valley more than they already have. I would say there is plenty of meat for the griswells for days to come. I suggest we load some onto the Morries and take them to the griswells tonight before it gets dark," Morsian said to the waiting men.

As the men set to the task of lifting the heavy grorachs onto the Morries, Morsian went about looking to see if any mastel or man was injured in the fight. Only a few lacerations and minor scratches were found. Tyleed and Morsian mended the minor injuries, and smiles spread across their faces as relief set in. A disaster was avoided for both men and mastel due to the warnings from griswells and the Jade Harbinger to allow a plan and to activate the strategies that saved their lives.

Morsian noted that many of the men were busy field dressing the grorachs. Smoking the meat and tanning the hides would take time, and Morsian decided to deliver as many of the carcasses as possible to the village to be processed. Time was essential. The meat would spoil if not processed quickly. Even though it was a long, hard day, the work was not yet done. All the field dressed grorachs not taken to the griswells or smoked for the camp's consumption would need to be loaded and taken to the village tonight while it was cool. No groans were heard as Morsian conveyed this thought to his men. All agreed it was necessary.

Throughout that day and night, more and more of the newest arrivals were finding that they could read minds, especially during the stress of battle. Aloftin was, at first, disappointed when he discovered his great abilities with the jounce were not only his skill but the modifications Morsian made to the jounces with phyrium. After thinking for another moment, Aloftin decided he liked being able to communicate with the weapon as well. He could see the significance of hitting a target even on an off day.

"You are by far the best jounce marksman in the camp," Morsian said for all to hear. "The fact that I made modifications did not take away from your skill. The modifications may have enhanced it a bit. You were spectacular in your treetop perch. Taking down the leaders of the pack is what helped to scatter the remaining grorachs and make our victory complete. In fact, I must tell you how proud I am of every single one of you men and every mastel. Rydor echoes my praise. Three cheers to all of you!"

Morsian wished he had something special to celebrate the victory since none of the men were very interested in eating grorach this soon after the battle. The left-over food from the satchels was eaten slowly while each man recounted the highlights of individual fights. Morsian was not sure that there were many highlights, only moments of respite when someone or some mastel was saved. The killing of any living being was not something Morsian relished. Saving the beloved mastels did fill him with a sense of pride. If there were more time to figure out another way to keep the mastels safe without destroying a species, he would have done so. Now, he needed to concentrate on the remaining threat.

He wanted to scatter the surviving grorachs to the badlands and keep them there permanently. He hoped they would never need to battle them again. They were fortunate this time...

Enjoying the excitement of the newest young men experimenting with their new-found telepathy, Morsian reached out to Rydor. He sensed stirrings from the mastel herd as well. Gratitude was not a big enough word to describe how the mastels were feeling towards the men who saved their lives and the lives of their foals. Morsian watched as young stallion and mare alike came closer to men, they felt particularly grateful towards. Muzzles were lowered for a soothing touch, and often, a new bond was formed.

Morsian began to realize it would be he who would be taking the Morries to the village tonight. He didn't mind. He could take a much-needed nap on the way, knowing the Morries would not stray from the path to town. Besides, Morsian wanted to see if Lalaya was packed and ready to return with him.

When the Morries were loaded, Morsian reached out to Rydor to let him know he would be back no later than two days from now. Rydor came to his side to bid him farewell and to get the pats and praise he felt he deserved.

'You are by far, the greatest stallion in this or any herd. Without you, our battle strategy would not have worked,' Morsian praised. 'Watch over the newest men as they settle into their bonds. You know how crazy men can be when they feel the first thrill of bonding. Make sure they go to their camps to eat and sleep. I will leave Tyleed in charge. You can communicate with him through Teetawn while I am gone. I will miss you as I always do when we are apart. I must go if you are ever going to know Lalaya. She makes the best biscuits on the whole planet.' Morsian added a mental wink.

Giving instructions to Tyleed, Morsian sat upon the lead Morry and headed towards the village. One thought went quickly through his mind as he started down the road. 'What if the smell of the dead grorachs caused river monsters to attack me on this trip?' Looking down at the platform, Morsian took inventory of how many crossfires or piercers remained on the Morry. Finding none, he commanded the Morries to hasten into a faster pace.

Fairly sure the river monsters would not venture on to the road to the village, Morsian settled down to a nap. Before sleeping, Morsian decided some small deterrent would make his sleep more restful. Picturing the sides of the platform curving up and over the entire load of grorachs, Morsian felt quite sure he would not be in danger.

Traveling through the night at a quick pace, Morsian awoke to see the village in the far distance. Early as it was, people were already milling around to set up booths to sell their goods, or to get an early start in the fields. The sight made Morsian feel relief and excitement that he would soon see his wife.

Pulling the Morries to a stop in front of the butchers and processing compound, Morsian hopped down from his seat and knocked loudly at the door. When a burly man answered the door, Morsian gave him a bear hug, happy to see his old friend, Volger. Asking the phyrium platform to return to its original flat state, Volger let out a howl of surprise.

"My gosh! What in the world have you brought to my door?"

Morsian laughed. "Not only have I brought three Morries full of grorachs, but I also am not going to charge you a cent. You can have all of them free if you would not mind tanning some of the hides for our use. We might enjoy a little of the smoked meat as well," Morsian said as an afterthought, "The rest is for you to butcher, and sell.

"Morsian, that is too generous. I will employ several young men to get the work done quickly. I feel I should pay you something for all that meat and hides. There is a small fortune there," Volger said, unable to believe his good fortune.

"We were blessed not to have a single fatality. We want to pass on that blessing. Maybe you can pass on the blessing as well. I don't know of anyone who is hungering in our village personally. You may know of a family or two who could use a little extra. I will leave it up to you. If you could hire some of those young men quickly and get the Morries unloaded, I would be grateful. I am not sure how much stuff Lalaya intends to bring with her. I might end up needing all three Morries for her clothes and shoes alone," Morsian laughed.

Laughing with Morsian, Volger said, "I know your Lalaya. She is a practical woman. I know she will only load up one Morry or maybe two. You will have plenty of room to take some other supplies to your new mining community." With a more serious note, Volger continued, "When do you think you will start to send phyrium to our village? I am amazed at the properties of the mineral. I am hoping I can use phyrium with my tools to make my day easier. I am not getting any younger, you know, and those hides and bones seem to be getting tougher and harder to cut through all the time."

Responding, Morsian said, "We have a few minor kinks to work out in the mining process. I feel comfortable in saying that we can have a shipment of phyrium here by next moon or two moons at the latest. I will send Branley with the first shipment to make sure you know how to mix the phyrium in the proper proportions. He will get you started, and then you will be fine. If not, I will make whatever tool you might need. How does that sound?"

Volger was pleased. Seeing the mounds of carcasses waiting to be processed, he cut the conversation short. Yelling for his son to come out, Volger placed his son in charge of finding young men who wanted to work. Morsian walked away to his home, where he hoped to find Lalaya packed and ready to go.

Walking through the front door, Lalaya sat at the breakfast table, sipping her warm beverage. Startled, she dropped her cup, and it shattered into many pieces and shards spread across the floor.

"Morsian, you scared me to death! I didn't know you were coming home this soon. I thought it would be many days yet before you arrived. I have much to do," Lalaya said as she scurried into his arms.

"Don't fret. I will help you pack whatever you want to bring to our new home. Once we get there, I will make cups and dishes for you that will never break. In fact, I will invent ovens that will do all the cooking with only a thought from you," Morsian said while hugging his wife close to him.

"Look at our son grow. It has only been a short time, and already your belly is swollen," Morsian said while patting Lalaya's lower abdomen.

Lalaya stood back and looked down at her belly. "Our son is getting big. I have chosen a name for him. I want to call him D'Hantin after my father. Is that alright with you?"

"I think D'Hantin is a wonderful name. Your father was a great man. I will be proud to have our son named for him." Morsian said. Seeing tears starting to form in his wife's eyes, Morsian quickly changed the subject. Even happy tears made Morsian uncomfortable. "Where shall I start with packing?"

In the time it took to have the Morries unloaded and washed down, Morsian and Lalaya packed everything Lalaya felt she would need to settle down in her new home. Anything else that remained in the home could be left for whichever young couple might want to move in. Many items Morsian told Lalaya to leave since he would make new items out of phyrium that would work much better than what she would be leaving behind.

Loading the Morry with the belongings Lalaya could not part with and having the other two Morries loaded with more supplies and hay for the mastels, Morsian mentally thought of home, and the Morries moved under their own power. Lalaya gave a backward glance at the home she was leaving behind. Placing one hand on her stomach, she took Morsian's hand with the other and smiled contentedly. She was looking forward to raising her son with mastels. All that Morsian relayed to her was like a wonderful dream, and she wanted that for her son. She saw how happy her husband was now that he was linked forever with a mastel, and she knew D'Hantin would find a reason to live and work side by side with a mastel of his own.

Humming a song quietly, Lalaya watched the countryside go past quickly as the Morries picked up speed. Chuckling, Lalaya knew Morsian was using his mind to increase the Morries speed. She knew how badly he wanted to get home.

CHAPTER TWENTY-FIVE

All nineteen young men were bonded with mastels. Rydor was stern about making sure that the men went back to their cabins to eat and sleep as each was more than willing to lay under the stars by the side of their new partner. Rydor saw how goofy the new bond could make both man and beast and was grateful that he and Morsian had more sense than their lesser counterparts. When they bonded, it was special, Rydor admitted. There were more mature and settled ways to approach bonding. The young mastels and young men were outrageous, according to Rydor's imperious thoughts.

Several of his minor stallions were now bonded with men like Kobart, Breckon Junyn, and B'hant. The men who first bonded understood how euphoric the newest members of the mining company felt since they had a hard time leaving their newly bonded mastel as well. Morsian tolerated no silliness from his workers and made them return to their cabins each night for food and sleep.

The mastels who bonded earlier like Biscuit, Lattee, Fonrah, and Teetawn flaunted their superiority over the other mastels. They each felt that they were more special since they bonded first. Rydor tolerated their foolishness only because it seemed to bring the other mastels down from the clouds. Sea Foam and Frisky identified with each group since they landed somewhere in-between. Neither acting arrogant nor mindless, the two found comfort in each other's company. They knew that the extreme emotions following the life-threatening battle caused the others to bond more readily than they had themselves. Both Frisky and Sea Foam admitted that the looming threat of the grorachs' attack predicated their bonding as well.

Euphoria was the only word that could explain the feelings of both man and mastel in the valley. Even the grumpy old griswells exhibited some playfulness in the caves at the thought of none of the mastels dying in the battle with the grorachs. Memories of losing griswells from many previous seasons of the grorach invasions and knowing this would never happen again now that the mastels were staying in the valley caused griswells to send excited messages to their bonded mastels.

The mastels ran in large circles through the valley and up boulders and trees alike. A harmony of colors swirled throughout the valley as mastels raced along, blurring their coats complexities into prismatic hues of breathtaking beauty. The men sat in awe as the mastels spirited, prancing to their delight.

As the Morries came into sight, cheers went up from the men. Leaving their seats, they raced towards Morsian and Lalaya to offer their assistance in unloading the Morries. Lalaya stood spellbound by the view she witnessed before their arrival interrupted the exhibition.

"They are even more beautiful than you said," Lalaya said out loud suddenly aware she was the only one using spoken words.

"Oh, I am sorry, my dear. I will make sure your diet has plenty of phyrium. You will soon hear our thought in your mind, as well. I am sorry I did not think of leaving you a large supply after my last visit. I feel ashamed of myself for not thinking to do so. Don't worry, you will be part of this silent and wonderful world in no time," Morsian said as an apology to his wife.

"In the meantime, men, would you mind using spoken words so Lalaya will be included in your discussions?" Morsian said as a reminder of how things used to be only days before.

"Let me help you down," Branley said as he offered a hand to Lalaya. "You are going to love it here. We will get all your belongings unpacked, and you can settle in."

As Rydor approached, Lalaya backed close to Morsian. Seeing a mastel up close was intimidating, and Lalaya found herself afraid.

"Don't be afraid, my dear. This is Rydor, my bondmate. Isn't he the most beautiful thing you have ever seen?"

'Thing? I am not a thing!' Rydor snorted loudly, sending Lalaya scampering behind Morsian's back for protection.

'I apologize. Sometimes there are no words for how incredible you are,' Morsian said mentally, chuckling quietly to himself as he watched his stallion accept his reasoning for using such an inappropriate word as 'thing.'

First asking permission from Rydor, Morsian encouraged Lalaya to come out from behind him and feel how silky soft Rydor's fur felt to the touch. With trepidation, Lalaya inched forward with her hand tentatively outstretched to touch the velvety coat of the brilliant red stallion.

The men worked quickly and efficiently at unloading the Morries as Lalaya made Rydor's acquaintance. Sturjen and Branley maneuvered the Morry filled with hay to the mastel cave to unload. Before long, Lalaya and Rydor were comfortable with each other, and the cabin was filled with Lalaya's belongings.

The mastels in the meadow were in high gear and continued to run and frolic. With unified precision, all running ceased as Rydor made his desires known. Sending a message to Morsian as well, soon, all the men and Lalaya were sitting on a Morry as it became seats for the exhibition to follow.

"What is going to happen?" Lalaya asked Morsian.

"I have no idea, my dear. Rydor wishes to show us a display of the mastels agility and skills in celebration of the successful grorach battle. We are going to need to sit and watch to find out. From what I understand, I am to move the Morry to allow us to see each spectacle from a better viewing advantage. I have a feeling this is going to be good."

At first, the celebration looked as if it was going to be competitive races. Morsian explained to Lalaya that the mastels lining up for the first race were juveniles. Any mastel under the age of one season was invited to race on the flat ground of the meadow. Morsian explained the small bright red mastels would someday become stallions, and the other colors of mastels, including strawberry, beige, cream with stripes, were the females. However, Morsian pointed out that some females had red manes or gold manes or even snow-white manes. He also pointed out that each mastel had two sets of buds on their foreheads and explained the purpose of those buds.

"You are joking me. Those tiny buds can become huge spiraling horns in seconds? I won't believe that until I see it," Lalaya said, looking at her husband as if he was teasing her.

"I hope you are not obliged to see it anytime soon. Those buds only become horns when they must fight to defend themselves. I would like to believe that we have no dangers anywhere near. This is a day for fun and frivolity."

With a sudden ear-splitting vocalization from Rydor, the race was off with small mastels running at full speed. Blurs of color breezed past the Morry as the spectators watched in amusement as some mastels lost focus and began to wrestle playmates to the ground, tumbling end over end, while the more mature young mastels focused on the finish line. Cheers went up as a red male crossed the imaginary line Rydor had set as the final goal.

Without hesitation, older fillies and colts took the starting position, and with a second shrill bellow, the next race was ready. Again, the race seemed to be over almost before it started. Another red male finished in the lead.

Soon mares were at the starting line, and many new miners stood to cheer on their new bondmates in the race. Fonrah gave Lattee the race of her life, but soon the strawberry mare with the red tail and mane inched Fonrah out of the first-place position with Kellyn jumping from the Morry and running to his mastel's side, bursting with pride.

The stallions formed the line with Rydor pawing up the ground. Geselle, as Rydor's favorite, squealed the start of the race. No stallion could match the pace of the mighty leader of the herd, and Rydor finished without even breathing hard.

"No fair!" shouted Breckon when his stallion finished several paces behind Rydor. "There is no way any of the stallions can compete with Rydor. Why don't we even the playing field a bit and put more weight on Rydor's back?

Rydor snorted, 'Get on my back, Morsian. I will win even with your added weight!'

Morsian reluctantly slid off the Morry. Climbing onto Rydor's back, he was given one instruction from his stallion. 'Hold on, and don't let go.'

With all stallions on the line once again, Geselle started them off with another high-pitched squeal. Rydor leaped to the lead with Morsian holding on for dear life. Tears streamed from Morsian's face as the wind lashed his eyes. Unable to see through the tearing eyes, Morsian only knew they won the race by Rydor's prancing and vivid mental visualizations of his victory.

'To make the rest of the events more even, I will carry Morsian on my back for each,' the stallion trumpeted to the other mastels who conveyed the challenge to their bondsmen.

Morsian, uncertain about his own abilities, became concerned when the herd headed for the forest, and the Morry followed with the spectators. Seeing the tree where Aloftin perched to pick off the lead grorachs, Morsian began to tremble. 'We are going up that tree?'

Aloftin caught Morsian's fear and laughed. Out loud so Lalaya would not miss out on what was happening, Aloftin said, "Frisky and I made it up that same tree. I am sure you and Rydor will have no trouble at all."

"Why don't you and Frisky join us in this race?" Morsian sarcastically fired back at the young man.

"Frisky can't compete with Rydor with the extra weight of my being on his back. I think my agile young mastel will do fine without me holding him back," Aloftin shouted to Morsian.

"Wait! How many mastels can climb that tree at the same time? Shouldn't each have their own tree? I don't know that I like the idea of many mastels scratching and clawing their way up the same tree that I will be in," Morsian said without jest.

"That could make it fairer. How about if the younger mastels have smaller trees to scale while the older, more powerful mastels climb the larger trees? It will be a race to the top," Aloftin said. "In fact, if Frisky and I have a smaller tree to climb, I will join in on this event. I do have some experience with the tree climb, after all."

It was decided that any mastel who had a bondsman who wanted to try to compete in this event was encouraged to come forward.

When fourteen of the men rushed to the trees with their mastels in pursuit, a new contest formed. According to sex and size, the mastels picked a tree to climb while their team members sat on their backs.

With one last word to the competitors and a chuckle, as well, from Aloftin, the racers were ready to begin. "It isn't as easy as you think!"

Again, Geselle sounded the start of the tree climb, and mastels leaped to the lower branches and continued to jump from branch to branch making their way up the tree. When branches were too far apart, claws dug into the bark of the tree, and the mastels continued the climb. Several riders misjudged the leap and found themselves tumbling from the backs of their mastels, grabbing limbs to break their falls. Knowing immediately that they had lost their riders, the mastels leaped and spun in the air, making grabs with claws or teeth for their team members. This maneuver kept the men from serious injuries. Even with the rescue from their mastels, many young men sported bruises and scrapes from their descent.

Frisky and Aloftin made it to the top before Rydor and Morsian mainly because the highest limbs of the larger tree could not bear the weight of the larger mastel and his rider. Whoops of joy sounded for Aloftin as he and Frisky scrambled down the tree in neck-breaking speed to bask in the admiration of the crowd for besting the dominant stallion.

Rydor beamed with pride at his son's abilities as he descended the tree. His own failure at not winning, he blamed on the fact that Morsian ate too well and weighed him down. Morsian laughed, knowing that Rydor was saving face and because it was true. He was eating too well.

The next event made Morsian more confident. It was the boulder climb. Once again, any mastel who wanted to join in the competition with a rider on his back was welcome. Younger mastels could compete without a rider to build skills and confidence.

Once again, Morsian sat on Rydor's back as he bounded from boulder to boulder. He knew Rydor would visually show him which rock he planned to leap to in advance; that way, Morsian could adjust his weight and position to make the leap easier for his stallion. The difficulty with climbing to the top was there were few good paths to take up the cliff, and knowing which route to take in advance could be complicated by another mastel making the same choice. Morsian felt he and Rydor had the advantage since Rydor was incredibly powerful and could leap greater distances to achieve the same goal.

With a start being trumpeted, the mastels leaped to the boulder that would give them the greatest gain. Rydor outdistanced the others and was in the lead up the cliff. When two young mastels made the decision to leap to the same boulder at the exact same time, one mastel lost its footing and started to fall. Barely before hitting the sharp rock directly below, teeth sunk into the young mastel's hind leg, stopping the fall.

Rydor gripping the boulder he now stood upon, gently lowered the young mastel to the rock below, not loosening his grip until the mastel had all four paws on the boulder. The race continued to the top without the stallion.

Morsian shook with terror at the experience. One minute he was racing up the cliff, and in a split second, he was free-falling with Rydor to make the rescue. Morsian's head continued spinning from his body, shifting from up to down in a matter of seconds. How Rydor managed to keep Morsian from falling while saving the young mastel below was beyond Morsian's comprehension.

With his feet firmly on the ground, Morsian was soon joined by several of the other men. Slaps on the back and congratulatory comments were made. All comments were high praise for the stallion's feat.

Rydor almost seemed irritated with the praise. Licking the young mastel to reassure him, Rydor reached out to Morsian with annoyance. 'Would you humans not do the same for your young if they were in danger? I don't want praise for doing my duty,' the stallion's mind sent out visuals to his bondman.

Morsian soothed Rydor by explaining that the men were in awe of his prowess and ability to act quickly when danger loomed. He noted the mastel stallion relaxed his stance and turned to watch the other mastels on the cliff.

Once the mastels were back down from the boulder climb, many of the newest bonded men said they wanted to try the boulder climb as well. Rydor agreed only if two mastels climbed at a time and used different courses to make sure no one was hurt. With inexperienced teams of riders and mastels wanting to compete, Rydor knew he must minimize the competitive element for now.

Once every man who wanted to try the boulder climb had a turn, the merriment continued with each trying the tree climb. When all the teams were exhausted, they returned to the meadow, where they were surprised to see a table set up with fresh-made biscuits and jam that Lalaya made while the young men engaged in the festivities.

"Where did you find fruit to make jam?" Morsian asked while slathering a large amount of the jam onto a biscuit.

"I used those left-over berries that you placed on the Morries during the battle," Lalaya beamed.

"Well, no one should get sick for a very long time," was Morsian's only comment.

"Don't you like my jam?" Lalaya asked in bewilderment.

"It is delicious, but those berries are for healing," Morsian explained.

"Oh...I should have asked, shouldn't I?" Lalaya said, repentantly.

"It is alright, my dear. You and I will go on a berry hunt tomorrow to replenish the stock of berries. It will be fun. We can pack a picnic, walk to the bushes, and make a fun day out of it. Besides, I know of some bushes not too far away."

Lalaya's mouth dropped open. "You mean, I need to walk? Why wouldn't we use one of the Morries."

"I never thought about using a Morry. Of course, my dear, we can use a Morry. The terrain is not difficult," Morsian said to dispel his wife's distaste for anything physical.

Soon the joyful enthusiasm of the younger men drew Morsian from the biscuits and jam, and Morsian joined in with other games the men invented. Finding sticks, the men placed them on the ground at equal distances from each other and were taking turns seeing who could gather the most sticks while riding at breakneck speeds on the back of their mastels. Morsian watched, feeling way too old to try to slide to the side of Rydor to reach sticks on the ground.

As the daylight faded and the men and mastels were quietly resting, one young man declared that they should engage in the games every year on this date. He said it would be their first holiday as a mining community, and the men and mastels should get the day off from work. Everyone agreed, and names were thrown out as to what the holiday should be called. Names like Grorach Day, Bonding Day, and finally, one man suggested Morsian's Day that was meant with gales of laughter.

Acting offended, Morsian said, "Why not Morsian's Day. I brought back the weapons to fend off the grorachs, didn't I?"

The next day found the teams of men and mastels entering the caves cautiously to test whether the griswells would tolerate the men in their domain. Finding the beasts snarling and grumpy yet allowing the men to gather the phyrium that the griswells excavated, Morsian felt hope that the mining community would flourish. Digging the new tunnels to mine would be difficult for the men. It would be necessary, though, to find the new veins of mineral.

Months went by, and all was working well. The first shipment of the phyrium was sent to the factory village along with Branley to show the villagers how to use the mineral. Many of the wives of the older miners were already settled in the mining community, making Lalaya happy to have female company.

Morsian made an incredible discovery when Rydor conveyed a communication he had with Flint. 'It seems Flint is over one hundred seasons old.'

'How can that be?' exclaimed Morsian in mental excitement.

'It seems phyrium has other properties that we know very little. Flint visualized me as an old but very robust stallion. Flint showed me that I will live a long life barring an unfortunate accident and what more, she showed me that you would live to a very old age as well,' Rydor expressed with vivid mental pictures.

Morsian was flabbergasted. He never dreamt that Aztara would change completely. What would this mean to the planet? Would it become overpopulated as new life was born and the old did not die?

'I never said you would not die,' Rydor interrupted Morsian's thoughts. 'I only said you would grow quite old and stay robust.'

Morsian dismissed Rydor's last visualization. The fact that he would die someday did not stay the fact that Aztarians would need to make some changes in how the population was managed. Aztara was too small of a planet to allow overpopulation.

Sitting outside watching the magnificent display of colors as the sun started to set, Morsian was joined by Lalaya. Placing Morsian's hand on her swollen belly, Lalaya conveyed something new and strange. 'I can communicate with our baby.'

'You are kidding...," Morsian's thoughts conveyed his confusion about what his wife gently placed in his mind. 'What does our son say?'

'It isn't words, dear. Our baby boy sends feelings of warmth and love. It is hard to express... I know he can read my thoughts. He reacts to my words of love and pictures of the world I am showing him. I feel as if he knows who I am already. I tell him all about you, the mastels, and the community into which he will be born. I even show him my memories of my family and my life before coming to this valley. When I call him by his name, D'Hantin, he jumps for joy.'

Squeezing Lalaya's hand, the two sat in silence. Rydor's thoughts intruded on the quiet scene. 'I think you are going to enjoy being a father. It will change your whole world.'

With a faraway look, Morsian responded to Rydor. 'Your world has really changed with men coming into your valley, hasn't it?'

'No, your world has changed since coming into my valley,' Rydor corrected.

Morsian thought for a moment and replied in a mental picture. 'Our world, Aztara, will never be the same.'

To be continued...on Surtees, Science Rules, Volume I

MASTEL KINGDOM GLOSSARY OF TERMS

Allsight *(all-site)* – A telescope with day and night sight capability.

Aloftin *(a-loft-tin)* – Expert with various weapons, especially the jounce. Bonded with Frisky.

Aztara *(az-tare-a)* – The purple planet in the Ursa Draconis Galaxy.

Aztarian *(az-tare-e-an)* – Refers to the original inhabitants of the planet Aztara.

B'hantalion *(bant-al-lion)* – Nicknamed B'hant. The second apprentice to Morsian.

Biscuit *(bis-cut)* – A young playful, mischievous, and beautiful cream-colored female mastel. She craves sweets. Bonded with Branley.

Bog *(baa-oog)* – A young male griswell, bonded with Teetawn. Off-spring of Flint and Greyble.

Branley *(Bran-lee)* – Young, tall, and willowy man. Apprentice to Morsian. Bonded with Biscuit.

Breckon *(brr-reck-on)* – One of the original miners.

Cawwen *(caw win)* – Beast of burden like an ox but broader and shaggier.

Crossfire *(cross-fire)* – A weapon. Capable of firing multiple arrows at the same time.

D'Hantin *(dan-tin)* – The son of Morsian and father of Tymorian and inventor of many items, including the SoundBlaster.

Diviak *(div-ee-ak)* – Is the factory village blacksmith and carpenter.

Feigons *(fee-ja-uns)* – Insects that are used medicinally to clean deep wounds and for stimulating through their saliva, new cells needed to replenish lost blood.

Flint *(f-lint)* – The main female griswell, bonded with Rydor. Mother of Sunshine and Bog. Flint's mate is Greyble.

Fonrah *(fawn-rah)* – A young deep strawberry—almost red colored filly with prominent cream stripes and green eyes that bonded to Sturjen.

Fremits *(free-mits)* – Insects that live under rocks and boulders. Food Source for Larters.

Frisky *(frr-isky)* – Bright red colt with gold mane and tail. Rydor and Geselle's offspring. Also known as Three-Legs. Bonded with a griswell named Sunshine. Bonded with Aloftin.

Geselle *(jez-elle)* – Strawberry Mastel with stripes and green eyes. Rydor's favorite mare and mother of Teetawn.

Glemee *(glem-eee)* – Sheep like animals. Food source for griswells. Mastels hunt these creatures and feed them to the griswell in trade for phyrium.

Greyble *(gray-bell)* – a griswell male, Father of Sunshine, and Bog. Greyble's mate is Flint.

Griswell *(grr-is-well)* – An irascible creature. These animals are necessary for finding the mineral phyrium. Their sharp claws allow for digging. The miners must be able to stop the griswells before extraction as the mineral is extremely fragile, and these animals are not particularly concerned about the integrity of the mineral. Unfortunately, the miners are not able to use interspecies telepathy to communicate directly with the griswell. However, mastels can direct the griswell, keeping them calm, as griswells tend to be excitable and easily provoked. The interspecies telepathic trinity between miner, mastel, and griswell is critical to the existence of the planet Aztara.

Grorach's *(grr-roar-ack)* – A strong massive beast with sharp teeth and two pairs of tusks on either side of its jowls. Cloven hooves that act like scissors.

Gurlion *(gurr-lion)* – Tree dwelling animal with long limbs and a prehensile tail. A noisy creature that swings from limb to limb as they chatter.

Jade Harbinger *(har-bin-ger)* – A beautiful small jade-colored bird, much like a hummingbird. Bonded with Rydor.

Jicerian trees *(ji-sear-e-an)* – Fragrant trees found in the forest south of the capital city of Aztara, often chipped into pieces to provide aromatics, and used to build fragrant furniture. Morsian tapped the tree for its sap. When combined with Phyrium, it made a polymer.

Jounce *(jown-ce)* – An airfoil-shaped weapon with razor-sharp edges. It is thrown like Australian boomerangs.

Junyn *(june-yen)* – One of the original miners.

Kellyn *(kell-kyn)* – Always straight forward and to the point. One of the young men who become a miner. Bonded with Lattee.

Kobart *(ko-bart)* – One of the miners that is a good man.

Hyddle *(hi-dell)* – Small animal that lives in the rocks on the river bottom with sharp pinchers like a crayfish.

K-rod *(kay-rod)* – A unit of distance measurement equaling 3.125 miles or 5 kilometers.

Lalaya *(la-lay-ah)* – Morsian's wife, who is pregnant with D'Hantin.

Larters *(lar-ters)* – The larters are half the size of Rufus, the German Shepherd Dog. They are rock-dwelling creatures that live in dens. They have long sharp claws for digging and for scratching out fremits from under rocks and boulders. They are puce colored, which helps them blend into their surroundings, and they smell musky.

Lattee *(latt-tee)* – A female mastel, strawberry colored with subtle cream striping and a red mane and tail. Bonded with Kellyn.

Levitation *(lev-ah-ta-shun)* – The Phyrium mineral is modified to create a super-diamagnetic torsional gravity system by which a transporter or another object can be held aloft, without mechanical support, and in a stable position.

Mastel *(mass-til)* – The mastel is a creature that looks like a cross between an Earth leopard and unicorn. They have two buds on their forehead that spiral to golden horns when ready to fight. They have large padded paws with sharp retractable claws in the place of hooves. They move like a leopard leaping from boulder-to-boulder and can climb trees. They graze like a horse. Bonding with miners, mastels can direct the griswell, keeping them calm, as griswells tend to be excitable and easily provoked. The inter-species telepathic trinity between miner, mastel, and griswell is critical to the existence of the planet Aztara.

Mind-Voice – Inter-species telepathic communication.

Miners *(my-ners)* – Each miner works in a complicated inter-species telepathic tri-team. The miners work down in the mines with an irascible creature called a griswell. Unfortunately, the miners are not able to communicate directly with the griswell. Mastels, however, can direct the griswell and keep them calm. Luckily, inter-species telepathy between man and mastel and mastel and griswell takes milliseconds to complete the circuit.

Mining Compound – A mining business twenty K-rods south of the capital city of Aztara. This business was started by Morsian. It contains the phyrium mines, the mining community, the medical center, and a research lab. It is also the place where one can find the unique inter-species relationship between miner, mastel, and griswell. The large meadow to the west of the mine is where the initial Morsian Day Festivities were held. The hills to the east are where the mastel's hunt for the griswells food in exchange for the phyrium in their diet.

Morry *(more-eee)* – Uses a super-diamagnetic torsional gravity system made from phyrium. This transporter was invented Morsian to haul hay and mining equipment.

Morsian *(more-cee-ann)* – Lalaya is his wife, who is pregnant with D'Hantin. Bonded with Rydor, the leader of the Mastel kingdom. Discoverer of the mineral Phyrium. Discovered the relationship between the griswell and mastel's. The inventor of the Allsight instrument. Discoverer of the longevity and telepathic effects of Phyrium when consumed by humans and creatures. The inventor of building structures. Machinery and appliances using the mineral Phyrium. The inventor of the intelligent home using the mineral Phyrium. The inventor of super-diamagnetic torsional gravity system for levitation and propulsion. The designer of the Morry. Morsian literally changed everything about the way people eat, think, communicate, work, play, and sleep.

Morsian Day Festivities – An annual mining community competition held on the west meadow in honor of Morsian. Large fair with food booths, inter-generational games, and major competitions for miners and their mastels. Aztarians travel from all over the continent to attend, camp-out, or stay in the mining compound hostels.

Orange River – The orange river is in the western and southern regions of Aztara. It flows from the Northwest downriver on the southern side of the hills into the badlands in the eastern region. The fast-moving heavy storms leach minerals and metals out of the rocks and crevasses along the path of the river. This effect causes the river to turn orange and toxic. Only monsters can live in and around the river. A very dangerous place.

Piercer *(pierce-er)* – A long-shafted weapon that has a pointed double-edged serrated blade at its tip.

Phyrium *(phy-ree-um)* – A mineral only found on the Planet Aztara. This mined mineral enhances the 'Longevity Gene' (FOXO3) and the 'Telepathy Gene' (semaphorin 5A). It decreases aging while allowing telepathic communication between humans, creatures, and building structures, and machinery.

Qu'bees *(que-bees)* – Very tiny insects that live in the soil or on plants and emit a pleasant aroma.

Rod – A unit of distance measurement equaling 3.3 feet or 1 meter.

Rydor *(rye-door)* – Brilliant red stallion with gold mane and tail. Leader of the Mastel kingdom. Bonded with Morsian and mated with Geselle. Teetawn is one of his off-springs. Bonded with Flint a griswell.

Sea Foam *(See-foam)* – Snow white female mastel. Bonded to Timrick.

Sturjen *(stir-jen)* – He is an opinionated, large frame and strong. Must see to believe. One of the young men who become a miner. Bonded with Fonrah.

Sunshine *(sun-shine)* – A young female griswell, bonded with Three-Legs, aka Frisky. Off-spring of Flint and Greyble.

Teetawn *(tea-tawn)* – Bright red colt with gold mane and tail. Rydor and Geselle's offspring. Bonded with a griswell named Bog. Bonded with Tyleed, the veterinarian.

Telepathy Gene' **(semaphorin 5A)** – The Telepathy Gene increases one's ability to communicate telepathically with another being, species, or even a compatible machine or building. The gene allows one to transmit, receive, block, speed up, or slow down the delivery or acceptance of images and information. The consumption of phyrium enhances this sixth sense.

Teleetheric *(tell-la-eth-ric)* – Is the ultimate form of the telepathy gene involving our entire spiritual being, encompassing our mind, body, and soul.

'Tersherkin Rivbin' *(ter-shure-kin)* *(riv-bin)* – Means 'Dreaded River,' the ancient name of the 'Orange River.' Translated from old Aztarian Language.

Three-Legs *(three-legs)* – Bright red colt with gold mane and tail. Rydor and Geselle's offspring. Also known as Frisky. Bonded with a griswell named Sunshine.

Timrick *(tim-ric)* – The tallest miner that is as broad as a young cawwen. Bonded to Sea Foam. **Trechor** *(tray-core)* –

River dwelling monster with spikes protecting its entire body and tail.

Tyleed *(tie-lead)* – The mining village veterinarian. He is a very thoughtful and kind man. Bonds with Teetawn.

Volger *(vol-jer)* – Factory village butcher.

Weilks *(well-ks)* – A rock dwelling creature smaller than griswells, but not as aggressive. Found in the terrain of the Eastern and Southern Hills. Hunted by Aztarians, on occasion, for food.

Wildflower *(wild-flower)* – Young filly mastel saved by Teetawn and Frisky.

Yuari *(you-r-ee)* – Fierce tree-dwelling creature. Found in many regions on the continent.

Carole Walker Carter

Carole Walker Carter

Starting life in a small town in Nebraska, Carole and her family frequently moved across the USA, Carole met many fascinating personalities that inspired characters for her many stories. With a vivid imagination, Carole expressed her love of story-telling in Children's Literature, Mystery, Science Fiction, and Fantasy books as platforms for her expressive writing. Carole lives presently in the Pacific Northwest with her husband, Don, her childhood sweetheart and partner, their pet dogs, several chickens, and a few fish. Carole's career involved working with children from pre-school through high school, dealing with special needs, and "at-risk'" children as an Occupational Therapy Assistant and Educational Assistant.

Aztara, Mastel Kingdom, the prequel to the *Aztarian Series*, providing insight into the lore of the creatures on Aztara. Surtees, Science Rules, the first volume in the *Aztarian Series* describes the narcissistic protagonist that abused both Surtarians and Aztarians for his own personal needs. Aztara, A Galactic Love Story, is the first published book and the second volume in the *Aztarian Series*. Aztara, Secrets Revealed, the revolt where Aztarians take their planet back. Carole announced in the summer of 2017 a mystery book series, *Evers and McFarlan Detective Series*. Final Alumni, Shadowy Faces, and Nine Points of a Circle all are available today. Carole also started a *Fantasy Series* in the fall of 2017 for young people. Little Dragon is the first book in the *Child Rowanda Series*, Return to Arolsen, The Underworld and the Dragon Princess will be available in the winter of 2019/2020. Please watch for additional volumes in the *Aztarian Series, Evers and McFarlan Detective Series, The Child Rowanda*, Series, and Carole's many children stories on her website www.walkercarter.com and www.amazon.com.

Aztara, The Mastel Kingdom
By
Carole Walker Carter

Aztara, The Mastel Kingdom, tells the background story of the mastels before entering into a bonding relationship with the miners of Aztara. The setting for this book is two generations before the plague that killed all the Aztarian women during the time frame for Vol II *Aztara, A Galactic Love Story*. Idyllic as it might seem, the mastels are nomadic, dependent upon the weather and growing cycles for the food they eat.

The bond between the griswells and mastels seems destined to failure, until Morsian, an inventor from the eastern factory villages, creates a symbiotic relationship that will change everything on Aztara…forever. Explore the early world of Aztara and enjoy Mastel's unique story. This book will be available on Amazon, Kindle, Nook, and Barnes & Noble in the winter of 2019/2020.

Surtees, Science Rules
By
Carole Walker Carter

Surtees, Science Rules is the First book in *Aztarian Series.* In Surtees, Science Rules, we discover how ruthless a utopian society can be when the ruling power is Scientists.

Ananaya's family are the Oligarchs in this society. His father and mother are obsessed with increasing longevity to keep their power and wealth. Ryndor, Ananaya's father, set up several of his senior scientists as the leaders of scientific research centers.

Hoygazor became the leader of the Astro-Scientists that travel the universe. Eyutho lead research into Marine Science. Doyfear founded the Agricultural research centers. Kaycee'na, wife of Ananaya, developed Neurochemistry research.

Ananaya's sinister plans will become known as he maneuvers his way through the Oligarchy.

This book will be available on Amazon, Kindle, Nook, and Barnes & Noble in the winter of 2019/2020

AZTARA, A Galactic Love Story
By
Carole Walker Carter

In AZTARA, A Galactic Love Story, the second book in the *Aztarian Series* centers on two main characters and their magical creatures that they share a unique bond. The two main characters are caught up in their own personal grief.

Shayla, an Earth woman, who finds life on Earth hardly worth living after being deceived by her husband, and having her only son die, is close to suicide.

Ty, having lived through a plague that killed all the females on his planet, finds refuge in his work, mining a mineral instrumental to all aspects of life on Aztara, including telepathy, longevity, and levitation. Scientists from Surtees, a dying planet, relocate to Aztara to receive the benefits of phyrium. In their attempt to rebuild the Aztarian population, they import Earth women who carry a specific gene, the warrior gene, to mate with the Aztarian men.

The story is about finding love, trust, and internal strength as well as romance, intrigue, and thrills while the two main characters come to grips with a situation, not of their own choosing.

Find this book on Amazon, Kindle, Nook, and Barnes & Noble Now!!

AZTARA, Secrets Revealed
By
Carole Walker Carter

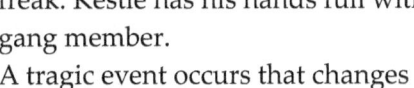

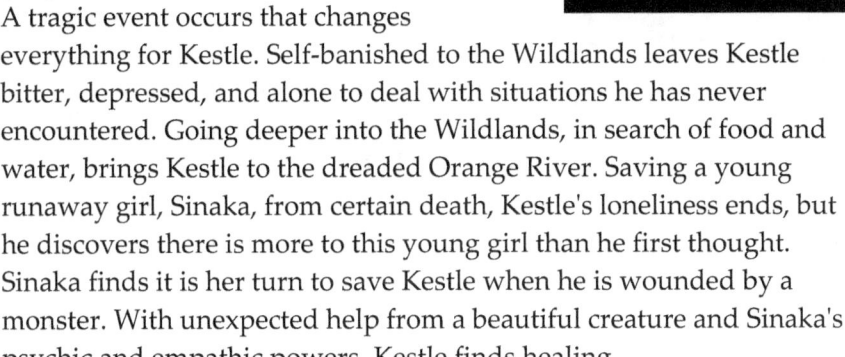

AZTARA, Secrets Revealed, the third book in the Aztarian Series, opens with Shayla's and Ty's love for their twins, Nayela and Kestle. Nayela, the only interspecies girl who communicates telepathically with a mastel, finds others her age calling her a freak. Kestle has his hands full with being a gang member.

A tragic event occurs that changes everything for Kestle. Self-banished to the Wildlands leaves Kestle bitter, depressed, and alone to deal with situations he has never encountered. Going deeper into the Wildlands, in search of food and water, brings Kestle to the dreaded Orange River. Saving a young runaway girl, Sinaka, from certain death, Kestle's loneliness ends, but he discovers there is more to this young girl than he first thought. Sinaka finds it is her turn to save Kestle when he is wounded by a monster. With unexpected help from a beautiful creature and Sinaka's psychic and empathic powers, Kestle finds healing.

The Surtarian Chief Scientist, Ananaya, accelerates his plan to genetically modify the Aztarian/Earthling boys' Warrior Genes, with performance-enhancing injections. Ananaya's plot is to create a daunting army of new Enforcers.

All hell breaks loose when the usually passive Aztarians decide to fight to get their boys back.

Find this book on Amazon, Kindle, Nook, and Barnes & Noble Now!!

Final Alumni
By
Carole Walker Carter

The Final Alumni is the first book in the *Evers and McFarlan Detective Series.* This series follows two high school best friends who join forces to solve multiple cases. Tish, haunted by a childhood experience, enables herself with many disciplines of martial arts, while Scotty falls back on his sharpshooter training and physical prowess as a football hero. Together they make an unstoppable team.

Now living in Chicago, Illinois, and mentored by a well-respected couple who owns a detective agency, Tish and Scotty are enlisted to assist Aileen and Patrick Jamieson in solving cases in Chicago while pursuing a series of unsolved murders in their own hometown as well. Find this book on Amazon, Kindle, Nook, and Barnes & Noble Now!!

Shadowy Faces
By
Carole Walker Carter

Shadowy Faces is the second book in *the Evers and McFarlan Detective Series.* In Shadowy Faces, Tish and Scotty are confronted with the lives of three young women who have been ruined. Each young woman deals with lost weekends where all they can recall are vague faces tormenting them. These shadowy faces become the focus of the investigation of Evers and McFarlan along with the Jamiesons and the Chicago Police. The team works methodically to discover what happened to each of the women to bring the criminals to justice.

Tish needed to lean on a discipline her Grand-Master taught her even with the warning of what could happen to her if anyone should learn of her new martial arts fighting technique. Scotty also faces the threat of losing the love of his life

Find this book on Amazon, Kindle, Nook, and Barnes & Noble Now!!

Carole Walker Carter

Nine Points of a Circle

Evers and McFarlan Detective Series

Nine Points of a Circle
By
Carole Walker Carter

Nine Points of a Circle is the third book in the *Evers & McFarlan Detective Series.* In Nine Points of a Circle, Tish and Scotty are now husband and wife, owners, and licensed detectives in the Evers & McFarlan Agency. Even though the Jamison's are retired, they will continue to consult with Scotty and Tish.

Captain Jones hires the Evers and McFarlan Agency for what appears to be a serial killer. Four deaths have occurred over the past two years, and the bodies were dumped on different streets in downtown Chicago. At the same time, Tish and Scotty are approached by a well-known Chicago business executive regarding his missing daughter.

Both cases will take all of Scotty's technical expertise and Tish's detective skills to solve. Follow them as they delve into the seedy depths of the Chicago underworld.

This book will be available on Amazon, Kindle, Nook, and Barnes & Noble in the summer of 2018.

The Child Rowanda, Little Dragon
By
Carole Walker Carter

Twelve-year-old Rowanda lives with her mother in the lush garden country of Neslora. Seemingly an idyllic world with endlessly blooming flowers, buzzing bees, and birds chirping, Rowanda and her friends are confronted with the horror of the abduction of their mothers.
Rowanda finds herself confronted with the daunting task of finding and rescue her mother and the mothers of her friends. A tyrant king abducted and transported the mothers to a desert world where they are being held as slaves.
Armed only with four talismans, chosen from many by mystical means, Rowanda goes through a portal to Arolsen where her fate is intermingled with two desert dwellers. Together they join forces to brave the desert, defending themselves from nomads, terrible creatures, and scorching desert days and frigid desert nights to rescue Rowanda's mother.
The Palace City reveals the true identities of Rowanda's traveling companions and the reasons they accompanied her on her quest.

Find this book on Amazon, Kindle, Nook, and Barnes & Noble Now!!

The Child Rowanda, Return to Arolsen
By
Carole Walker Carter

When Rowanda and the Elder Sorceresses become aware that the charms left in Arolsen are causing destruction in Neslora, Rowanda, her best friend, Nalivia, as well as Beirimor, Rowanda's father and his mother, the Elder Sorceress, must return to Arolsen to set things right. Many adventures await all four of the Neslorians. Boultori, the wicked king's brother, is being held captive in the palace prison. The Neslorians plan is to rescue Boultori and place him on the throne so he can make Arolsen a safe, flourishing, and blissful world…

Rowanda finds Arolsen more fascinating as two new talismans chose Rowanda. A tiger's eye and an animal's tooth manifest their magic by controlling the most feared creatures of Arolsen. These creature's aide Rowanda on her quest for justice.

Nalivia, a new and untrained sorceress and Rowanda's childhood best friend, joins this adventure as she is tasked to find charms that will aide Boultori when he battles his evil brother, King Nashua. With help from Anarigar, a young goat herder, the two youth finds themselves in trouble.

Magic abounds in this second book of the Child Rowanda series as good battles evil to rescue a world from slavery and hardship and to keep Neslora from the same predicament.

Find this book on Amazon, Kindle, Nook, and Barnes & Noble Now!!

The Child Rowanda, Underworld
By
Carole Walker Carter

Trying to rid the world of Neslora of the evil wizard, Nashua, Rowanda finds herself dragged into the Underworld with the evil sorcerer.

Navigating the terrifying darkness of this new world, Rowanda finds a mysterious and mystical guide who reveals that Rowanda can only exit the Underworld the same way she came in, with the evil sorcerer at her side. However, Nashua must be truly repentant of his depravities before he is allowed to leave, which means Rowanda cannot leave if he does not repent.

Trying to find Nashua in the darkness and convince him to repent, becomes a difficult process. Making matters worse are the demons, intent on making both Nashua and Rowanda one of them that would mean living an eternity in the Underworld in agony.

Find this book on Amazon, Kindle, Nook, and Barnes & Noble Now!!

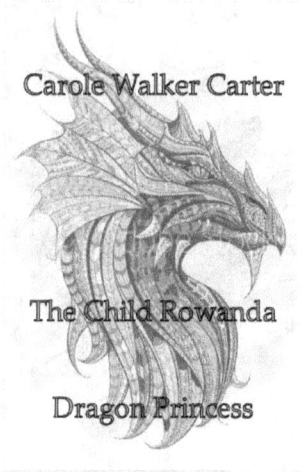

Carole Walker Carter

The Child Rowanda

Dragon Princess

The Child Rowanda, Dragon Princess
By
Carole Walker Carter

Leaving the Underworld through another portal, Rowanda finds that she has not returned to her home-world of Neslora but finds herself on another parallel world with the devious Nashua, where she is elevated to a princess.

Friends and members of her family are in this world, but they are not as they should be. They are doubles with a different personality and…no recollection of Rowanda.

Rowanda finds herself at odds with her look-alike parents, the king, and queen of Soleran.

Rowanda's magical talent of charming animals allows Rowanda to help the enslaved citizens of this world by joining the rebel army in opposition to the king and queen.

Wanting nothing more than to return to her own world, Rowanda seeks the aid of a fire-breathing dragon.

Find this book on Amazon, Kindle, Nook, and Barnes & Noble Now!!

Childhood Stories my Dad Told Me
By
Carole Walker Carter

Growing up on a farm in Nebraska during the Great Depression was difficult, but for two young boys, it was also filled with fun and adventures.

These stories tell about the amusing antics that my father and his younger brother found themselves in during these hard times.

The stories are filled with insights about rural schools, country social events, and harvest time, as well as the day-to-day chores of a working farm.

Find this book on Amazon, Kindle, Nook, and Barnes & Noble Now!!

www.ingramcontent.com/pod-product-compliance
Lightning Source LLC
Chambersburg PA
CBHW070817180626
46818CB00001B/307